WAHIDA CLARK PRESENTS

URBAN ISIS PART 1: REVOLUTION

A NOVEL BY

WILLIE GROSS JR. WITH WAHIDA CLARK

Wahida Clark Presents Publishing
60 Evergreen Place
Suite 904A
East Orange, New Jersey 07018
1(866)-910-6920
www.wclarkpublishing.com

Library of Congress Cataloging-In-Publication Data:
Willie Gross Jr with Wahida Clark
Urban Isis Part 1
ISBN 13-digit 9781947732377 (paper)
ISBN 13-digit 9781947732421 (ebook)

LCCN: 2017904240

1. Sex - 2. Lies - 3. social - 4. African American- –
5. futuristic - 6. Violence - 7. Relationships

Cover design and layout by Nuance Art, LLC
Book design by www.artdiggs.com
Edited by Linda Wilson
Proof-reader Rosalind Hamilton
Printed in USA

Introduction

Let us, reader and writer, agree on only what's real, numbers, and reality, primarily because they don't lie! Tragically, the drug usage among our teenagers of today has steadily increased year after year after year. The problem with this reality is it infringes upon the productivity of our expected torchbearers of tomorrow—the dreamers, the inventors, the pioneers of new technologies that'll spearhead breakthroughs in scientific research, futuristically enabling this nation to remain ahead of and relevant to every other nation.

Yet, as a nation, it seems as though we won't decide which of the two is more important: the drugs or the torchbearers. It is one thing to say we are who we say we are as a nation; yet, we steadily and with regularity, do the opposite. So, we ask ourselves, those confused and concerned by these truths . . . *What's the plan?* Or, *who's doing the planning?*

Yes, politics, greed, economics, fear, arrogance, and hate . . . All recipes for the gradual destruction of a nation and its torchbearers! These are critical components designed to suppress the brilliance, idealism, and productivity of our young, bright minds. The critical thinkers in possession of solutions to common problems plaguing our society, our neighbourhoods, our schools, and ultimately . . . our generations!

But, today, we're thinking critically! We'll start designing what our minds, hearts, and souls are in total agreement with. It's the right thing to do. We won't fool ourselves into selfish decision making cantered around who's right. We're thinking long-range, making decisions for the whole, predicated on solid advice in doing what's right!

Yes, it's fiction—only because we're living in a society controlled by a few—and their only concern is always *their* needs. So, to do what's right in this society would be to them, fictitious. Now, we've established that their fiction is really a reality in the real world, so let's talk building! No hidden agendas . . . hands on the table . . . real-life, drama-type of building.

Let's dream again; let's rewind our memories; let's go back to when all of us knew as pre-schoolers and young grade-schoolers what we wanted to be in life. Let's heal instead of kill the dreams of tomorrow. Feel me? Let's build this dynasty alongside James Johnson. Let's come together in our minds, then think critically about our tomorrows . . . our hopes, our struggles, our accomplishments, our defeats, our victories, and, yes, even our demise. But more importantly, let's leave something good behind. Let's do *that*!

Let's resolve to understand why we struggle, get it all out of our system, then never look back, because the struggle isn't our identity. It was only made to look that way. That's why we accepted it!

In essence, we tear down the fake, then replace it with the real. Let's not automatically think defeat when we go up against the powers that be! Remember, *they're* the reason why we're in this mess! Look, we're building in this book, the right way too, reality!

Let's realize our propensity to be a great people first; *then* we can talk that great nation stuff. Keep turning pages; you'll see, we're people building. This way, we can't lose because we must be a great people before we can be a great nation. You agree? But it's not going to be pretty. Old habits die hard! But they *do* die, and that's James Johnson's only concern!

Now, let all of us envision ourselves in powerful positions, just like the powerful people of today, then ponder . . . If *I* ruled the world, what would *I* do? Who would *I* be? What, then, would be *my* contribution to society? Imagine *that*!

Let's face reality . . . No matter how much good we do in life, it'll never be enough to satisfy the haters. It's what they do best. So keep turning pages to see how James dealt with those haters. How he masterfully played a game they invented.

Let's look at the big picture—the future! Let's all agree . . . Tomorrow is for those who prepare for it today. Let's begin with the real . . . "Urban Isis, Part 1: The Revolution"!

CHAPTER 1
The Blueprint

The dark, chilly night and semi-deserted parking lot provided a perfect canopy for mischief. The clean-shaven Caucasian male acknowledged this as he walked with deliberate haste en route to his vehicle. He looked every bit the part of an ivy leaguer: starch white shirt, blue tie, and blue duck head slacks. His expensive leather briefcase swung in time with his steps. A quick glance toward the small end of the parking lot revealed an open Krispy Kreme doughnut shop. The wonderful smell of deep-fried sweet dough floated in the air like clouds.

As he approached his vehicle, an Arab dressed in traditional Muslim attire, slipped behind him and wrapped his right arm around his victim's damp neck and placed his left arm behind his head and squeezed. The Ivy-leaguer put up a struggle, kicking and twisting but his body went limp, and the offender relieved him of his briefcase.

The attack reminded the carefully observant James of poetry— a concentrated imaginative awareness of experience, chosen and arranged to create a specific emotional response. James too had been stalking the victim for the past two days, but for different reasons, it seemed. The briefcase was supposed to have contained a large amount of money. The information he possessed came from an employee at the tech company who was dying for his attention. She estimated it to be well over $200,000. They agreed on a ten percent split, provided the information checked out. So, here he was parked for a second night ducked down in a stolen black Regal.

Wearing all black, and his favorite black New Orleans Saints cap pulled down snug on his head.

With plans of only retrieving the briefcase, and by any means necessary, if it came down to that, James followed the van. It was now 11:35 p.m. on a Friday night. The Arab's final destination was a warehouse in New Orleans east. Hastily, James exited the Regal and crossed the dark, deserted parking lot with his Glock 40 planted against his leg.

At first James leaned up against the building, but now circled it in search of an entrance. He found none. On his second search, he located an air conditioning ventilation grill. It was approximately four feet by four feet. *Perfect.* He immediately began kicking it in until he was able to peel enough of an entrance to climb through.

The hole was behind a crowded room of big barrels of liquid he held no concern for, as he slowly crept about the room blindly. He could now see a lit entrance. The smelly fumes made James assume that oil was inside the barrels.

From the shadows, James peeped out into the hallway and into the warehouse strategically arranged like an air traffic control tower on one side, and a torture chamber on the other. The kidnapped victim was seated in an iron chair fitted with iron bracelets that secured his hands and legs to the chair. The kidnapper was seated directly in front of the victim.

"What business did you have in my country other than as a missionary worker?" the Arab asked evenly.

"None, sir. Please," the Caucasian male nervously answered while sweat leaked down his face. "Please . . . I swear. I was just trying to help your people."

"I'll ask this another way. What business did you have in my country other than missionary work?" The kidnapper never raised his voice, exhibiting the utmost control as an interrogator.

After subtly leaving his chair, the Arab returned with a long sparkling sword. He placed it on a table nearby that also held the briefcase James had come for.

Ivy Leaguer danced in his seat, then cried out, "Okay, okay. I'll tell you . . . I provided a . . . a location," the victim frantically spoke with nervous candor in an attempt to right his perceived wrong. "I'm sorry. I had to . . . They-they made me . . . Oh my *God* I'm so sorry! Please, please don't!" he begged.

Slowly, the Arab walked over to the wall, then flipped a switch. From the ceiling, a thick braided rope with a noose at the end mechanically descended. The victim pleaded, wiggled, and cried out, but to no avail—the noose was now fitted around his neck.

James watched in amazement as the Middle Easterner held up the sword, then chopped off both arms of the victim to the elbows, then his legs to the knees. The victim screamed in agony as blood splashed, skeeted, and oozed out of the wounds. But before he could faint, another switch was flipped, and the victim was sprung into the air by the rope, breaking his neck instantly. The body twisted violently in the air, causing it to rain blood.

The man with the long gray and white beard placed the sword on the table and was now accessing his computer system. James looked from the Arab to the briefcase, trying to determine how he could get what he wanted, then live to enjoy it. After determining (1) they were alone, and (2) he had the ups and planned on keeping it; he slowly eased out into the opening with the gun in his right hand, still lying comfortably against his leg.

Sensing his presence, the man calmly scratched his head through his black turban. He turned in the chair, and then stood to fearlessly face James. James stared back at the man, but couldn't get a read on him.

"As salaam Alaikum," James offered as his greeting.

"Wa alaikum as salaam," the Arab responded.

They both seemed to relax.

"May I help you?" the man questioned, in the most respectful of manners.

"I've been staking out your victim for a couple of days in regard to that briefcase over there." James nodded.

"Do you know of its contents?" the man asked.

"I know what's *supposed* to be there. My inside connect has never been wrong."

"And if what you seek isn't there?"

"Then I've been misled."

"I've been surveilling this person for two months. So, how do we determine *who* has the rights to the briefcase?"

James tapped the gun against his leg. Closely taking in the man's visage from head to foot, he'd made out the Arab's true identity. He now possessed the ups and the deal-breaker. "Aren't you aware of the $25 million bounty on your head? Dead or alive. Osama bin Laden."

Osama smiled and shifted his gaze toward the gun being patted against the young black man's leg. "I'm *very* aware of it," he confessed.

"So, can I have my briefcase now?" James tilted his head slightly.

"And that's it?" The man shrugged lightly.

"That's the only thing I came for."

Wrinkles appeared in Osama's forehead. James knew Osama was both intrigued and puzzled. Now he wondered if the man was bold enough to express the better move.

"So, what's his transgression?" James focused on the guy still twisting slowly in the air.

"He's a double-agent. By day he was on our front lines appearing to be a missionary to our people, and by night he's feeding the United States coordinates to launch their drone attacks."

"What will you do with his body?"

"You really must know?" Osama asked.

"Flatter me," James stated.

"Dispose of it after I take pictures to post as a warning to other spies." He paused briefly before speaking. "You do know our countries are at war because of your country's occupation of my country?"

"Don't follow politics. I focus on my survival," James stated firmly.

"And what exactly is your true goal in life besides survival, which is a basic animal instinct?" He placed his thumb and forefinger on his bearded chin.

"To be in a position to one day make a difference." *Where is this conversation going?* James wondered, but nevertheless, he kept his eyes on the briefcase the entire time.

"Then that is your purpose. Now, how do you intend on reaching this feat?"

"I need . . . a break in life. Just one . . ." he emphasized, pointing the gun toward the briefcase.

"No," Osama reasoned. "You need structure, strategy, and faith. With those qualities present, it gives you the best chance to succeed." Osama grabbed his blood-stained sword to pick up the briefcase by its handle. It slid down on the sword's sharp incline toward Osama's clasped hands on the grip. He left the briefcase there, dangling against the guard, just like the body above their heads.

"I have none of those qualities, and heart isn't on that list, so that makes me doomed, right?" Instantly, James stepped forward and got a good grip on the briefcase's handle. The two men locked gazes.

"If what you say you have is true, then the qualities I spoke of are already present, and you need only to hone your skills." With one forceful jerk of his sword, Osama broke the intruder's grasp on the briefcase.

"And how does all this *honing* occur while I'm struggling to take care of my family, stay out of the penitentiary, and stay alive?" James asked, with a face void of emotion. He was getting pissed with the line of questioning and the fact that $200,000 had just been knocked away from his fingertips.

"Where are your parents, if I may ask?"

"I'd rather not speak of my parents," James stated in an almost threatening tone with a hardened glare.

"Any other family?" Osama asked, now pointing the sword at James' chest.

"Kinda sorta," James said with reluctance, careful not to divulge too much info. Not knowing how the present situation would play out, he raised the gun at a thirty-degree angle, prepared to deliver a shot to Osama's heart.

"Do you know what a network consists of?" Osama looked

down at the gun briefly, unfazed.

"I hate guessing, so why don't you explain."

"I'd rather you tell me what you think it is," he insisted, lowering the sword so the briefcase slid toward James.

James let his right hand holding the gun, rest at his side. He released a small sigh. "In street terminology, I'd say it's a group of people working to achieve the same goals."

Osama half turned and set the briefcase and sword back on the table and began clapping. "Your definition was better than mine, and I'm prepared to offer you access to this network, as well as the briefcase you desire. Being it is reasonably clear that you're a man of principle, and we also have a common foe."

"And who would that be?" James narrowed his brows in genuine curiosity.

"The ones in control—the powers that be."

"And how did you come to that conclusion?" James asked.

"Simple. You never seriously considered collecting the bounty on my head, even though the opportunity presented itself."

"And?"

"And it's clear you oppose killing without a reason, or for the powers that be. You've acknowledged our plights are different, yet we're fighting the same system."

"How could you know about my plight?" James' nostrils flared.

"Because I knew of your people's struggle throughout history. You are no different than the last generation of young black males still experiencing racial bigotry even as adults."

Instinctively, James stole a quick glance at the hangman.

"That should never be you," Osama stated, after observing James' brief gaze at the victim.

"Why's that?"

"Because you possess loyalty to your cause and to those cut from the same cloth. But you must remember, every man confessing loyalty isn't who he says he is. I can teach you to spot them, test them, and destroy them." He picked up the briefcase and held it toward James.

"Then *that* sounds like a winner," James stated, placing the

Glock 40 in his waistband. He gripped his $200,000 bounty, then walked over to embrace Osama. "You must really love your countrymen, braving your chances here in America." he asked, breaking their contact.

"It is because of that love that I took the chance of coming here." Osama folded his arms across his chest.

James thought about Osama's answer, then focused on the body still suspended in mid-air. *Damn, I hope this isn't a trap,* he thought. "My mother was that type of person to the community. She instilled in us the love of our neighbor and country. But she could not be to her country what she was to her community. She was just a hardworking, loving pillar in the community. I want to succeed where she could not."

"You must become just as big as your country in order to succeed on that level, my friend."

"Is that a realistic goal?" James smirked.

"When you think of my country—who do you think of?"

"That's easy! Osama bin Laden," James stated.

"So, it is possible—no matter in what way you're thought of."

"Yet, being America's Most Wanted isn't the recipe for the changes I'd like to make."

"Then you must become America's most loved," Osama insisted.

"And how would I succeed at that?"

"You begin with the deadly venom in order to get the antidote. That my friend, will be your task, and my duty is to help you realize this goal is realistically possible."

"The world all of a sudden has gotten much larger," James stated, taking a few steps back to begin making his exit. He wasn't crazy enough to turn his back on Osama.

"Then your vision must do the same. Remember, a true visionary gives us a glimpse of the future in his work today," Osama assured him. "We will meet again."

James never envisioned abandoning his mother's vision of what a community should be. But what could he do to affect not only his community, but every community in the country? In order to determine the solution to the problem, he'd have to definitely identify the cause. He knew in most communities he would try to help, that cause would be drugs. And many days he'd sold these same drugs in order to feed his family—a real life catch-22. Yet the real trick would be to win with drugs and build stronger communities all over the world in light of this union.

CHAPTER 2
The Tragedy

"Please, James. Please come to the hospital quick. Momma has been calling your name. Something's wrong with her," Deon said frantically.

"What's wrong, Deon? And slow down," James stated calmly into his phone. He gave his younger brother Troy, who was also his passenger, a quick glance.

"I don't know. I'm not a doctor."

"What did the doctor say?" James closed his eyes briefly when Troy tugged on his shirt to ask if their mother was okay.

"He hasn't said anything, but they're hooking all types of machines to her, along with tubes and IVs."

"But what is Momma doing, Deon! Damn!" James yelled through the cell phone as he held up to his ear. He was navigating the brand new stolen Impala through traffic as if he were law enforcement.

"She's crying out in pain," Deon stressed.

"Miss, you're going to have to leave the room," a stern voice stated.

James was sure the voice belonged to a nurse. He knew Deon would snap and give the nurse a hard time. She would never leave their mom alone.

"Deon?" James called.

"That's not going to happen, *Miss Nurse*," Deon stated aggressively. "That's my momma lying there. Would you leave your mother?"

"Deon, what's happening now?" James asked.

"Very well, but you must move to the side while we tend to the patient."

James sighed with relief, glad the nurse allowed Deon to stay.

"Oh my God, James! Momma just had a seizure. I gotta go. Get here ASAP!"

James heard the dial tone and pressed harder on the accelerator. He arrived at the hospital within minutes of Deon's frantic call. With Troy at his side, they bolted through the door and entered to find their mother's room full of medical equipment.

The staff began rolling the IV poles and the bed as Ms. Bertha continued convulsing.

James grabbed the doctor's arm. "What's going on, Doc?"

"Sir, there's no time to talk right now—I'll be back to see you."

With that, everyone in uniform exited the room. James, Deon, and Troy were all instantly on their knees praying in a family huddle. After offering individual prayers aloud, they rose in unison.

"What happened?" Troy asked.

"I was seated beside her bed talking to her after her chemotherapy, then she began convulsing non-stop."

"Was she upset about something?" James pressed.

"No, none of that. She was just weak."

"Is that all we need to know, Deon? Think . . ."

"We were just talking. Well, mostly me."

"Did she say anything about hurting?"

"You know Momma, James."

"You're right, she wouldn't tell us anyway."

"She did say she was tired."

"Was it before chemo or afterwards?"

"Before. Why?" Deon asked curiously.

"Just wondering," James lied.

He knew those were the magic words of the sickly whenever they were ready to stop fighting the inevitable. With that in mind, James sat back in the chair beside Troy, who was staring out the window in space. Truth is, they all knew, yet none of them was willing to accept it.

It took the worst of situations for them to finally admit their mother into Charity Hospital. They tried their very best to tend to their mother with around-the-clock care. She'd began losing the battle, plus weight, and then her mind. Their decision was predicated on economics. There was no real breadwinner in the home. Their father's sudden disappearance and their mother falling sick, set the present in motion. Charity Hospital was the only option available.

Deon and Troy were still in high school. James was in the streets robbing and petty drug dealing to barely pay the bills. Their mother, Ms. Bertha was the picture of nobility. She loved everyone in her neighborhood, helped anybody, and accepted no charity. She raised everyone's kids and never turned away a hungry child, no matter how little they had for themselves. Whenever she needed more money, she took on extra houses to clean, and never, ever complained. After her husband left, she simply did what she had to do with dignity and grace, as she always did.

James knew his father Wayne's unexpected disappearance weighed on her. She seemed to age faster since that day. He thought of all the family time they spent together, and couldn't understand why he left them. Every morning he'd tell them he loved them. Then when night came, he'd tell them bedtime stories and always expressed his love again before he turned out the lights.

Shortly afterward, Ms. Bertha developed breast cancer and Type 2 diabetes, which didn't help the situation. Things could not have gotten worst.

The hospital was freezing cold as usual and smelled of rubbing alcohol. Troy and Deon had dozed off by the time the nurses were wheeling Ms. Bertha back into her room. Ten hours had passed. It was now 2:00 a.m., and James was up to greet her when she returned. Ms. Bertha was awake, but barely. The medication made her drowsy and her usually bright caramel skin tone now appeared dull. James pulled up a chair next to her bed, then grabbed hold of her cold, bony little hand. Her eyes opened and she smiled. He smiled back, like when he was a child. Suddenly her light brown eyes peered over at Troy and Deon. Wrinkles appeared in her forehead, signaling concern.

Ms. Bertha was still graceful as ever, even in the cloth blue hospital cap which covered her baldhead as a result of the radiation treatments. The crows' feet in the corner of her eyes revealed exhaustion and aging. She attempted to speak. James grabbed the pitcher of ice water, then poured a cup. She took a sip.

"Take care of my babies," she whispered, as James held his ear to her lips. He nodded. "You finish school and find success wherever it may be," she squeaked out. Again he nodded.

"Life isn't always fair, but you're never without opportunities to shape it as you see fit."

"Okay, Momma," he whispered.

"Be to your community, what you are to your family—be to the world the gift God created you to be."

"I will, Momma."

"I did my best with what I had, son, but I'm tired," she confessed.

"I know, Momma, and thanks for being the best mother we could've hoped for." Ms. Bertha smiled at her son, but she gradually weakened.

At 5:00 a.m., Troy and Deon awakened James, Their mother had passed away. Deon and Troy were in tears.

James' mind was not a stable one at this point. He hugged Troy and Deon, then assured them that their mother loved them dearly. He started thinking how politics and poverty dictated who lives and who dies, and what his mother had told him: "You're the best of me and your father; go on to do great things and do us proud."

"That won't be a problem," James whispered in her ear, then finally fell asleep. He figured the best way to do that would be to bar none, and do it by any means necessary!"

* * * * * * *

People from multiple communities gathered inside Rhodes funeral home in remembrance of Ms. Bertha Johnson. The building held 300 and every seat was taken. The choir sang the most beautiful gospel songs in her honor as she lay peacefully in a pearl white and gold-trimmed casket draped in white roses. Ms. Bertha's spectacular white and gold dress reflected the classy woman she was. The stories told by people touched by Ms Bertha's undying love and service to the needy, had to be cut short, as the line grew longer than the day possessed hours.

James, Troy, and Deon sat on the front pew dressed in all black with their heads held high. Irvin, James' childhood friend stopped to dap it up with James. He hugged Troy and Deon and gave them all words of support and encouragement. "I remember Ms. Bertha favorite saying, 'It's not always—" Irvin said, before Deon cut him off.

"What you have in this life, but it's what you *do* with this life that matters. That was my momma all right," Deon said, reminiscing on her mother's words and another conversation they'd had.

"But why are others blessed more than everyone else?" she had asked.

"The knowledge of God's plan is with God, not man not woman, sweetie," Ms. Bertha assured her.

"It isn't fair, Momma."

"Nor when children die not having lived; yet, who knows but the Creator, why their lives were taken," Ms. Bertha countered.

"So, you getting sick was a part of God's plan?"

"The universe is God's plan, and everything and everyone in it, can do no more than nature requires of it, or them. And yes, everything and everyone has an expiration date. Yet, God in his mercy to us, sometimes warns us of that date."

"I love you, Momma," Deon said, with tear-filled eyes.

Ms. Bertha had prepared her children for this moment every day of their lives. They also knew how loved their mother was, a testament to the many testimonials. They'd miss the wisdom of their mother's words and deeds, for sure. Plus, they knew having her was a blessing in itself, and remembered what she taught them about blessings.

"Who knows better when your blessings will arrive than the one who believes, then prepares for one?" Ms. Bertha would ask.

Deon thought about these words as she curiously glanced around at the attendees. During the initial meeting with the funeral director, to her brothers' and her own surprise, their mother's funeral had been paid in full, although they hadn't the slightest clue who had footed the bill.

* * * * * * *

The man seated in the back of the funeral home was Wayne Johnson's best friend. Also he was the person responsible for paying for the entire funeral. And he too was oblivious to Wayne's whereabouts, contrary to what Ms. Bertha thought.

Tray King and Wayne Johnson were as tight as fish pussy. They were local hustlers always looking for an opportunity to feed their family. Tray was part responsible for James, Troy, and Deon being born. He introduced Wayne to Bertha way back in the game when they were in high school. They were together ever since. He remembered Wayne always saying he would one day be able to take his family from the slums. Wayne was always worried about his wife Bertha working so hard, cleaning white folks' houses just to get by. He never did keep a job very long and felt like the wages were no better than slave labor. He would come home from slinging hundred pound sacks of potatoes on ships all day, then go straight to bed. His back was always hurting. Bertha would tend to his aching back, and he'd tend to her sore feet till they both fell asleep.

One day, Wayne strolled onto the corner during the time he'd normally be at work, surprising Tray.

"Man, I thought you were working on the river?" Tray asked.

"Man, fuck that river and all the ships docked there," Wayne stated. "The only muthafuckas making money over there are the owners. The rest of us ain't doing shit but digging our own early graves working like damn fools. They'd better find some machines to lift that shit, 'cause I ain't the one," Wayne admitted. "Shit, I can't even spend time with my kids anymore. I find myself peeping into their room once I get home, only to find them asleep. The only time I spend with Bertha is when I'm massaging her sore feet, and she's massaging my aching back. Man, we can't expect to live long under these conditions," Wayne complained.

"Sounds like you're done with that job shit. So, what's on your mind?" Tray inquired.

"Hustling pays the bills, too, so let's get back to what we do best. I told Bertha I'd give that legal shit a try, but that river busting my ass legally," Wayne said. They laughed.

"You know I'm down for the cause, my man," Tray said, dapping Wayne off.

Tray was glad Wayne did come back to the streets. *That nigga could spot a hustle a mile away,* he remembered. Two days after Wayne quit the riverfront, he made a startling discovery. Wayne had broken into a warehouse in a deserted part of Houma, Louisiana, defeating its security, only to find out it belonged to Colombians. Wayne searched the warehouse and discovered it was a major cocaine distribution plant. It was set up to look like a Gold Medal flour processing plant. The more he searched, the more he came across what indicated he'd hit the jackpot. It was 3:00 a.m., and Wayne had crawled out of the plant with a kilo of the best coke on the streets.

How Wayne had stumbled upon the plant was beyond Tray's understanding, but when Wayne knocked on his door at 5:00 a.m., then produced that kilo—he didn't care where it originated, on the block was where it was going. Wayne explained that there was a warehouse full of those kilos, all packaged in Gold Medal flour bags. He'd also run across some stand-up safes throughout the warehouse, but it made no sense tampering with them; he had a plan.

They agreed to peddle some of the coke on the low for a good month to acquire the money to purchase a moving truck equipped with a forklift, and enough money to keep their bills paid. Then on the perfect night, they'd empty the warehouse. Everything was working as planned. Wayne had Bertha thinking he'd gotten a night job, so now he'd be able to go watch the action happening in the warehouse.

The Colombians wore uniforms and drove vehicles stamped with Gold Medal flour logos. Wayne was impressed at how organized they were. They came in at 8:00 a.m., and then left at 5:00 p.m., as if it were a regular job. Eighteen wheelers pulled up with whole loads of product, and then some came to pick up product.

Wayne purchased binoculars and witnessed employees

stocking the safes with money. There were three thousand kilos per pallet on the floor at all times. Wayne would leave the warehouse, then go straight to the block. Then two hours before Bertha would leave for work, he'd come home. He made her cut back on working so many hours, as he now gave her money more frequently. He would come home dressed in his janitor's uniform, then hand her all the money he supposedly made. He then made love to her before she left for work.

A month passed. Wayne and Tray sported their mover's uniform, along with matching baseball caps and were driving the big truck down the long dark road. They pulled up to the warehouse. Wayne inserted a key made from an impression he'd lifted off the shipping entrance lock, and then raised the door. Tray backed the truck into the warehouse. Everything was quiet, with only crickets chirping in the nearby woods. Tray exited the truck, then they went to work. The truck came with a forklift that enabled them to empty the warehouse twice as fast. Once they loaded the ten pallets onto the truck, they then went for the safes. There were four of them, all full; the two heavy duty dollies were all they needed. The last of the safes were on the lift, when Wayne took out his towel to wipe sweat from his face. He accidentally knocked off his cap, revealing his identity to the hidden cameras recording the entire episode. Wayne grabbed the cap and placed it back on his head, then continued loading the safes into the truck. So they left, thinking they'd pulled off the perfect heist.

They made it to New Orleans East on America Street in two hours. The truck was parked inside old man Papa Joes' junkyard. He agreed to sell the junkyard to them for twenty grand. Papa Joe would've jumped through the roof had his health not been an issue. He was very thankful to get rid of the junkyard anyway.

The truck had been parked at the yard ever since the heist. Tray or Wayne would come periodically to feed the vicious pit bulls guarding their stash. Two weeks passed with the two men seeing less and less of each other. They were doing their own thing in separate places, with what was left of the original kilo. They decided if the two of them were together pumping dope all of a sudden, it would raise suspicion. Word on the street was the Colombians were seeking all information with big reward money readily available. Tray and Wayne still purchased dope from other pushers, so everyone thought they were still small-time hustlers. The Colombians were looking for big suppliers, not buyers.

The Colombians had been working behind the scenes with top technicians to enhance the video surveillance that captured the burglary. The video wasn't clear, but with help from their police friends, the face shot of Wayne was entered into a computer databank. It came back with five possible matches in Louisiana. They all were in New Orleans, and Wayne was one of them.

Lieutenant Ryan, of the New Orleans police department, immediately received a call from his buddy, Sergeant Browning.

"Lieutenant Ryan speaking. How can I help you?"

"How have you been, Mike? This is Sergeant Browning over in Houma. I'm investigating a burglary, and the video surveillance shot we have has come back with five possible suspects, all in your area. I need you to take a look at the video along with suspects."

"No problem. Send it through."

"I've sent it to your email. Look at it, then give me a holla back if you notice any familiar faces," Browning stated, then hung up.

"Lieutenant Ryan, you have a meeting in two hours," his secretary said as he checked his email. He shook his head, now looking at the two-minute clip of the burglary. He studied the video, then looked at the suspects, he recognized all five, but one in particular caught his eyes. Lieutenant Ryan picked up the phone and called Wayne.

"Wayne, this is Mike. I need to see you. Now! Meet me at the We Never Close restaurant in the east. Whatever you're doing, drop it!" The phone went dead.

Wayne wasted no time debating his uncle (his father's brother), and when his Uncle Mike spoke, it usually meant to listen carefully. Within seconds, Wayne was speeding down Chef Menteur highway with all types of paranoid thoughts running through his mind. Everything came back to the burglary or the drug selling. He pulled in beside his uncle Mike's unmarked patrol car, and then jumped in.

"You know any of them?" Mike asked, handing him the laptop computer with the two-minute clip playing. He then tossed five pictures in Wayne's lap.

Wayne dropped his head. "So, where do we go from here, Unc?"

"I heard a lot about this burglary before I received this information. I don't want nothing from you. But if you're smart like I think you are, you'd leave here and don't plan on coming back. And for your family's sake, do *not* take them with you. These people have unlimited resources. They'll track you easier with a family, and hunt you all down like dogs, and they'll die right alongside of you. Right now, they don't know anything for sure, but don't think they're not watching. I'll try to knock the scent off your trail by telling them it's not you in that video. But they basically want me to say a name, and they're coming. That leaves only two suspects, because two are already dead. Look, let Tray take care of your family—you need to leave now, and do not look back. Do you understand me?" Lieutenant Mike Ryan asked.

Wayne shook his head. He was supposed to meet Tray later that day, but decided it would be best to do as he was told. He thanked his uncle, then went to the junkyard to stack up on enough product to begin another life. Wayne cried continuously as he stacked his vehicle full of Gold Medal flour bags because he truly loved his family. He knew he'd finally got the break they needed in life, but it ended too quickly.

Once he finished stacking, there were 200 kilos in the trunk. He glanced at the safes and knew there would be no time to crack those open. Wayne trusted Tray to do the right thing, so he left with only the clothes on his back, 200 kilos, and a broken heart.

CHAPTER 3
The Promise

James had been crouched behind the large, foul-smelling blue garbage dumpster for the longest five minutes of his short life. But for the moment, it shielded him from the barrage of gunfire sent at him by a heavily armed crew of violent drug dealers. The Desire projects, in the heart of New Orleans, was their turf. And rightfully so, they were opposed to James' hustling there.

Pandemonium broke out like wildfire once James was spotted, and now his back was against the wall on foreign soil, once again. In his right hand was his trusted Glock 40, with the extended clip. His left hand was anchored to the ground for balance as he pivoted back and forth, peeping, then repositioning from behind the bullet-ridden dumpster.

To his right, five yards across from his position, was a young black male with a snap back New Orleans Saints cap turned backward on his head. He looked to be eighteen years old. James did not know him. The unidentified young man was seated against the same wall he'd just slid down when hit with James' return fire. A puddle of blood circled the young man like the rings around the planet Saturn. The concentrated smell of fresh blood lingered in the air. Periodically, James peeped from behind the dumpster at the young man, still struggling to breathe. His last look found the young man with his chin planted in his chest. Dark red blood now spewed from between his lips like lava.

The night air was hot and humid amid the hundred-degree heat index New Orleanians were accustomed to. This fact also created a litany of other problems. Gun powder lingered in the air from the automatic gunfire like chem-trails in the sky. The powder found its way into James' eyes, mouth, and skin. Without a doubt, a by-product of discharging his weapon from a confined space. Still, he remained boxed in his position inside the Desire projects, contemplating an escape route. To his delight, police sirens were wailing from the north end of the projects. Gunfire was now replaced with fear of a first-degree murder arrest that convinced everyone to abandon their foxholes. Seconds later, James slowly stood from his crouched position, then commenced to sprinting in the opposite direction of the sirens.

Tonight, he had dodged a major blow by entering the most dangerous project in New Orleans for that mighty dollar. Sadly, he'd taken another life, one he'd never be proud of taking. *This can't be life,* he assured himself. *There has to be more.*

The beat up, white, stolen 1972 Ford Falcon was now in James' view. It took him longer to find it, considering the high volume of police presence. He made several detours in order to wipe clean, breakdown, then ditch the now infamous murder weapon. *Good riddance.*

Cautiously, James crept the speed limit along Interstate 10, en route to Aunt Joyce's house. A couple blocks away, he turned into a lighted lot occupied by tall weeds and burned out stolen vehicles. Quickly, he shed the all-black attire full of sweat and gun powder. He grabbed the gray hoody and sweatpants, completed the change, then exited the vehicle en route to the trunk with lightning speed. He returned with a red five-gallon can of gasoline. Working with extreme haste, he doused the interior of the car, discarded the black uniform, then set the old rusty Ford aflame.

In two minutes, James reached the little white shotgun house on the corner of Martin Luther King Boulevard and LaSalle Street. Aunt Joyce's red Honda Civic wasn't parked in the yard, so that meant they were still at Bible study.

James unlocked the front door, then slid into the home he'd occupied for almost a year. The smell of lavender was forever present as were the many family portraits strategically hung on the walls. He hesitantly stepped toward the portrait, reached out and touched his mother's lovely face, bowed his head, then headed to his room. *Damn I miss her so much.* After gathering a change of clothes, he slid into the bathroom to soak his aching body. Shortly afterward, he heard his aunt's boyfriend's car pull into the yard with music blaring. *So disrespectful.*

It was nearly a year after his mother's untimely death, and James was still ravaging the deadly streets of New Orleans like Hurricane Katrina. But who would've thought in the process he'd meet America's most wanted fugitive, Osama Bin Laden?

Straight out of business school graduation, immediately the streets became his haven, and he, a predator who stalked them. The diploma was to honor his mother's wishes. *The next promise would likely lead to many more autopsies,* he contemplated while drying off, and then exiting the bathroom. Feeding his two siblings wasn't just a priority, it was a promise that must be fulfilled regardless of the cost, he vowed.

Deon, James' youngest sibling, was fifteen and a freshman in high school. Troy was seventeen and a senior in high school. Since Mrs. Bertha Johnson's death, the three lived with their mother's sister, Joyce. But the transition would not be an easy one. Aunt Joyce was older than their mother by three years at forty-nine. A lovely low-key Christian woman, and a habitual victim of domestic violence. A major sticking point where James drew a line in the sand.

Aunt Joyce's boyfriend Frank was a thirty-five year old with no job or life outside of preying on women who were hard-up and willing to accept his bullshit in the name of love.

"What's up?" James asked, leaning against the kitchen wall where Frank was attempting to pass. Many times he had schemed for the day in which he would catch Frank alone. Like a blessing from Allah, that day came like death and judgment day—on time!

"You tell me," the slim, light-skinned, pretty boy insisted, in an effort to match the intensity level of his possible opponent.

"What I have to tell you, you may not be ready for," James shot back with a crooked frown. He stood four inches taller than Frank at six feet four inches, like his father Wayne.

Frank shot him the same twisted grimace. "Seems as though

you're looking for some trouble." James' 200-pound athletic body, clad in a traditional gray wife-beater and matching gym shorts, put no fear in Frank's heart. Slowly raising his hands, Frank took a step back, as if hoping to lay a trap.

James chuckled. "Doesn't look like you're wanting any trouble."

"What makes you think that? You definitely do. Got your dreads pulled back specifically for this occasion, huh?" Frank scoffed.

"First of all, I know a coward when I see one. Secondly, any man that beats women isn't a man at all. And last but not least, had I begun looking for pussy, I would not have passed you up." James gave a wicked grin that reached his caramel-colored eyes.

Frank pivoted as if he was going away, then shot a straight right hand that caught James on the chin. "Guess I can look at this as a bright side. I finally get the chance to put my money where my mouth is. Prepare to receive a well-deserved ass whooping." Frank began dancing around, ready to rumble. The punch had little effect, other than upsetting James.

Instinctively, James scanned his memory bank full of lessons Osama had taught him. *Strategy is similar to art. If you're unsure of a course of action, do not attempt it. When you execute, move effortlessly, as if your best is yet to come.* It was much too late for James to counterpunch, instead he spat on the floor looking for blood or teeth. James knew the many months of physical and mental training with Osama twice a week placed him light years ahead of his opponent. *And only in cases of the enemy posing a serious threat should you use a fatal move,* Osama reasoned. Frank was not the exception, so the mental approach to his fight should be sufficient, James figured. *The best deceptions are the ones that seem to give the other person a choice. Set a goal, and when you reach it, stop,* Osama once advised James.

Frank made setting a trap for him as easy as breathing. James' goal was simple: Get him out of his aunt's home for good. He knew Frank would have to feel a certain degree of humiliation first.

"You *pussy ass coward!*" James stated firmly, knowing those words would do the trick. As expected, Frank retaliated by sucker-punching him.

With pin-point accuracy, James slapped Frank twice before he could attempt to block the strikes. Like a raging bull, Frank charged through the doorway leading to the small kitchen. James pivoted left, then tripped Frank, who took a nose dive onto the wooden floor.

"Mighty clumsy of you," James joked.

"Fight me like a man!" Frank insisted, while peeling himself off the floor.

"You're not a man, remember? Coward ass pussy!"

"Bullshit!" Frank threw a flurry of punches at James with none finding its mark.

"I told you, you're pussy, so accept it," James said as he slapped him four more times, like a bitch.

Gradually, Frank lost all energy and hope from swinging at air and getting punched to the floor. Frank, once gung-ho about the idea of fighting a twenty-five-year-old homeless nigga, dissipated real quick. Now on hands and knees, he was reluctant to raise himself from the floor again for fear of more punishment. James decided to seize the moment.

"Look, pussy nigga," James said. "I could've long ago ended your useless life. Consider this a warning that many others wish they would've gotten. And from now on, whenever you enter these doors, show me the respect that comes with being the man of the house. And if at any time I hear you've laid your dick-beaters on my aunt again, I'll kidnap your pussy ass, pour scalding hot grease all over your body, cool you off with a Bengay bath, then repeat the process until you die. Do I make myself clear?"

"Nigga, fuck you and this house!" Frank exhaustingly stated.

"Is that supposed to mean something to me?" James cracked his knuckles.

"That means you can have this dump and everybody in it for all I care."

"You don't have to leave, pussy, but you do have to respect my gangsta."

"Nah, nigga. You can have this dump, like I said. And from the looks of things, you need it more than me," Frank stated, in his weak attempt at saving face.

"Well, I accept your resignation, pussy. So, push on up out of here before I get mad about you leaving without telling my aunt good-bye."

"She'll be all right—ahhh!" Frank cried out in pain, as he began to pick himself up. He peeled himself off the floor as James closed the gap between them in the blink of an eye. He threw a flurry of punches and followed it up with a vicious leg sweep that made the floor a stretcher for Frank.

"What the fuck—nigga!" Frank exclaimed.

"Don't *ever* disrespect my aunt in my presence again!"

Once again Frank peeled himself off the floor. This time he exited the door without another word being spoken. Afterward, while sitting in his car he gave James a death stare.

CHAPTER 4
The Robbery

"How can we get Rick to let us borrow the car for the game?" Troy asked his best friend Luqman while seated at the kitchen table.

"Rick's cool," Luqman stated. "But he's most likely going to miss another one of our games, unless we go at him with a gangsta guilt trip."

"And he did say that he'd make this next one, right?"

"*I promise*, were his exact words," Luqman reminded Troy.

"Sounds good. So then that's our angle," Troy stated. "Now, who's negotiating?" He jumped up from the table, excited.

"You'll have a better chance than me," Luqman said, leaning the chair back on two legs.

"And you base that on what?" Troy rested both hands on the table.

"I'm the pesky little brother," Luqman insisted, not really wanting to expound further.

"And you said that to say what?" Troy scratched his head.

"You know brothers fight a lot."

"Sure they do." Troy shrugged. "But what else aren't you saying?"

Luqman sighed. "Sometimes it takes longer to make up."

"And?" Troy pressed.

"And sometimes it's not entirely the other brothers' fault," Luqman confessed.

"Man, c'mon out with the rest of the story."

"Look, Troy. You know I have mad love for Rick, but his drug using has gone too far, and I may be too hard on him for it. I should've chose better words to call him out on it."

"Well, that's a start. So just tell him that." Troy poured milk into his bowl of Frosted Flakes.

Luqman looked as if he was pondering Troy's advice while they both sat facing each other with bowls of cereal in front of them. "Okay, you're right. But I'll do it after our game. Cool?"

"As long as it gets done and soon," Troy agreed.

"Go ahead, he's in his room," Luqman urged.

Troy took a deep breath, rose from the kitchen table, and then crept through the two-bedroom house toward Rick's room. In the hallway, boxes were labeled whites and blues, as if they were makeshift dresser drawers. Thus, bringing to his attention the gradual deterioration of the home's cleanliness. Roaches scurried across the walls and floor to their hiding places as Troy approached. Big spots resembling oil slicks blotted the beige dingy carpet. The rank air wasn't a pleasant smell either.

Troy made it to the door, then knocked. After a few seconds, Rick stated, "Come in." Movement could be heard from behind the door as Troy peeked in and found Rick peeping out of the window.

Rick turned to face him. "What's up, Troy?"

"Damn, man! What are you cooking in here? Skunk guts?"

"Nah, man. You trippin'. What's up?" Rick asked, as if he was just in the middle of giving a lecture at a prestigious university.

"Okay, if you say so," Troy stated, pulling his shirt over his nose. "Look, Rick, we need to borrow your car for our basketball game the day after tomorrow."

"Now you sound like *you* been cooking something," Rick joked.

"Oh, it's like that?"

"Yep! Shit, nigga, do you know how much money I have in that car?"

"I have no idea, but are you coming to the game with us then?"

"Nope, I have plans."

"You told us that the last time. Man, you've been slippin' big time!"

Rick smiled. "Ol' clever ass niggas. Where's Luqman?"

"Doing something, why?"

"Look, do you have a driver's license?" Rick asked.

"Yep, do you?"

"Fake ones, but at least I got some," Ricked joked.

"Damn, nigga. That test was easy. What happened?"

"Ever heard of the wrong answers?" Rick asked.

"Ever heard of studying?"

"Whatever. Look, how much money you donating?"

"Really? I'm in high school, Rick."

"Yeah, that's right. My bad. When y'all need the ride for again?"

"Day after tomorrow."

"All right, but take care of my shit and wash that bitch when you finish."

"You got that. We owe you one," Troy said with a huge smile.

"You sure know what to say, and I'm gone want that favor, too!"

Troy hurriedly left the stinky room before he fainted and rushed back to the kitchen.

"Everything good?" Luqman asked.

"Yep, we're on!" Troy dapped Luqman. "Oh, yeah, I think your brother's cooking skunk."

"That's them drugs."

"Wow! We need to team up on his ass—that shit gots to be dangerous."

"Now you see what I see, and smell, and deal with daily."

"Has he always been strung out like this?" Troy questioned.

"For as long as I can remember—he just hid it really well in the beginning. Take for instance, the nice vehicle and pretty decent clothes."

Troy took a good look around the small cluttered house. He now noticed the slow transformation from tidy into a complete smelly dump.

Ever since kindergarten, Troy and Luqman had been friends, so he knew how unfortunate his friend had been over the years. They were in their teens now, both six feet tall, slim built frames, and high expectations on eventually reaching the NBA. The beat down tattered blue and white house, with a porch that leaned from the cracked foundation was over sixty years old, and held the only memories of Rick and Luqman's grandparents.

"Man, I hope Rick keeps his word about us using his ride," Luqman stated.

"He sounds like he will."

"I don't know, man. If my grandparents were alive, they'd be devastated by the condition of this house. Hell, Rick's condition especially. Man, those drugs, Troy . . . Sometimes I feel like Rick's getting farther and farther away from me, man . . ."

"Yeah, I feel you. I got you though."

"I'm going to hold you to that, bruh. 'Cause I don't know what's going to happen to me if Rick ends up dead somewhere."

* * * *

Rick was James' age, twenty-five. He once was a high school basketball phenomenon. A six foot tall point guard with mad ball handling skills until an Achilles tear derailed a college scholarship. Drugs were his escape for the moment.

After Rick's grandmother died five years ago, there was a gradual transition from hard working man to hard working hustla. He quit his UPS job two years ago, then took to the streets full-time like the bubonic plague. Not knowing his actions would later lead to the destruction of the last beautiful aspect of his life.

Rick walked past Luqman and Troy as if they weren't seated in the front room. He was locked in on a major hustle. He'd been casing a hardware store on Peters Road for a couple weeks.

The old man, Mr. Barlow, owned the store for over thirty years, and Rick knew there was some major cheese in those safes that Barlow's ten-year-old grandson, Bobby, spoke about.

Bobby was Doug's son, and Mr. Barlow loved his son Doug dearly, but he just couldn't keep him out of jail, or off drugs. Mr. Barlow agreed to take custody of Bobby, being that his mother had four other kids and was also a drug addict.

Little Bobby often sat outside the hardware store, out of the way, unless his grandfather called for him. One day, Rick approached Bobby, then gave him a brand-new slingshot. Bobby really appreciated the gift and continued to get closer to Rick as time went on.

Rick, being the shrewd thinker, was slowly and methodically bleeding little Bobby out of vital information about Mr. Barlow and where he kept things, mainly his gun and money. Showing Bobby a brand-new pellet gun, they went for a walk and Bobby killed his first bird. Caught up in the excitement, Bobby revealed the whereabouts of his grandfather's gun, as he figured he could now trust Rick.

Bingo! Rick thought. That was the most important piece of information Rick would ever need. His plan worked like a charm. Rick gave little Bobby the gun as a gift.

While Bobby was sitting at his dope-fiend mother's house visiting his siblings, Rick crept out of the shadows and inside the hardware store after Mr. Barlow had closed the store doors.

"How'd you get in here?" Mr. Barlow asked, as he stepped from behind his desk with clenched fists.

"That's not important," Rick replied, with his ski mask on, tightly clutching a 9-millimeter pistol leveled at Mr. Barlow's chest. "What's important is that you hand over the money in that safe so I can be on my way."

Mr. Barlow studied the intruder a second with a sneer etched into his face. Then to make the matter worse, Mr. Barlow mumbled, "Got-dammit! Gotta hand over all my hard-earned money to this nigger who got the ups on me." He made his move for the pistol, but Rick fired his gun with pin-point accuracy into the chest of the old Klansman.

"Stupid muthafucka!" Rick shouted, then sprang into action, going to all the money spots little Bobby spoke of. He then trotted into the office to find the safe wide open. "Yes!" he stated, sliding the three nice stacks of money into his bag, then he headed for the door.

Once outside the store, Rick glanced around before heading in the direction of the Monte Carlo ducked off alongside the road. He sprinted a half mile in the direction of the vehicle, making it there in two minutes. He jumped into the car, then pulled off, removing the bloody shirt. Rick wiped down the pistol, wrapped it into the shirt, and then stuck it under the seat. He then made a mental note to pull over and toss the gun and shirt into the water. But right now, he had to purchase some drugs to get the gorilla off his back. Anxiously he counted the money while driving to see his drug connect. It came up to $5,600. He immediately called his connection, ordered a half ounce of cocaine, and a half ounce of heroin. At discounted prices, he copped both for $2,500. Soon after, Rick dropped the Monte Carlo off at the house for Luqman and Troy, hid $1,500 in cash, then dashed out the door.

CHAPTER 5
The Set-Up

Luqman and Troy both scored career highs in the game against Abramson High. The gym was packed with spectators from each side. With thirty points from Luqman, and twenty-eight from Troy, the bench only needed fifteen points for the 73-69 victory. Both played for Kennedy High for the last four years and were very popular. Both young men were very smart with 4.0 GPAs and scholarship offers. After the game, they managed to get plenty more phone numbers from the prettiest young ladies in attendance.

Rick's 1984 Monte Carlo was as clean as a whistle with a European grill, a forest green candy coated paint job with the pearl and peanut butter baby gator interior and top. The rims were 24-inch Davin floaters that made it seem as if the vehicle was traveling in slow motion.

Luqman and Troy left the school, then headed across the river to the West Bank, which is across the bridge from New Orleans, divided by the Mississippi river. The music was pumped up as they floated across the interstate. The fifteen-inch woofers sounded like four gorillas trying to break out of the trunk. Tupac could be heard as clear as a whistle inside the vehicle.

♪ *I won't deny it I'm a straight ridah, you don't want to fuck with me.* ♪

They both were bobbing their heads as they approached the Lafayette Street exit. Luqman turned down the music, knowing Jefferson Parish law enforcement would hook a nigga up as fast as the KKK.

A couple days earlier, Luqman met a lil honey in Jefferson Parish who also said she had a friend for Troy. Luqman made a left on Lafayette Street. A patrol vehicle pulled behind him.

"What did I do?" he asked Troy.

"Nothing. Just be cool and drive regular."

"You sure I didn't violate any traffic laws?" Luqman asked, second-guessing himself.

"Yeah man. I'm sure. Just keep on driving."

Luqman continued to drive and switched on the blinkers, indicating he was turning left. The patrol car did the same. Suddenly, the patrol car activated the red and blue lights.

Both young men cursed and Luqman pulled over, then told Troy to retrieve the insurance and registration out of the glove compartment. It was now 9:30 p.m., and Luqman cursed himself for being caught in Jefferson Parish at this time of night, even though it was 2008.

Suddenly, the officer shined his light through the rear window of the vehicle, then stated, "Driver, step out of the vehicle with your hands in the air. Passenger, place your hands on the dash." The officer exited the vehicle and pointed his gun at Luqman, who exited the Monte Carlo.

"Put both of your hands on the car, son," Officer Rositti stated, moving tactically. He searched Luqman, then placed all the contents from his pockets onto the patrol car. "Passenger, exit the vehicle with your hands on your head," the officer commanded, pointing his gun at Troy as he carefully moved toward the patrol car. At that moment, three other vehicles turned the corner with lights and sirens blaring.

"What's this? A traffic stop, or a robbery in progress?" Luqman asked, growing agitated.

"It's whatever we say it is. Now, what exactly are you doing over here this time of the night?"

"Why? Is it a crime to be out at night, or to be in Jefferson Parish at night?"

"Like I said, what's your business over here?"

"McDonalds on the east bank didn't have hot fries, so we came over here knowing y'all take care of the rich, predominantly white neighborhoods," Troy reasoned.

"Ohhh, you boys looking for trouble, huh? Well, you've come to the right place," Officer Sanchez assured them.

"No, Officer. We're trying to figure out why you pulled us over in your great parish of Jefferson," Troy said, visibly laughing.

"Let's see . . . basically, you two fit the description of fugitives believed to be in this area," Officer Rosotti lied.

"Did they just leave a high school basketball game in which at least 200 witnesses would attest we participated in? And were they driving a Monte Carlo?" Luqman asked.

"Not exactly, son, but I'll tell you what. We're going to go ahead and search this vehicle—with your permission, of course—and if things check out, you boys can be on your way," Officer Sanchez offered.

"Bullshit! Unless you got a search warrant, or something resembling one, we're going to decline that offer," Luqman shot back, mad as hell about the violation of his constitutional rights. The officer gritted his teeth, mumbled something under his breath, then pulled out his baton and wacked Luqman upside his head several times. Luqman cried out and covered his head as he fell to the ground after several blows rained down on him.

Crack! Pop, pop!

"Hey! What the fuck he beating on him for! Get off of him!" Troy shouted, witnessing Officer Sanchez hit Luqman with the long black flashlight, as if he were a runaway slave. Sanchez retreated after his fellow officer pulled him away. Luqman slowly stood to his feet. His face was now a bloody mess, leaking from multiple places as if holes had been poked in it.

"That there is because you resisted arrest," Officer Sanchez said to Luqman. "Now we got the right to search that there vehicle to see if you boys are hiding something that may in fact, be harmful to us. We're officers and law-abiding citizens of this great parish of Jefferson," he concluded, then spat tobacco juice in the direction of Luqman.

The other two officers were now tearing the Monte Carlo apart. They shined their lights into every crack and crevice of the vehicle, and then, those magic words were heard: "Bingo!" An officer

40

strolled over to Officer Sanchez, then whispered into his ear.

"Cuff 'em, now. These boys are going for a little ride," Officer Sanchez stated with a satisfied grin, walking toward the vehicle.

Officer Weatherspoon strolled over to the patrol car, then placed the clear bag marked "evidence" on the hood in front of Luqman and Troy. A gun and a bloody shirt were visible, along with the smirk on Officer Sanchez's face.

"Looks like you boys should've waited them ten minutes for those McDonald fries on the East bank," Officer Rositti stated. The other officers began laughing. "Is there anything you boys would like me to know before we take this ride downtown?" Officer Sanchez asked.

"We ain't got shit to say to you or your Klansmen!" Troy angrily stated. "Pussy muthafuckas!" *Where the hell that shit come from?* Troy thought as he remembered the conversations he and James used to practice in case the police ever had him in custody.

"Rule #1: Don't say shit about nothing, but have your attorney present for any questioning."

Rule #2: "Same as rule number one!"

"Well, boys, I guess we're going to have to place y'all under arrest," Officer Sanchez said.

"On what charges?" Troy asked.

"Oh, well, we'll think of a few things along the way," Officer Rositti said.

* * * * * * *

The officers brought Luqman and Troy to the investigation bureau. They separated them, then offered them cigarettes and food. Both declined. Two detectives were assigned to each young man, as Officer Rosotti went digging for information of any kind that may involve the commission of a crime with a gun lately.

Detectives Jamison and Royal entered the room that Luqman occupied.

"How are you doing, son?" Jamison asked.

"How would you be doing?" Luqman answered.

"This isn't about me, boy. Now, if you want to make it to jail before feed up, I suggest you get to cooperating."

"Man, fuck feed up! Actually, since you think so highly of the meal, tell them to give you mine. Furthermore, until you explain what charges I'm on, there's really nothing to talk about."

* * * * * * *

In the other interrogation room, Detectives Curry and David were having the same problem with Troy. "How many cops does it take to throw a suspect down the stairs? None. He fell," Troy said, void of emotion. "How many cops does it take to screw in a lightbulb? None. They just beat the room for being black. I've got about twenty more of these."

Detective Curry took a swing at Troy. Troy ducked and Curry swung again and missed. His partner Detective David pulled him away and held him in a strong grip. "You cool?" David asked. Curry nodded yes.

"What part of lawyer don't you hillbilly muthafuckas understand over here?" Troy insisted with a grin.

"Let's get out of here before I do something I'll regret later," Detective Curry stated to his partner.

"You've already done that, with your stupid ass. Thought you were going to crack me— the little nigger, huh? Fooled that ass! Oh yeah," Troy continued. "Where'd you get them badges? Dummy dot com?"

"That's it, you black muthafucker!" Detective Curry rushed back into the room, and then slapped Troy so hard, he spun around in the chair. Blood leaked from his bottom lip. Troy tasted the blood. He smiled at the detective who was now being restrained by his partner.

"That's all you got, pussy? Bet you couldn't do that with these cuffs off!" Troy challenged.

The detective was tempted, but realized he had too much at stake to risk it on a nobody. They quietly left.

"That's what I thought, girls," Troy continued.

* * * * * * *

All four detectives met up at the coffee pot. "No luck for you guys either?" Curry asked. Jamison and Royal shook their heads in disgust. Officer Rosotti continued writing his report, then thought about entering the license plate into his computer. The detectives now strolled to his office.

"Find anything?" Jamison inquired.

"No, nothing yet, just about to enter the license plate numbers into the computer to see what surfaces," Officer Rosotti stated. "Bingo!" he shouted.

All the detectives set their donuts and coffee down and hurried over to the computer.

"What do you have?" Jamison anxiously asked.

"Remember the murder/robbery that happened at the hardware store?"

"Mr. Barlow's store?" Jamison questioned.

"Exactly!" Rosotti said.

"Hey, I interviewed the guy who claimed to have seen two guys jogging away from the direction of the store. They jumped into a vehicle matching the description of these guys' vehicle, come to think of it. But only half of the plate was verified in the statement."

"Good thing you entered it under the partial plate also," Rosotti remarked.

"Let's go see what these boys got to say about this," Curry suggested.

"Look, I'll pick up our eyewitness, so we can positively identify our prime suspects," Jamison volunteered.

Detective Curry strolled into the room occupied by Troy, confidence illuminating through his sneaky grin. He leaned against the wall for a second, just staring at Troy. He yawned as he prepared once again, to ridicule the detective.

"I must give it to you, detective. You're made of titanium, or that shit the Terminator's made of, but that still don't make you smart! Shit, they don't make hillbillies like they used to. You take a licking and keep on ticking, with your stupid ass. What the fuck you want now? These nuts?" Troy broke out into laughter.

"That's real funny, my nigger," Detective Curry shot back. "I came to let you know we figured out where that gun was used."

"So, fuckin' what! Whooptie doo! Whatchu' want? A cookie?

No, no, maybe a cracker, Cracker!"

"That's some nice joke you got there, Toby! However, the joke I have is much funnier, depending on who's telling it. Anyway, we got this witness that saw two nigger boys running from the scene of a murder. That's right. This witness identified the getaway car as a green Monte Carlo with the same license plate on you boys' car, ya' heard me?" Curry mocked. "Oh, you didn't like that one? No problem. I got more, it's a double header." He smiled. "Okay, okay, back to the joke. Well, it seems we're about to play a game called peek-a-boo when the witness gets here. Feel me?"

Troy sat there steaming, but said nothing.

"What's wrong, my nigger? You don't like my jokes? Maybe it's because it isn't a joke, huh?" Curry inquired.

"Maybe you don't only need surgery to correct that unusually small brain of yours, but it seems those ears don't work much either," Troy stated seriously. "Bitch, you still not scaring shit, and what part of 'suck my dick' don't you understand?"

"Keep that attitude, lil nigger. You're going to need it when you get to Angola State Penitentiary, and then become somebody's whore!"

"Just like your momma, with her ugly ass," Troy shot back.

Detective Curry walked out of the room laughing, now feeling like he had the upper hand, finally.

CHAPTER 6
The Snitch

Wendal Law, the crack-head who swore he saw two men running from the direction of the robbery, and then jumped into a car, was standing in a room occupied by Detectives Curry and David. He'd been shown pictures of Luqman and Troy earlier, then told detectives he wasn't sure of their identities. That's when the detectives threatened to bring him to jail on an outstanding warrant for theft over five hundred dollars—a possible ten-year bid.

"Okay, officer. Let me take another look at those pictures. It could be them, but I haven't had my medicine yet, if you know what I mean."

"Are you trying to shake us down for drugs, Wendal?" David asked.

"That depends, Detective."

"On what?"

"On how bad you want these fellows to be the ones who robbed that store," Wendal replied, with a buck-toothed smile.

Detective David grinned, then shook his head. "I see. So, what's it going to cost?"

"Depends on what I have to do." Wendal licked his lips as he looked through the window across the street at a liquor store, wishing he could get a drink.

"First, you must identify these two pieces of shit we have at the bureau as the two seen running to the getaway car. Then you're going to testify in court to make sure justice is served for Mr. Barlow."

45

"That sounds dangerous, Detective," Wendal suggested as his nerves began to unravel from the lack of alcohol and crack. He twisted his head as if it was on a swivel, looking for a bump of cocaine or a swig of alcohol. "If I can't get you to look out for me until this is all over, I'll have to decline," he suggested.

Detective David looked at Wendal a few brief seconds, then walked out the room and outside to his vehicle. He looked around to make sure he wasn't being watched, then popped open his trunk and retrieved the ounce of crack. He waved for Wendal and Curry to come outside. He then walked around the car, opened the door for Wendal, and told him to get in. The three men pulled off, now headed to the detective's bureau.

"Let me assure you, Wendal, if you fuck me on this—you're a dead crack-head! From time to time, I'll give you something as I get it. But you get it through your head, this ain't a free crack party, understood?" Wendal nodded in agreement.

Detective David tossed the ounce of crack to Wendal. Eyes bugged wide, Wendal gripped it and pulled it close to his heart as if it was a defibrillator. He almost caught a heart attack from the excitement of having so much to smoke! Detective David looked through the rearview mirror at Wendal. "Don't smoke it all in one place," he stated.

They pulled into the bureau's parking lot, then exited the vehicle. Once inside, the only people in the room were Troy and Luqman, with Wendal Law on the opposite side of the two-way mirror.

"That's them," Wendal stated as he stared at Troy and Luqman.

"Are you sure?" Captain Juarez asked.

"Two hundred percent sure. A hundred for each of them," Wendal said, then wiped the sweat from his forehead.

"Book 'em on one count of second degree murder, and one count of armed robbery," Captain Juarez commanded.

"No problem, Captain," Detective Curry gladly said. He walked into the room occupied by Luqman and Troy.

"Well, my niggers. We have a little problem. Seems our lil game of peek-a-boo has gotten you boys in a lot of trouble. That means our witness has positively identified you boys. So, let's take a ride downtown, fellas."

Luqman looked at Troy, then shook his head.

"You crackers will try anything under the sun to get two niggas off the streets, huh?" Troy questioned.

"No comment, my nigger. We got everything we need, unless you want to talk to us about something else," Curry offered.

"If you got everything you need, then what else is there to talk about?"

Just in case you boys want to confess," Curry added.

We must get out of this shit! How stupid could Rick be? He left a murder weapon in his car. This doesn't look good, Luqman thought.

* * * * * * *

James and Deon stood at the courtroom door of section G, in Jefferson Parish waiting for the doors to be opened. They were there before the crowd, and even the press. Every news station in Jefferson Parish had a representative waiting to get a glimpse of the two men charged with the murder that sent shockwaves throughout the parish. Primarily, because Mr. Barlow was respected throughout the parish.

Janet and Doug Barlow stood in the hallway, also waiting. Janet, Mr. Barlow's widow, couldn't understand why her husband would be the target of these killers. Doug stood beside his mother with his hands balled into fists resting at his side; his thoughts were of pure hatred. Nothing or no one would prohibit him from seeking justice.

The bailiff opened the doors, then everyone filed into the courtroom. The family and media all strolled to the left side of the courtroom, seated behind the Assistant District Attorney. Also tagging along were the greedy lawyers hustling more clients to swindle.

Chatter resounded all around the courtroom as the inmates were brought in on the chain gang. Troy and Luqman led the pack. Deon waved at her brother, but James stayed focused on his surroundings. He hated seeing Troy in this situation. He also never felt comfortable around the racist crackers in Jefferson Parish. Therefore, James hired Luqman and Troy the best damn lawyer in New Orleans, Mr. Johnny Jackson.

Seated on the front row, James and Deon heard all the insidious remarks about their brother Troy and his friend. James looked around at all the family and media talking amongst themselves as they stared, then pointed at Luqman and Troy. Suddenly, as he scanned the courtroom, his eyes locked with Doug Barlow. James looked at the white boy with death in his eyes, but he knew it only activated the hate within Doug because he'd lost his father. *That boy doesn't know what he's dealing with, and he probably doesn't care either, but he should,* James thought. His mind instinctively began constructing a plan to punish the young man for disrespecting him. Then his mind eased up as he thought about the boy acting without the benefit of his intellect. He would spare him this time.

The lawyer walked into the courtroom, spoke to James, then went directly to Luqman and Troy seated in the box with the other nine inmates. He was five feet eleven inches tall, clean shaven, and a handsome fifty years of age. He stood tall and dignified in his brown pin-striped suit, of proud Haitian heritage, and with his Tulane law degree as his proudest accomplishment.

"I'm Johnny Jackson," he stated, introducing himself. "James has paid me to represent both of you. Today is a bail hearing, nothing more. The state will oppose bail, but you have a constitutional right to bail. However, the judge will not see it that way, but I'll do my best."

"All rise in the court!" the bailiff ordered. "Judge Riley's court is now in session!"

The Assistant District Attorney, Vinney Pachero strolled up to the podium.

"First order of business is the bail hearing of Luqman Shabazz and Troy Johnson, Your Honor," the DA stated.

"Johnny Jackson representing the defendants, Your Honor."

"The state is opposing bail, Your Honor. Primarily due to the defendants possibly being flight risks, as well as the aggravating circumstances surrounding the case." The DA stated.

"Your Honor, the defendants have no prior arrests of any kind, both are still in high school, maintain 4.0 grade point averages, with employment," Attorney Jackson stated, stretching the truth. "And, as a matter of their eighth amendment right, they are entitled to bail that is reasonable, no matter the charges, nor the circumstances surrounding them. The defendants by law are presumed to be innocent until proven otherwise, Your Honor."

Judging by the way Judge Riley looked around the courtroom at the media and family of the victim, James could sense the judge's thoughts of political dread. If he allowed Troy and Luqman bail, he'd lose his seat in the next election six months away. *Damn!* James thought.

"Gentleman," Judge Riley began. "I have weighed in on this matter, and due to the magnitude of this case, I feel it's in the best interest of the case going forward in a timely manner, and without delays, that these young men stay incarcerated. My ruling is that bond is denied."

"Note our objection, Your Honor, and we'd like to take a writ to the appellate court," Mr. Jackson stated.

"Very well, objection and appeal noted. And I'll see you back on the issue in thirty days," Judge Riley ordered. The chatter inside the courtroom grew louder, and the judge yelled, "Order in the court!"

James and Deon stood up and headed for the door. He was not pleased, but the thirty thousand dollars paid to Mr. Jackson to represent Troy and Luqman put a dent in the two hundred grand he negotiated with Osama.

* * * * * * *

Osama and James were at the warehouse in New Orleans East training.

"What are your plans for the $200,000 you have?" Osama asked.

"The truth?" James asked.

"That's a good place to start."

"I'm going to score a few kilos of cocaine, take over a few money spots, then invest."

"That's it?"

"That's what I know."

"There are a lot of problems with that plan."

"Doesn't mean it won't work."

"Your plan means war," Osama reasoned.

"Yours too," James countered.

"But I don't wage war against my own people."

"But, bringing war to your own people is okay?" James questioned.

"Look at it this way—war isn't the answer, it is the result," Osama expressed. "There lies the fundamental difference in our plans. Within your plan, war is the answer in order to acquire turf, in order to sell drugs. Within my plan, war is the result of me standing against others imposing their ideas, religions, and thievery upon my people."

"That's deep. And one day I hope to implement that type of plan, as well as be the person in position to stop the war against my people," James emphasized. "But today, I'm not that person."

"Tomorrow, perhaps, if that is what you truly desire."

"Look, Osama, I desire a lot at this time, and survival is at the top of my list. Family is the next, and getting in position to make some real changes in the future is the best I can do right now."

"I can't argue with you, James. I am not in your shoes, so I'll not act as if I am. But, we have enough time to come up with better solutions," Osama suggested.

"I look forward to your input, Osama. But one last question. What makes Al-Qaida different from ISIS?" James asked.

"Many things. I think from a tactical standpoint, both Al-Qaida and ISIS employ different ways of showing the world their effectiveness. ISIS' agenda has everything to do with power and wealth to support the acquisition of land and its resources to ultimately combine it all to create its own Islamic state. They have created a resemblance of ethnic and religious cleansing comparable to that of Hitler's holocaust. Al Qaida has no such agenda. Yet we do strategies and prepare to fight the same hate-filled war being thrusted upon us. We have a collection of foreign militaries occupying our sovereignty, waging war against us in the name of saving who? Us from ourselves? But although there seems to be a lot of senseless deaths, it happens to be the way of the world, as it pertains to war."

"Do you mean by way of the carnage we witness on the news?"

"Not necessarily. But consider it's your news station because it serves their purpose in renaming our war as terrorism and us terrorists. Make no mistake about it, Al-Qaida is at war, but consider this. It's in our own regions, yet against foreign warmongers. We are not waging wars in the United States, or army rebels to fight against their countrymen. America has an agenda; they have always had agendas. Just as they did when America armed me and my fighters to fight for them before the collapse at the World Trade Center."

"I'll have to chew on that for a while. I'll see you tomorrow," James said, ambivalent as to how he'd pull everything together concerning his own plans.

CHAPTER 7
The Bought Testimony

Wendal Law crept up on the witness stand decked out in his brand-new Brooks Brother's three-piece suit, courtesy of the district attorney's office. The DA's office managed to take the case to trial in record time, no doubt, anxious to get it over with while their crack head star witness was still breathing. Wendal had been living high on the hog for the last few months. He was given a nice, cozy hotel room miles away from the neighborhood in which he once dwelled, smoking his life away. His habit had gotten worse. He was now averaging an ounce a week. The detectives created a monster. Wendal knew things were coming to an end, from the way they now talked to him when he called them for more dope. But he also knew they needed him, so he didn't give a damn!

All motions filed by Luqman and Troy's attorney were promptly denied by Judge Riley. He continued to move the case forward as if it were his only one, as promised.

James and Deon were seated in the front row as usual. Now, James wondered why he didn't just kill the redneck judge. He glanced at Luqman's brother, Rick, who was seated beside Deon. He apologized for the mistake he made in having the gun in the car. At the request of Luqman and Troy, James spared his life. Rick had not touched any drugs since the day James snatched him from the motel.

"State your name for the record," Assistant District Attorney, Vinny Pachero stated.

"Wendal Law," he replied.

"Mr. Law, on the night the hardware store had just been robbed—"

"Objection, Your Honor," Mr. Jackson interrupted. "Mr. Law never knew at that time a hardware store had been robbed."

"Objection sustained."

"I'll rephrase the question, Your Honor," the DA insisted.

"Mr. Law, on the night of June 28, 2008, you told detectives you witnessed two men running from the direction of Mr. Barlow's hardware store. Is that correct?"

"That's correct," Wendal stated, trying to avoid eye contact with anyone but the District Attorney.

"So, as you look around the courtroom here today, do you see those two men present?"

"Yes sir," Wendal replied.

"Are you one hundred percent sure of the identifications you are making today?"

"Yes sir."

"Do you remember anything else about that night, what the suspects may have did, or said, that would make you remember them?"

"I just seen them jump into that older model green car," Wendal claimed.

The DA strolled over to his table and picked up some photos. Once he approached the defense's table, he showed Mr. Jackson the photos, and then slid them on the projector. Rick's green 1984 Monte Carlo appeared.

"This is State's exhibit number six, Your Honor. Mr. Law, is this the vehicle you saw that night?"

"That's the vehicle, sir," Wendal stated, loud and clear.

"What makes you so sure?" the DA asked, sensing blood in the water.

"Because I also remember the first three numbers on the license plate in that picture."

"How are you only able to remember those numbers?"

"Because them boys were in a mighty hurry, shooting all that dirt and rocks in my face as they sped away."

Vinny smiled. "Ladies and gentlemen of the jury, note that Mr. Law has identified these two men running from the scene of the crime."

"Objection, Your Honor!" Johnny Jackson was on his feet instantly. "That's pure speculation that my clients were running from a crime scene."

"Objection sustained. Mr. Pachero, we have crossed this path. Move on," Judge Riley ordered.

"One more question for the witness, Your Honor," stated Vinny.

"Did you have any idea the weapon that killed Mr. Barlow was inside this vehicle you've identified today?"

"No, sir."

"Your witness, counsellor," Vinny stated confidently, as he strolled back to his table.

Mr. Jackson stood up from the defense table with notes in hand, then strolled up to the podium.

All eyes were on the high-priced attorney, impeccably dressed in a gray suit, gray tie, soft leather shoes, with a starched white handkerchief that accentuated the 24-carat gold Rolex.

"Mr. Law, do you wear glasses?"

"No sir," Wendal replied.

"Do you have any problems with your vision?"

"Not that I know of," he admitted.

"How long were you staked out before you saw those men jump into that car?"

"Maybe twenty minutes," Wendal said, looking toward the ceiling before answering.

"What exactly were you doing in that area?"

"I was resting a little bit."

"Was it because you were smoking crack at that time?"

"Objection, Your Honor!"

"Objection overruled. You may answer the question," Judge

Riley ruled.

"I was earlier," Wendal admitted.

"When was the last time you smoked, before you started resting?"

"About thirty minutes," he stated, looking at the ceiling.

"Do you also drink?"

"Yes sir."

"Had you been drinking that night?"

Wendal looked over to the DA, Vinny Pachero.

"Your Honor, could you instruct the witness to answer the question?" Mr. Jackson stated.

"Answer the question," Judge Riley commanded.

"Yes sir. I had a little something."

"How much is a little something?"

"About a pint of Heavenly Hill," Wendal confessed.

"So, were you tired because you were drinking an eighty proof bottle of alcohol?"

"No sir. I wasn't drunk; just tired."

"Did you go to work earlier that day?"

"No sir. I don't work."

"Okay, so where exactly were you hiding?"

"In some bushes," Wendal replied.

"Now, let's see," Mr. Jackson stated, looking to the ceiling like Wendal. "You expect us to believe that you didn't fall into those bushes after smoking crack and drinking eighty percent proof liquor on a hot sunny day. All day!

Vinny sprang to his feet. "Objection, Your Honor! That's not a question. The witness doesn't expect the defense to believe anything but their side."

"I'll rephrase. Mr. Law, what time did you begin drinking and smoking that day?"

"Early, I guess. About nine to ten in the morning."

"And you stopped at nine p.m. that night?"

"That's about right."

"So, you're telling us here today, that you can drink from sun up to sun down and not be drunk?"

Wendal looked around for help from the DA, but he remained frozen-stiff and scared to look at Wendal.

"I wasn't drunk, sir."

"Okay," Mr. Jackson said with sarcasm. Then you smoked crack all day and ended up in bushes on the side of the road. And you were not affected from the use of drugs, neither by drinking, that you could clearly see two men running to a car at full speed. Is that your story?"

"That's what I seen," Wendal stated, now looking at the floor.

"Your Honor, could we please have a recess? The witness has been on the stand a very long time," Vinny pleaded.

"Just a few more questions, Your Honor," Mr. Jackson lied. He wasn't going to let Wendal off that easy.

"Very well, counselor. You may proceed," Judge Riley ordered.

"Mr. Law, what color clothes did you say these men had on when you saw them?"

Wendel searched his mind, wondering if he said a color in his statement. "Ummm, I think they had on black sweatshirts with hoods."

"Are you one hundred percent sure about that, too?"

Wendal looked at the district attorney again, who was sweating bricks, sensing his case was going down the drain.

"Yes, I'm one hundred percent sure."

Mr. Jackson smiled at the answer, then he strolled over to the defense table. He retrieved a photo, then showed it to the DA, whose body sank a little lower into his chair.

"This is exhibit number two, Your Honor," Mr. Jackson stated, and then slid the photo on the projector. The jurors were now looking at a white shirt stained with blood.

"Mr. Law, does this shirt look familiar?" Mr. Jackson questioned.

Wendal's beady eyes searched for any remembrance of the shirt, then satisfied with his statement, he stated, "No."

"Well, Mr. Law. This shirt was worn by the person who robbed, then killed Mr. Barlow that night." Mr. Jackson let the first part of the bad news sink into Wendal's mind. Then he stated, "So, if the suspects had on black sweatshirts, the blood from Mr. Barlow and the gunpowder shouldn't be on this shirt right here, am I correct?"

Wendal shrugged, not knowing what to say.

"Furthermore, Mr. Law, what are the chances the suspects somehow shot Mr. Barlow, then had a sweatshirt handy to put on after the robbery?"

"Don't seem like that would make much sense," Wendal stated.

"You are correct, Mr. Law. So considering the person who committed this crime had on that white shirt on the projector, instead of the black hoods, is it safe to say that maybe these two may not have robbed that hardware store?"

"That's a possibility," Wendal agreed.

"So, Mr. Law, you are testifying today that you don't know who actually robbed then killed Mr. Barlow, and you are only identifying these men because they were running from the direction of the store."

"That's correct," Wendal stated.

The DA sprang into action. "Your Honor, if we could take that recess now." He ran his fingers through his hair in frustration.

"Mr. Jackson, are you done with this witness?" Judge Riley asked.

Mr. Jackson stood, knowing he'd proven reasonable doubt, and any more poking around would be overkill. "Yes, Your Honor. But I reserve the right to call the witness again, if the state wishes to have a rebuttal of this witness, considering my cross examination was interrupted by a break," Mr. Jackson insisted, then glanced over at the DA, Vinny Pachero, daring him to put Wendal back on the stand.

"The state's finished with this witness, Your Honor," he immediately interjected.

"Very well. This court is now in recess," Judge Riley stated, then banged his gavel.

Thirty minutes later, everyone filed back into the courtroom. James, Deon, and Rick sat on the front row, as usual.

"Your Honor, the state rests."

"How about you, Mr. Jackson?" Judge Riley asked.

"The defense rests as well," Mr. Jackson stated.

Subsequently, Judge Riley read the jury its instructions, and the bailiff sent them into the jury room.

Mr. Jackson assured James that there was nothing more he could add to show reasonable doubt. They had done that, and then some. There simply was nobody who could place them at the scene of the crime, not even their star witness.

* * * * * * *

As usual, Tray and Jaafar had been seated all the way in the back of the courtroom watching and waiting on justice for Luqman and Troy.

Tray was also convinced that Mr. Jackson had exposed the state's case. Their star witness worked against them more than he helped. Yet Tray knew from the past, Jefferson Parish possessed an accomplished history of racial discrimination against its African American citizens.

However, the Parish's crown jewel was achieved on August 29, 2005, when thousands of evacuees attempted to cross the greater New Orleans Bridge to escape the rising waters and devastation of Hurricane Katrina. They were denied access to Jefferson Parish. At the foot of the bridge, barricades were set up, along with armed law enforcement officials to prevent many sick, elderly, and dehydrated New Orleaneans from getting help and shelter from the storm. Many men, women, and children would ultimately die on that same bridge, with nowhere to go, thanks to Jefferson Parish.

On many occasions Tray attempted to buy land in Jefferson Parish, but was blocked by other residents. Places like Old Metairie were full of older residents, politicians, and retired law enforcement. They all had one thing in common: Racism!

Tray's businesses were located in New Orleans rather than Jefferson Parish. It was not by choice, but what could he do? He was a businessman and learned to avoid Jefferson Parish for anything. Besides, his clothing stores were all making good money, and he was able to give back to the communities. He provided jobs, invested in affordable housing, and sponsored youth programs throughout the New Orleans area.

He was the only child of working class parents. Mrs. Rosano King was a nurse, and her husband, Mr. Lawrence King, was a welder. Both parents were able to retire, due to Tray's success. They now enjoyed traveling and spending time with their granddaughters. Tray's eldest daughter, Kelley, was twenty-five and the youngest, Laura was twenty-two.

Kelley graduated from Southern University, and was now a registered nurse. Laura, followed suit, attending Southern and graduating in business. She was also a model. Kelley and Laura both enjoyed spending time with family and living in California. Both of their careers were successful.

Other than Wayne, Jaafar was Tray's closest friend, and he was also a man of exceptional character and martial arts skills. Jaafar was a lethal force in every sense of the word. The fact was made evident when Jaafar rescued an employee who was at one of Tray's stores. A masked robber entered the store armed with an automatic weapon while Jaafar was shopping.

The gunman held the assault rifle up to the employee's face and demanded money from the register and safe. Jaafar was still inside the dressing room. Instinctively, he sprang into action by dropping to the floor and crawling underneath the half door and into the open area. Now he was able to see the lone robber and to judge distance. He slowly slithered into position directly behind the robber, whose attention was trained on the employee emptying the safe. That would prove to be a costly mistake.

Jaafar crept up to the robber as silent as a ninja and grabbed the barrel of the gun with one hand, then the banana clip with the other. He wrestled with the robber for the gun, and in the process, dropped down into a vicious leg whip that made the robber scream from the pain. Once the robber hit the floor, Jaafar ripped the gun from his hand. The amateur robber was allowed to leave empty-handed. The employee called Tray who made it to the store within five minutes. Tray and Jaafar had been inseparable ever since.

He and Tray had taken a one-hour break and returned to the courtroom. The bailiff informed the lawyers, the DA, and the media that a verdict had been reached. The courtroom was still packed in anticipation of a quick verdict.

Judge Riley looked around the courtroom. "Bailiff, bring in the jury," he stated.

One by one the twelve jurors and two alternates filed into the courtroom. The jury was comprised of ten whites and two blacks, with the alternates also being white. The typical racial makeup of a Jefferson Parish jury. It bolstered racially motivated mass incarceration and upheld a 10-2 verdict concocted to take the place of a unanimous verdict; thus, eliminating the black vote all together.

"Ladies and gentlemen of the jury, have you reached a verdict?"

The foreman stood up. "We have, Your Honor." He passed the slip of paper to the bailiff, who then handed it to the judge, who read it, nodded, then stated, "Very well."

"May the defendants rise?"

Troy and Luqman rose.

"We, the jury, find Luqman Shabazz and Troy Johnson, guilty on all counts of murder in the second degree and armed robbery."

The courtroom broke out in cheers and applause as Mr. Barlow's family and the media were in a frenzy about the verdict.

Neither Tray nor Jaafar were surprised when James casually stood up, looked around the courtroom, and then stated, "So be it!" He then pledged a lifetime of war against Jefferson Parish and its court system. All three of them strolled out of the courtroom.

Troy and Luqman had to be restrained. Troy stated to the judge, "You must be a fool if you think Troy Johnson is going to spend his life in prison."

Luqman spat in the DA's face as he was being escorted out of the courtroom.

Tray, who remained seated in the back, expressed to Jaafar, "Today is the start of a war that will rage on for many years with James. Revenge will be taken against Jefferson Parish. We will need to be there raging war right alongside our young friend," he suggested.

Jaafar nodded, then placed his hand on Tray's shoulder.

"Let's go, my friend. We have a call to make."

They strolled out into the hallway, away from the drama inside the courtroom. Tray pulled out his cell phone, then dialed James.

* * * * * * *

Seeing that Deon was still in tears only added to James' boiling anger. He walked silently through the halls with Deon and Rick beside him as they headed for the elevator. The ride to the lobby was silent with the exception of Deon's sniffles. The doors opened with a ding, and they stepped off.

"Hello?" James said curiously to the person calling from a blocked number. He had just exited the courthouse and was walking toward the parking garage.

"Just listen," the caller stated. "When you get to your car, there will be an envelope on your driver's side front tire. It will contain a key to a room at the Family Inn Hotel on Chef Menteur Highway. This is only a band aid for a very deep wound that has been inflicted upon your family. But it's a start toward the healing process."

"Who are you?" James inquired.

"All you need to know right now is, I am a friend who has been around a very long time." The caller hung up.

Traffic was very heavy as the news began reporting that the jury had convicted Luqman Shabazz and Troy Johnson of the hardware store murder. James and Deon rounded the corner, then entered the parking garage, now picking up speed as he thought about what the caller had said.

"What's wrong?" Deon asked.

"Nothing much. I just received a call from someone claiming to be a friend and left something at the car."

"Did they say what it was pertaining to?"

"He said it's a band aid for a very deep wound."

The 750 BMW appeared as they rounded the final corner inside the garage.

James deactivated the alarm, then slid his hand under the wheel well of the car, retrieving the envelope off the tire. He flipped it a couple times curiously, analyzing it.

"Gone get in," he then told Deon and Rick.

James scanned the parking garage carefully for anyone suspicious. He noticed nothing, so he started opening the simple white envelope. There was a note inside along with the key. He read the note, then handed it to Deon.

"Just a temporary fix," Deon read the note. "What's this, a wild goose chase?"

James backed up the BMW, preparing to exit the parking garage. "Don't know yet, but I will soon find out," he stated.

CHAPTER 8
Sweet Revenge

"Stay here," James stated, after pulling the BMW into the Family Inn Hotel parking lot as instructed. He viewed each door until he reached number 68. He looked around for a second, then reached over Deon, retrieving his 9-millimeter Beretta out of the glove compartment.

"Oh no, you are not about to leave me," Deon stated, reaching into her purse and retrieving the .380. She cocked it back, sliding one in the chamber.

"I don't have no iron, but I'm coming too," Rick insisted.

"Okay, you just stay behind me," James demanded.

They exited the vehicle, then James strolled over to the room and knocked on the door. There was no answer, so he inserted the key, turned the doorknob, and then pushed it open. A chair was positioned in the middle of the floor with a man seated in it. His back was to the door, and he was duct taped to the chair. James immediately signalled to close the door, then walked around the chair to see who it could be.

"I'll be damned," James stated. "Look at this piece of shit, white-men-loving, ratting-ass nigga here."

Curious to know who it was, Deon and Rick walked around the chair to get a good look. Once Deon obtained a visual, she slapped Wendal so hard, you could momentarily see her hand impression.

"Oh yeah, you little bitch-ass nigga. I got your pussy ass now," Rick excitedly stated. "James, please don't shoot this sell-out. Can you let me do my thing?" he asked as he snapped out his switch blade. "I want this nigga to suffer, and both of you can have a ringside seat. Man, look," he continued. "I know I started this shit, but now I would like to end it." He pleaded further, "It doesn't erase the fact that I'm responsible for Luqman and Troy heading to Angola, but they sure would like this crack-head rat to do a whole lot of suffering."

James looked over to Deon. She nodded, then said, "Why not let him do his thing, whatever that is." James nodded.

"Y'all sit over there." Rick pointed toward the door as he pushed the bed in that direction, so he could have more floor to work with. He dragged Wendell in the chair across the floor to the spot the bed once occupied.

"Mmmm mmph!" Wendal struggled to get words out from under the tape across his mouth.

"I don't want to talk, muthafucka!" Rick shouted. "We about to do this shit the dumb way, you best believe that. I hope them crackers paid your stupid ass enough." Rick began cutting away Wendal's clothing with the razor-sharp knife. Wendal's terrified eyes continued to relay the message his mouth was unable to, but Rick was not listening. He knew Wendal was scared, and he should be. The nice suit Wendal once donned was being carved off him as well as chunks of his flesh, until he was naked, ashamed, and in intense agony. Blood gushed from the wounds like a fountain. Rick then slit the tape that held Wendal to the chair and kicked the chair out of his way. Once Wendal fell to the floor, Rick grabbed him and flipped him on his stomach. He straddled his leg in a way that he was facing his feet. Lightly, Rick ran the knife over both feet. Then he aggressively held them down and sliced one open from the top, then dragged the knife down to the bottom. Wendal moaned and groaned, trying to get free as blood gushed from the wound. Rick sliced open the other foot, then began carving off meat until they were both bloody bone. Wendal moaned and groaned through the entire ordeal, but it fell on deaf ears.

Deon and James sat there unaffected by the gruesome scene without turning away. Rick kept slicing meat like a butcher, until he was almost to the knee. The entire bone was visible after the calf muscle had been carved away. Rick then plunged the knife into the other half as Wendal wriggled in agony, then collapsed.

"Wake up, you sorry piece of shit!" Rick shouted, beating Wendal across the head with the butt of his knife. He jumped up, then hurried into the bathroom with an ice bucket, filled it with cold water, strolled back into the room, and doused it into Wendal's face. He slowly began to awaken.

"I'm not finished with you, muthafucka!" Rick shouted. Wendal tried to focus, but the blows to his face welded his eyes shut. "Open your fuckin' eyes, bitch!" Rick commanded. Wendal only groaned in pain. He grabbed Wendal by the neck and dug the knife into his eye sockets. Blood squirted into Rick's face. Within minutes of the brutal assault, Wendal's body went limp; he was teetering on the brink of death. After he released Wendal, he stood up and began laughing and crying at the same time. Suddenly, he fell to his knees thinking about the pain his brother would have to endure because of his foolish mistake.

Deon and James stood.

"It's time to go," James stated calmly to Rick.

Two weeks later, Luqman and Troy received life sentences. They were brought to the Louisiana State penitentiary in Angola, Louisiana.

* * * * * * *

With Osama's strategic input, James captured the entire 9th Ward and uptown area in the city of New Orleans. It took them ninety days to terrorize the street hustlers. James was always inclined to believe that whoever chose the game, inherits the cut throat provisions that govern the game. Once you sign up, there are no rules. Those were the rules!

James had never seen street corners so empty where hustlers usually roam, until Osama and his team of Taliban soldiers began kidnapping them, then dropping the mutilated hustlers' bodies back on the corners without their testicles or eyes. The sight of this paralyzed others.

"Are you sure you want my help?" Osama had asked.

"I can't do it alone, so yes," James said.

The torture machines inside the warehouse did everything to a human body that was unimaginable. There were skin strippers, eyeball pluckers, ear clippers, finger and toenail peelers, neck breakers, and tongue splitters. They were all utilized on those who were not on James' team, and who violated his turf laws.

James walked into the middle of the warehouse, then looked 'around at all the menacing machines. *Was it all worth it?* The repeated screams from the men who were strapped to the chair, then hung by the mechanical devices kept playing in his head.

"Are you okay?" Osama asked.

"Not really," James responded, now having second thoughts.

"Anything I can help you with?"

"You've done enough, Osama."

"Are you sure? There's plenty more tactics I haven't implemented."

"Look, this torture shit has become the problem," James stated, menacingly.

"Has it not helped you accomplish what you set out to do?"

"Yes, but my problem is that I'm executing the same people I'm in the struggle with. How does that work?"

"A rise will always be tied to casualties. However, our mission is not about how many are killed, it's how many we have frightened. This is what these machines are designed to do. This is the blueprint to your success." Osama gestured toward the torturous devices.

"No, I have other blueprints that are not tied to the destruction of my own people," James emphasized and refused to look.

"Then why haven't you implemented it?"

"Because I'm not in position to do so."

"Well, until you are, get used to death. You are not going to just slide into a world controlled by superpowers, a virtual nobody, then acquire the type of power needed to make a difference without death and more death. There can be no plan on this scale without war, and yes, there will be times when your enemies will look like you. The same ones confessing undying love for you, will plot against you. You must be prepared to not be surprised by anything. But prepared to do everything. Now, does this sound like what you've planned for the future?" Osama questioned.

"Not yet," James admitted.

"Then we must go back to the drawing board, my friend."

"Look, once I get enough money to supply the territories now under my control, then my plan can be implemented."

"Do you need my help with that?"

"Nah, with all due respect. You have done enough for now."

"I just don't want you painting pictures devoid of reality."

"Meaning?" James asked.

"When you are in a game you can't win, plan to transcend."

"Why can't I win, when I intend to create the game?"

"My friend, there will be nothing new created in the game of power. Trust me, power has been obtained in many different ways. Sure, it may seem like it may be all about you, but it's also bigger than you. Your struggle is part of a worldwide struggle. What makes you different?" Osama questioned.

James thought about the flurry of knowledge from Osama that ended with a basic question. Yes, there were many different ways to answer it. But he needed to pose his own question as to show how he'd create a different path.

* * * * * * *

The next few months James learned much from Osama in the acquisition of land and the development of businesses. His business degree proved to be effective in the structuring of his string of dope houses. He recently acquired a Chevron gas station to use as his unofficial headquarters through Osama's friends.

The last decade was a very good one for Osama with the acquisition of gas stations and stores owned by his Arab brothers within the United States, Osama assured James, indicating how vast their network had become.

"My network is now your network," he insisted.

On the heels of Osama's departure to Pakistan then Afghanistan, James exited the Chevron gas station.

"What's your name, homie?" a Hispanic male asked.

"Why? Are you the police?" James questioned.

"That's a good one," the man admitted with a sinister grin. "Ordinarily, I would have shot you down in these streets like a dog, had I not known you didn't know better."

That's what you think, James thought, with his finger clutched around the trigger of a hidden sawed-off pump. "Well, ordinarily, you wouldn't have gotten this close up on me to shoot me, had I thought you were a threat," James shot back. He then slid open his jacket to reveal the sawed-off pump in his hand.

"Oh, it's like that, huh?"

"From the cradle to the grave." James did not crack a smile, with eyes that said he was down to die today.

"First of all, I'm not a pig," Julio began. "It's also obvious you have not been hustling very long to not know who I am. My name is Julio, and I'm who your friends wish they had in their corner. "I am the difference between who you are now and who you want to be. You can only dream about the riches I can make possible. I'm what the streets call a *connect*. Only once in a lifetime a man in the game gets to actually deal with someone like me who possesses unlimited product. I can also add four letters to your name, instantly," Julio boasted.

What's this nigga talking about? Four letters? "What you mean, add four letters to my name?" James inquired.

Julio paused a second to admire the sexy young lady entering the store. "What's your name, lil homie?" Julio asked.

"James."

"Shit, you already have a famous name. But if you fuck with me, you'll be known as King James," Julio stated, with total confidence. He was dressed casually in expensive silk socks with matching button down shirt and brown soft leather Bally sandals. Clean cut, he was approximately thirty years of age, and his appearance screamed drug connect.

"King James, King James, King James," James kept saying, now wondering if the man could deliver on his promise. "What's the catch?"

"There is no catch. This is a business proposition, take it or leave it."

"Why me?"

"Let's just say, I make it a habit of picking winners."

"What are your prices?" James questioned.

"That depends."

"On what?"

"On what I front you, or how much you want to buy."

"What's the numbers on both?" James insisted.

"Let's take a ride, then talk about this further," Julio suggested.

Julio hit a button on his keypad, and the alarm chirped on his silver Maybach. Both men got into the vehicle and rode off toward New Orleans east.

"What type of music do you enjoy?" Julio asked as he opened the digital screen with various artists.

"I like the sounds of money counting machines." James had gradually flipped what was left of the two hundred thousand dollars enough times to invest two hundred thousand dollars of product into each of the five dope houses spread out over New Orleans. Since there was little competition to worry about, mismanagement by his manager was his only dilemma.

"Good answer. Let's talk money, then you give me a number of kilos you are prepared to purchase at let's say, fifteen a piece."

James did his own numbers at the rate he was copping. At twenty a piece and twenty kilos every transaction, he would save a hundred grand if he dealt with Julio, or purchase twenty-seven kilos at five grand more because of the savings. However, if he scored more, the prices should get better.

"How about fifty kilos? What can I get those for?"

"You playing with that type of money?" Julio questioned, with raised eyebrows.

"You playing with that type of dope?" James countered.

"How long would it take you to move those fifty kilos?"

Between each of these dope houses splitting the twenty, it would take no more than a week. So, he could do fifty in two weeks. James worked it out in his mind.

69

"Two weeks tops," James assured him.

"Bullshit!" Julio stated. "Do you mean in New Orleans?"

"That's right."

"Okay, give me an address to drop off a hundred kilos, and a number where I can reach you."

"For how much?" James asked.

"If you move those hundred in a month, they are yours for ten a key?"

"Consider it done," James replied with confidence.

"Don't cross me, James," Julio warned.

"Don't fake me out." James handed Julio a piece of paper with an address on it.

"Don't count on it," Julio concluded with confidence.

CHAPTER 9
The Campaign

James and Julio went on to develop a business relationship like no other. Just like Julio had promised, the streets now knew James as King James. He had built an empire that was now responsible for 70% of the drug distribution in New Orleans, Kenner, Metairie, and the West Bank. Louisiana was on lockdown.

In just five years, James had become the most powerful black man in the south. He received his law degree from Harvard. He excelled in constitutional, civil, and criminal law, graduating at the top of his class. He passed the bar exam on the very first try. Prestigious law firms from all over the world had received inside information on his perfect grades, and sought to hire him.

James, however, had bigger goals. The next year he bought a building on Canal Street, in the heart of New Orleans, and then turned it into a law firm—his law firm. But the acquisition would not be an easy feat. The building was located in the historical French Quarters. Yet James would not take no for an answer. "I don't care if no one has ever been allowed to open a law firm within this district," he yelled at the state representative brokering the deal on the other end of the phone.

"Then don't tell them what we are intending to use the building for." He continued to ridicule the representative. "Fuck the permits. You let me worry about that! Can you just get me the damn building?" he asked.

"Thank you, Bryan, and don't ever give me your opinion unless I solicit it, okay?" James demanded. "I know you are sorry. But just do your job and do not concern yourself with anything outside of that. And you have a good day too, Bryan." James ended the call.

It had always been no nonsense with James and his rapid development as a businessman. As he methodically gained power and prestige, he rightfully set his eyes on politics, in order to push his ambitious agenda.

Frequently, James visited the Harvard campus to visit his sister, Deon, who was enrolled there. He smiled at the thought of how defiant she was, when he told her she would be attending Harvard instead of one of the local colleges."

"Mrs. Bertha Johnson tried to give us a better life, and for that, we are forever in her debt. And while other families enjoyed the best of things, we were forced to settle for second best. Now, in light of our history, if the opportunity to have the best presented itself, we should take it," he explained. James remembered consoling her at just the mentioning of their mother's name. "We owe her more than that, baby," he said. "We owe her much more than what you are willing to settle for today. And one day I will need you to lead this family when I can't." He wiped away her tears with his handkerchief.

"But you have to learn to fight like they fight, know who they know, and think like they think, to be a part of the things that can make a difference in our life and to our next generation. That is closer than you think, and we must not make moves that waste our time and money. We came from a mother who gave us her all. I think it's the least we can do. So dry your eyes, baby. Big girls don't cry," James assured her.

Deon nodded, and from that day forward, she excelled at Harvard, and afterwards went on to attend business school at James' urging.

While on campus, he met a future friend. Malik Quinn was a twenty-six year old from Baton Rouge in his final year at Harvard. He married his high school sweetheart, Janice, the day he was accepted into Harvard. James and Malik met often at the coffee shop on campus. Their focus was always on what the other felt was needed in urban communities.

"You do know we lack the platform to make these changes, James," Malik insisted.

"I have a plan," James shot back. "A *really* good one," he added with emphasis. James knew he could pull it off; he was sure of it.

"Okay, shoot." Malik took a sip of his coffee.

James leaned in across the table, then asked, "Have you ever thought about running for a public office?"

"Not really," Malik replied.

"Well, I think we can create our own platform with you being a candidate for change," James said.

"Man, I don't have the background for the political scene."

"That makes you the perfect candidate for the job. No baggage." James sported a huge smile. "That's the message we want to get out. It's time for us to get serious and change the people in public office. They're promising the same things every year, then nothing happens. Basically, what good is it doing us, continuing to have discussions on what to do about what needs to be done, then do nothing to further what we both agree on."

"I agree with you 100%, James," Malik began.

"But we do have issues such as finances, exploratory committees, campaign drives, etc.," Malik added.

"We can simply hire people like any other candidate would."

"I don't have those type of resources," Malik reminded him.

"That's why I have created some family businesses for you that will make plenty of campaign contributions," James insisted.

"So, what office do we go after?"

"Senator McDaniel's."

Malik whistled, took another sip of coffee, then leaned back in the patio chair. "That's a five-term senator."

"He sure is, and he has not done anything but smile for the cameras, as if he was posing for a photo shoot! I want to shake up the political scene in Louisiana, starting in New Orleans. Look Malik, at one time I was not sure this could be pulled off, mostly for financial reasons. But now that I have gotten my money up, it's time for war. McDaniel has to go, and you're going to unseat him," he assured Malik.

Over the next three months, Malik began touring and campaigning. He was gaining ground on the five-term senator's thirty-point lead. The Republican Senator was stunned. James continued to pour money into the campaign, as McDaniel could only watch the dismantling of the lead he once held. Journalists everywhere concluded that the people simply believed in the message of change that Malik pounded through with every speech.

* * * * * * *

"How in the world are we ten points down to a virtual nobody after a thirty-point lead?" Senator McDaniel asked his campaign director.

"He is campaigning feverishly, for one," Gene, the director stated.

"And what does that mean?"

"That means, he is where we are not, because of your schedule. And he is on the campaign trail, reminding the voters that if you are too busy now, you'll be too busy to hear them when you are in Washington," Gene expressed.

"What type of dirt you have on him?"

"Nothing," Gene insisted. "He has an impeccable record at Harvard, strong role as a community leader. He's flawless at the Bar Association, and happily married to his high school sweetheart. Should I continue?"

"Then what are you going to do?" Senator McDaniel questioned.

"We drop the ball," Gene conceded.

"How can you say that? I have carried the same voters for five terms. How can this be?"

Gene did not know how to tell Senator McDaniel that his priorities became more important than the people. Truth is, he did not have to. The people had spoken through their votes. Malik Quinn was the perfect American, and that made him the perfect candidate to defeat the senator. The entire planet knew who Malik Quinn was.

His popularity prompted top new stations such as CNN, Fox, and CBS to reference Malik running for the presidency in the future.

"This country is in need of change. Malik has as good a chance as any of the top republican or democratic candidates," they reported.

Malik officially unseated Senator McDaniel in his own backyard and solidified the platform he and James spoke of not so long ago. The big question was: Could he do the same thing when it one day came down to occupying the Oval Office?

CHAPTER 10
The Evidence

"James, we located the person and the evidence," Detective Myron stated through his cell phone.

"Have you viewed it?" James questioned.

"In its entirety."

"Is it clear?"

"Crystal clear."

"Is the person there now?"

"Yes, right here."

"Hand over the phone."

"Hello?" a feminine voice answered."

"Hello, I'm James Johnson. What's your name, Miss?"

"Temeka Thompson."

"Ms. Thompson, you're a hard person to find," James stated.

"I didn't know anyone was looking for me, and you can call me Temeka.

"Okay, Temeka, I would like to meet you in person."

"That's fine, we can meet. I'm in Florida."

"Why Florida?"

"Because I have a job, Mr. Johnson."

"Can you take off?"

"Can't afford to. People depend on me in Florida."

"I want to thank you for your help."

"You just did." Temeka chuckled.

"Sounds like you're really busy."

"Most of the time. Other times, I'm plain ol' busy."

"Sounds like fun," James said, knowing the feeling.

"You have no idea."

James glanced at his desk calendar for the week. He liked Temeka's vibe, and definitely could use a short vacation. Besides, thanking her for recording Troy and Luqman's basketball game the night of the robbery was a top priority.

It was also discovered within the district attorney's files that witness statements reported the filming of the game by an unknown black female. This information was never revealed by the prosecution. Under Brady vs. Maryland, that was a violation. It took three years to obtain the file under Louisiana law; and two years, three detectives and countless dead ends, to finally locate the witness.

To hear the voice of the woman holding the key to his brother's freedom, felt so surreal.

"Okay, you win. How about I fly down there today?"

"Suit yourself."

"That enthused, huh?"

She laughed sheepishly. "Sorry."

"Don't trip. I'll see you soon."

Myron was back on the phone. "Hey, boss."

"Don't let her out of your sight. I'm on my way. I should be there in a few hours," he concluded, then hung up.

James phoned his pilot.

"Hello?"

"Joe, get the plane ready for a trip to Florida. ASAP!"

"How long will we be staying?"

"That's not clear, but chart it for a return in two days."

"Any other passengers?"

"Just me."

"Any stops in between?"

"Straight to Florida, Joe."

"Okay, boss, we'll be prepared for take-off when you arrive."

"See you then," James concluded.

Still seated behind the massive mahogany desk, James fist pumped in excitement.

"Yes!" he shouted to no one in particular. He buzzed his secretary Barbara.

"You need something, James?" Barbara asked, peeping through the door.

"I'm going to be away for possibly a couple days in Florida."

"Anything I should know?" she asked.

"It's pertaining to evidence in Troy and Luqman's case."

"Is everything okay?"

"Yes, it's cool. That reminds me, in exactly an hour give the head DA a call and the number to reach me on the phone. Tell him he will want to hear this."

"That's it?" Barbara asked.

"Oh yeah, call the chauffeur and tell him to bring the car around."

James snatched his keys, phone, and his black leather attaché case and was out the door. He dialed Deon while riding in the elevator.

"Hello," she answered.

"Hey there, sis."

"Hi James. What's up?"

"We got a break on the video of Troy and Luqman."

"You sure?"

"No dead ends this time. I actually spoke to the lady, a very interesting person I must say," he added.

"Sounds like more than business."

"Her vibe sounds like more than business," he shot back, laughing.

"What about Barbara?"

"What about her? She's grown at thirty-five years old."

"You know she's madly in love with you."

"And I should return the favor?"

"Play on, player," she teased.

"I'll get at you on my way back," he promised.

"And, James."

"Yes, Deon."

"Be careful," she warned.

* * * * * * *

"How are you, Mr. Johnson?" District Attorney, Paul Chen asked.

"I am better, Paul. You're early," James answered. He had only been seated on the plane for thirty minutes.

"Your message sounded urgent. What do you have?"

"I have what I knew I'd find, that your office concealed. It will exonerate Troy and Luqman, considering your jurors in Jefferson Parish did not have the courage, or want to do what's right."

"So, what exactly did we discuss in regards to the proposed new evidence?" Paul asked, playing stupid.

"That doesn't matter anymore. From my perspective, there are two options. The first, would be for me to show you the evidence for authenticity reasons. Then you file to the court a motion to dismiss the convictions and sentences, in light of this newly discovered evidence. Or secondly, we can file our own motion, claiming actual innocence and prosecutorial misconduct. Now, my way may take longer because of your futile attempts to delay the inevitable. But I promise you, if you choose this avenue, it's going to cost you a pretty penny, along with personal and professional embarrassment."

"That's a pretty compelling argument, James."

"That's the mild version. I have yet to assemble the media."

"So, we get to admit no guilt connected to this prosecution, and call it, let's say, it's in the interest of justice," Paul reasoned.

"Admit to what you want. Just on your motion, it says release Troy and Luqman," James demanded.

"And there will not be any civil litigation or public lambasting of the district attorney's office connected to the case."

"I can do that," James agreed.

"Let me get it in writing, and you got a deal," Paul quickly agreed.

Just like that the wheels of justice finally began to turn for Troy and Luqman.

* * * * * * *

The plane dropped down in Miami, Florida, glided to a stop on the smooth tarmac, and then taxied into a private hangar. It was exactly two p.m. and a sunny eighty-five degrees. James exited the plane, then was ushered into a waiting limo. He called Detective Myron.

"Hey, boss," Detective Myron answered.

"Hey. Where is Temeka?"

"Right here."

"Hand her the phone," James demanded.

"Hello?"

"Can I have your address, or would you rather us meet someplace else?"

"My home is fine—it's 63429 Oak Ridge Drive."

"I'll be there soon," James stated, then ended the call.

James' first view of Florida through the window of the limo was a pleasant one. He decided on the way to purchase a home in Miami soon. The closer they came to the destination, the more eager he became. His instincts almost never failed him, and they insisted he meet this woman.

The limo pulled up to the modest home ten minutes later. It was a nice red and white brick home, equipped with a large yard and well-kept manicured flowerbeds situated behind a six-foot-tall wrought iron fence. The neighborhood seemed middle class and family oriented.

Temeka's home screamed privacy. One vehicle pulled into the driveway behind the gate, a Toyota Camry. Another car was outside the gate along the street. *Must be Detective Myron,* James figured. He dialed the detective.

Seconds later, the front door opened, and only detective Myron exited to meet James on the sidewalk.

"How was your trip?" the detective asked.

"It was interesting. Nice scenery."

"Here is the DVD." Myron handed it to James, who secured it inside the attaché's case.

"Good job. Where is Temeka?"

"She's in her office. Let's go meet her."

James' heart fluttered. *What was that for?* He found himself dusting off his clothes, as if waiting outside his date's home on prom night with a bouquet of flowers. He smiled at the thought.

Both men entered the home that smelled of roses. Various certificates and diplomas lined the entrance hall. The hall then led to a sunken den with wooden glossed floors and an adjacent kitchen. Two other halls led to other rooms. *Nice and cozy,* James thought.

"We're here." Myron called for Temeka.

Seconds later, Temeka appeared through the east hallway with documents in hand and a pen stuck through her hair. She looked Brazilian, 5-feet 7-inches, no more than 140 pounds, full lips, bleached white teeth.

James whistled in his mind. He smiled as they approached. She was sharp, he could tell. She wore dark green knit shorts with a matching Miami Hurricane shirt.

Quickly she extended her manicured hand. "I'm Temeka Thompson" she stated, looking quizzically into his brown eyes. "It's a pleasure to meet you, Mr. Johnson."

"It's my pleasure meeting you. Please call me James." Again he took in her visage, stealing a glance at her manicured feet. "Nice home you have here."

"Thank you. It was my parents' home before they passed."

"Sorry to hear that."

"It's okay. That was years ago."

James still bowed in respect.

"Can I get you anything to drink?"

"Water would be fine, but my trip here was to hopefully get to spend time with you and cater to you. Did that come out right?"

"Really?" he questioned, while headed to the kitchen.

"Subject to your approval, of course." He attempted to clean it up.

Her dark eyes gave James a once over as he followed.

"You don't owe me anything, James."

"I know, but it's not for you. It's for me."

"You don't say," she said, blushing.

Detective Myron broke his silence. "I'm going to get back to

Louisiana, James. If there's anything else, give me a call."

"Okay, and thanks again," James stated, then shook his hand.

"Nice meeting you, and be careful on your trip," Temeka added.

Myron left, headed to the airport.

More silence fell between James and Temeka, like a Mexican standoff. His instincts told him she was running through the rolodex in her mind trying to peg him according to her past pursuers. Perhaps she had been searching for a standard way to say "I'm good. Thanks, but no thanks."

"Don't do that," James stated, beating her to the draw.

She smiled.

"So, where do you go to eat in Miami?" he asked.

"You must think I can't cook." Her landline began ringing.

"I think you can do anything, from face value," he shot back.

"Why thank you, and you're partially correct. I will probably try anything," Temeka joked.

"Hey, are you going to answer that?" He nodded at the phone.

"No. It's been ringing like crazy over the last few months. I've decided to ignore it, actually. So, James, you already have your DVD . . ." Her cellphone began ringing once the landline stopped.

"Truthfully," James started, "my trip here is to show my appreciation and to get to know this wonderful person. Will you allow me this privilege?"

"Do you see all this paperwork I'm in the middle of preparing?"

"Yes, I do. Can I help you with finishing it so we can go?"

"Not unless you're a business major."

"You've got to be a psychic too," he said, grinning.

"Look, I can't let you do that. What do you have in mind?"

"Get dressed for a little R and R, then I will think of the rest afterwards." He gave a sly smile.

Temeka pursed her lips together. "Thanks for the offer, but . . . no thanks," she said as her landline began ringing immediately after her cellphone stopped ringing.

"All right then. Well, thanks again for your help," James said, still lingering.

"No problem. Let me see you out."

"Are you sure?"

"James, let me not beat around the bush here. For months I've been getting threatening calls about the DVD. My home has been burglarized three times, computer was hacked, and I made it home just in time to put out a fire started in my office. Several cars have been sitting in front of my home for hours at a time. Now that you have what you need, it's probably best for us both that you leave. Someone doesn't want that DVD to be seen. This is obviously about much more than a basketball game being at stake."

"More than you'll ever know," James replied, following Temeka to her front door. "Call me if you need anything," he said, passing her his business card. "Is law enforcement involved?"

"Yes. There's an unmarked car sitting out there right now."

"Keep in touch."

"I won't. But do take care, James. I'm glad I was able to help prove your brother's innocence." She gently touched James's arm, then opened the door.

"Me too." James stepped outside.

"It's crazy how wanting to help in such a small way has created so much trouble."

"Seems like with any good comes evil."

"Not for me. My good deed is done and evil isn't welcomed in here." James and Temeka locked eyes.

One last thing. If I need you to testify in New Orleans. Would you?" he asked.

"I don't know," Temeka replied.

James turned away just as she closed the door.

CHAPTER 11
Judgment Day

The courtroom was deathly silent as Judge Riley reviewed the motion filed by the District Attorney's Office. He flipped through the pages with raised eyebrows. Judge Riley looked up at the head DA, Paul Chen, then stated, "Have both sides reached this agreement?"

"Yes, Your Honor," Paul agreed.

"The defense also, Your Honor," Johnny Jackson stated.

"Very well," Judge Riley said, then signed the motion to dismiss along with the stipulations as required by law. Now, there was only one other thing left to do.

"Mr. Johnson and Mr. Shabazz, would you please stand?"

Both men, dressed in prison blue jeans and long-sleeve blue shirts with LSP stencilled in orange on the back, stood. They had been there for hours. It was now 12:30 p.m. Testimony from Ms. Temeka Thompson had sealed the deal. Her recollection of the game in vivid detail could not be refuted nor denied. The video of the basketball game they played corroborated their testimony five years earlier, and hers, given earlier today.

They were both assured they'd die in the Louisiana State Penitentiary, as if they should speed up the doomed process. Not that they believed them, but being teenagers when entering one of the bloodiest penitentiaries in the world took its toll on them mentally. To be truthful, seeing men die every day in a dormitory took its toll on every man there. The question always seemed to linger in those left breathing: "Will I be next?"

The judge cleared his throat. As much as he hated undoing what Jefferson Parish's beloved one-sided juries regularly do, today he had no choice. The day of the verdict, Troy and Luqman were very disrespectful. Judge Riley vowed to deny everything that came across his bench with either of their names attached. Merit or not! This one, however, was filed by the District Attorney, and was out of his hands. He was up for re-election next year, and didn't want to run without the support of the District Attorney's Office.

"After consideration of the evidence, the law, and the motion filed by the DA's office, I hereby reverse the convictions of Troy Johnson and Luqman Shabazz, and vacate the sentences attached to those convictions. You will be required to return to the Louisiana State Penitentiary to be processed out and afterwards, you are free men."

James, Deon, and Rick were the only people allowed inside the closed courtroom, besides the Attorney, DAs, Judge Riley, and his clerks. The hearing was one of those hush-hush sort of deals. But little did they know, the innocent men had made promises to Jefferson Parish that they planned on keeping.

* * * * * * *

"You will die by another prisoner's knife, or die trying to do these life sentences," Warden Canizarro had assured Troy and Luqman upon their arrival at the Louisiana State Penitentiary, five years earlier.

"Yeah, I remember that stupid ass statement," Troy said while he and Luqman prepared to be escorted to the front gate for release.

"I wonder how that plan is working for him?" Luqman questioned, as they waved at Warden Canizarro to get his attention. He looked up and they both held up their middle fingers.

Warden Canizarro stormed out of his office and into the hallway.

"Get these muthafuckas out of my prison!"

"That's not how you're supposed to treat your guests, Warden," Luqman joked.

He ignored Luqman. "Sergeant Rednick, what the hell is the hold-up?"

"Let's go, Johnson and Shabazz," Rednick urged.

"Oh yeah, Warden, you can do the rest of that life sentence. We outta here!" Troy joked.

"I'll be waiting on you fools, remember that," Canizarro promised.

"Then you're the fool, not us," Luqman assured him. They exited the prison, headed for the front gate.

They were both free men. Both were convicted of a murder in Jefferson Parish five years earlier. A murder they were innocent of. The corrupt judicial system of Jefferson parish, however, had once again lived up to its name: "Hang A Nigga, U.S.A."

Both men stopped, then took a quick look back at the prison that sat on 18,000 acres. There were four camps where approximately 1,000 men resided in each; none were visible from the front gate. Then there was the main prison, which held 1,000 or so, and the cell-blocks, and the infirmary made up the grand total of 7,000 plus. There was nothing but a long road leading from the prison, and land as far as the eyes could see. Cattle and horses along the side of the road were fenced in. Not a spectacular view by any stretch of the imagination. The camps were all painted dull gray.

Luqman dropped his personal property down on the dirt road that deposited them outside of the prison, looked to the sky, then said, "Insha Allah."

"If Allah so wills," Troy translated in English, as the two men embraced in front of the prison they were told would be their final resting place. They noticed the guard still standing with a smirk on his face, on the other side of the gate.

"Problem, officer?" Troy inquired.

"That's the question I should be asking you," Sergeant Rednick replied. "You act like you left something and need me to let you back in."

This dumb Down South hick must've fell off his rocker, Troy thought.

"Nahhh, you got the right game, but the wrong ones, hick," Luqman suggested. "But you're correct in assuming we left something."

"And just what might that be?" Rednick asked in a southern drawl.

Luqman and Troy smiled at each other. They turned to face Sergeant Rednick, summoning all the cold that their lungs would produce, then spat it on the hick's boots.

"That's what we left, you racist muthafucka!"

Sergeant Rednick just stood there and took it like a chump. He'd been through this shit before, but in his mind, he knew the upper hand was still his. There were over 7,000 other niggas he'd wreak havoc against right behind him!

"That's very good, boys. I wasn't expecting this out of you two." He smiled for a couple of seconds, then spat tobacco juices to the side. "You niggas just don't come back, you hear me?" he stated, then walked away from the gate, laughing as if he knew something nobody else did. And perhaps he did. The truth is, there were many places like Jefferson Parish out there waiting to cheat men out of their freedom. That's what Sergeant Rednick knew, and he was banking on the fact that Troy and Luqman would be back.

The chauffeur, Lonnie, was stood outside the stretch Hummer waiting for Troy and Luqman to finish letting off steam. Lonnie opened the door as the two men walked toward the Hummer. The air conditioner pushed cold air out, along with the melodious sounds of Anthony Hamilton's hit song, "Charlene." The door was closed once they entered the spacious vehicle. Troy's older brother James was seated inside sipping Moet, puffing a Cuban cigar, and sporting a huge smile. He grabbed his little brother, then pulled him closer.

"Look at you, all grown up and shit," James stated.

"All that plantation food will do that to you, big brother," Troy replied.

"What's up, Luqman? You ready to get it on and poppin' in Jefferson Parish?"

Luqman nodded. "You know it."

Truth be told, Luqman had developed a side that can only be compared to the devil himself. He was a ruthless killing machine! He was tried twice for murder, and twice the jury in Saint Francis Ville, Louisiana, failed to convict him. James would always provide the best of lawyers to defend him. Not to mention, there was nobody willing to come forward with information against him, for fear of what would happen to them. In many ways, the prison officials and inmates were glad to get rid of Luqman. They knew one night he'd slipped out of his dorm somehow, then killed an inmate on another yard. But Luqman left no evidence, so he got away with murder. Luqman and his victim, Tony-T had gotten into a physical altercation over a late hit on the football field the day before.

Tony-T was a cold-blooded killer in his own right. He received six consecutive life sentences for attacking a former attorney at his office. When the AK-47 stopped spitting shells, everyone in the building was deceased. *No witnesses, no case,* he thought. Six dead bodies lay still when he eased out of the back door. But, there would be audio and video of the entire episode presented at trial that sealed his fate. At twenty-six years old, he ran around the prison with a heroin addiction and no hopes of ever getting out—nothing to live for other than to do it all again the next day. "The Black Assassin" was tattooed across his forehead in remembrance of his crime.

However, Luqman would prove to be a formidable opponent. After their altercation, Luqman drugged both officers assigned to their dorm while Tony-T was asleep, his final mistake.

The officers had not updated their log books, and had not made rounds for two hours. When the officers were awakened by the Tactical Team, one of the officers was found in Tony-T's bed, and Tony-T was found seated in that officer's chair with his own penis cut off and stuck into his mouth. The words: "dick sucker" were written in blood across his forehead. Nobody had seen or heard anything, out of the two hundred inmates interviewed.

The tower guards were all fired, along with the two officers. Luqman smiled the moment they came for him. He'd just finished his salats and was reading *The Final Call* newspaper. He was taught Islam by brothers in the Nation of Islam. His vision was identical to theirs: building a community that reflects the moral, social, economical and spiritual teachings of The Honorable Elijah Muhammed and Master Fard Muhammed.

DNA samples were taken from Luqman. He continuously

laughed at the detectives investigating the murder. The authorities did manage to get a few words for the record.

Luqman stated, "My lawyers are amongst the very best in the whole world. Would you call them for me?"

Both men were now seated in back of the stretch Hummer focused on the update James was giving. "We're going to make sure Jefferson Parish feels our pain," James said.

"And exactly when does this began?" Luqman asked.

"Immediately. I don't play any games about business. This is what they and their evil ways have brought on themselves," James assured them.

"Then nothing else needs to be said about the subject, other than the method we'll be using," Troy insisted.

"However," James interrupted, "there are crucial roles within the organization I've placed you men into. The agenda I have is a very ambitious one, and I'll need you in the worst way. More education for you two isn't an option, it's a promise to me and our mothers that must be fulfilled.

Both men shook their heads in agreement.

"Another thing . . . I control seventy percent of the heroin and cocaine markets in New Orleans and its surrounding areas. I'll need you two to oversee the operation while I help Malik make political moves. But first, there is one thing I'll need you to do before this happens.

Both men stayed focused on James.

James continued. "I am introducing you to a game I'm actively trying to destroy; so of course, you'll need a back-up plan. You must devise your own backdoor to the game. I need a complete comprehensive business plan implemented and executed, before you two get the run of the streets. The product that is in my possession can carry me for years without me purchasing another kilo, and I won't once it's finally gone. We will then be transitioning into another stage of the overall plan. But in order to successfully implement these stages, there will be wars, there will be death, and there will be betrayal.

"You forgot one important thing, James," Luqman insisted.

"And what would that be?" James questioned.
"There will be a whole lot of body bags!"
James smiled like a proud parent.

CHAPTER 12
The Proposition

George McNamara was one of the most powerful men in the political game. His wife, Beverly, headed the best public relations firm in the country. When they spoke, everyone listened. They were a powerful political couple, responsible for seating judges, senators, governors, congressmen, and even presidents. George now had his sights on Malik Quinn.

With an estimated worth of twenty billion dollars, George and his wife built an empire. George was as grimy as they came in the political arena. He had ties to Colombian drug lord, Pablo Hernandez.

He attended West Point Military Academy as his father and his father's father, who told him he would attend West Point. He said: "Son, many great men have attended West Point: Eisenhower, Grant, and McArthur. They all went on to become great generals in their service to our country. You will also be mentioned amongst them as a West Point graduate. You will also be great!"

George graduated from West Point, then entered the military for four years. Then he decided the U.S. Marines wasn't what he envisioned for his future. He loved politics, and the power that came along with it. He then decided to build a public relations firm. Along with his wife, they set out to make good candidates, great candidates. They succeeded.

"Get Senator Quinn on the phone," George urged his secretary.
Moments later, George's desk phone beeped.

"Yes, Alice."

"Senator Quinn on line three."

"Hey, Senator," George cheerfully stated.

"How are you, Mr. McNamara?" Malik asked.

"I'd be better once you give me the word on launching an exploratory committee for your bid to become our next president."

"I'm flattered, but that's quite a jump in such a short period of time."

"On the contrary, it's just the right time!"

"I don't know, George. Let me get back to you on this. I assure you, I'll give it some serious thought after talking it over with family."

"Senator Quinn, just a reminder on how this process works. It's a popularity contest, and you're the most popular politician in the country. Launch now, and everyone prefers you over the present unpopular president enjoying a thirty percent approval rating amongst his own party; and even worst in a bipartisan poll."

"Launch now and I'll personally guarantee you the Oval Office will be your next office for the next eight years, and the White House, your home."

"That's a pretty impressive pitch, George."

"No, Malik, that's a promise from someone who's made politics his life. However, consider this. There are men and women on the campaign trail attempting to mimic what you just accomplished in unseating a five-term senator. That implies there is a small window of opportunity to get this done, or someone else will become the next best candidate," George concluded.

"I'll take all this in consideration, George," Malik stated, then hung up the phone.

* * * * * * *

Malik made no decisions without James' input, no matter how big or small. So, he gave James a call.

"Hey, James, I need to run something by you," Malik stated.

"Okay shoot," James responded.

"George McNamara just called me wanting to open up an exploratory run at the presidency."

"How convincing was he?"

"Very. Plus he all but guaranteed me the presidency, if we were to launch at the height of my popularity and the bottom of the presiding president."

"Not bad at all," James considered,

"Don't tell me you're buying into this too."

"Well, you have no one to blame but yourself. Look Malik, we ran a great campaign and people noticed. It's a brilliant strategy, and from what I know about George and his collection of political allies; they only bet on a fixed fight."

"So you've been doing your homework, huh?"

"Let's just say, George has been doing his also, and I hate being a step behind anyone with their eyes on me or my friends."

"Sounds like you know something."

"Nothing to be alarmed about. Let's just say I was anticipating that call."

"So where do we go from here?"

"You'll call him back, then tell him to launch his exploratory committee. It's their dime and our profit."

"But at what cost?"

"Campaign for the presidency costs in the billion dollar range nowadays. We're not there yet. But they are, and we promise at best, to listen at their suggestions, then implement ours."

"Sounds like some pretty dangerous maneuvering."

"Sounds like a helluva accomplishment toward that platform we spoke of building. The senate is only a springboard. The presidency puts us and our agenda in an entirely different stratosphere," James said.

"Let's do it!" Malik stated.

"Call me after you've notified George." James hung up.

Malik made the call to George and history was in the making. But little did he know, he'd just entered a lions' den.

* * * * * * *

The campaign trail for the presidency was a grueling one for Malik and his wife Janice. The drama unfolded early and often with death threats from white supremacists in every state. Although many opposed him as a Black man on a world stage so early in his political career, they just could not deny his delivery of his speeches. The genuineness he regularly displayed reminded everyone that this guy was someone who was above reproach.

Malik still strolled across the stages of talk shows like, Oprah, Jimmy Kimmel, and David Letterman. The internet buzzed presidency. Somehow his message steadily gained ground all over the country, then reached the world stage.

Today, Malik was a special guest on the political talk show, *Meet the Press*.

"We're joined today by presidential candidate and front runner, Malik Quinn," news anchor Lester Holt announced.

"It's a pleasure to be here," Malik stated.

"Senator Quinn, there are detractors on both sides of the political isles that think your campaign is less about experience and more about popularity. What do you say to those detractors?"

Malik smiled. "I say, that in order to become president, or to win any other elected office, popularity translates into votes, and if anyone is being elected without the voters, they don't reside in the United States."

"So what about the fact that you lacked political experience as a senator and now as a presidential candidate?"

"Fair question, yet if experience in politics was a requirement, there would be no first- time senators, congressmen, or presidents for that matter. If you're not elected, then when and how does the experience come?" Malik asked.

"Some would say by being around political arenas like campaigns and clerking for politicians."

"Some would also say that those opportunities are only afforded to a few. But the fact of the matter is that those opportunities never definitively made those candidates better than the next candidate."

"So, what is your message to the American people that makes you the better pick to become the next president?"

"My message hasn't changed. It's about the people, not the politics. Traditionally, it's the other way around. But the American people have had enough of traditional politics, and my presidency offers them alternatives."

Lester suddenly looked perturbed as the show abruptly went to a commercial break. "I'm really sorry Mr. Quinn. But I've just been informed that there was a recent threat on your life sent in to the station, and we'll have to end this interview for your own safety. Our security will escort you to your security detail to your vehicle." Lester removed his microphone, ready to end the interview.

Malik moved not one muscle. "Lester, I came here to do an interview to share my plans and intentions for the presidency. And that's just what I intend to do. If you're willing to stay and interview me, then I'll continue."

"Are you completely sure?"

"Absolutely," Malik said with a straight face.

Lester looked at Malik with both wonder and admiration. The producer counted down. Lester put his mic on and went back to business as usual, as if a life and death situation had never occurred.

"So, Mr. Quinn, can you give us some insight on your agenda, starting with your top priorities if you're elected president?"

"Sure, Lester. These happen to be my top two priorities that if we'll tackle, then we as a nation will gradually see change for every American. Health and wealth disparages amongst the poor and the middle class are absurd, when you consider the wealth of this country.

"I think everyone born in this country legally, should enjoy the American dream. We must get rid of the notions that skin color and inheritance entitles you to a better life. We'll never be *one nation under God* with the present state of mind. My administration will tackle these issues and change the status quo."

"Let's shift gears. Recently, you've been under attack by white supremacists, because of who you are. What are your sentiments on that issue?"

"To be honest, as a Black man living in America, my life has always been under attack. Yesterday when I awakened to the death threats and what have you—even on this very day—it was a normal day for me. Today didn't usher in a new kind of supremacists—they may have changed their names, but who they are to me are the *ignorant*. And a very wise man told me that you don't fight nor kill the *ignorant*. You teach the *ignorant*. You see, they don't know that my plight helps them the most. However, I won't get off the subject, Lester. This was expected and prepared for by my camp. They are who we thought they were: deaf, dumb, and blind."

"Well, I want to thank you for dropping by, Senator Quinn, and sharing your honest views and strategy in regard to your presidential bid. Do come back and see us again soon," Lester Holt offered.

Afterward, Malik Quinn's ratings soared. Whoever his future opponent would be had better come battle ready.

* * * * * * *

James was interrupted from his daydream as his secretary beeped in over the intercom in the executive conference room.

"Yes, Barbara."

"Sir, Mr. Jackson has made it. Should I send him up?"

"That'll be fine, Barbara. Thanks."

"No problem, sir."

James leaned back and thought about Barbara and the relationship they developed over the last year she'd been with the firm. She could've easily been a model, but her ambitions never were set that high. They started seeing each other, but nothing too serious. James would not allow it. Not just with Barbara. With any woman. He knew she was in many ways, a good woman, but that was not what he was in search of. James knew for him to truly make the change he envisioned, he would need only one thing that could give it to him: power! Everything about him should exude power, and that would bring the respect of powerful people. Nothing, or no one would be allowed to get in the way of him obtaining that power, or feeding his family—not even Barbara.

"Knock, knock," Irvin said as he entered the conference room. "How you feeling, big guy?"

"Never been better," James replied.

"Today is the day we've been waiting for, and it feels good that it's finally here," Irvin said.

Irvin and James were childhood friends. Mrs. Bertha loved

Irvin as she did her own kids. Irvin was adopted, and the only mother he ever knew, died shortly after Ms. Bertha. He was a few years older than James and very smart, street and book. He graduated high school, then went on to Southern University on a football scholarship. James would visit Irvin in Baton Rouge every month, then attend the Bayou Classic game he played in the Superdome each year. Once Irvin graduated, he obtained a degree in computer science, and that cultivated an idea to start a security firm. And not just any security firm. His was considered among the very best in the world. He protected banks, malls, celebrities, governors, senators, clubs, and corporations.

I-Max was one of the most dependable firms around, garnering an impeccable track record. Irvin built relationships with very powerful people all over the world. Those people also used his I-Max vault. Mainly because they could hide any and everything there. Paintings, jewelry, money, wills, or secrets about a killing, or secrets that could cause a killing. Every storage had its own coded key and could be passed down through generations. There were rumored to be hidden books of the Bible locked away in the I-Max vault. But if anyone attempted to break into a specific vault then succeeded, that vault would incinerate, the total insurance held in relation to its contents were paid out in full. There was a billion dollar policy on I-Max vaults.

"Irvin, have you made any progress toward plugging that leak within our organization?" James asked.

"Not yet, James. But I'm getting very close. What's puzzling me is the way my firm is set up. There's no explanation how someone could've obtained a Level 4 clearance, other than you and me. You see, my security is designed by tiers. None of the other tiers know what the others are working on. I set it up like that so if I lose someone, they wouldn't be able to leak information, nor gain access to the entire system."

"I need that leak plugged, like yesterday," James demanded. "And don't forget, we have clients that have secrets that can start nuclear wars. Trillions of dollars are at stake, and our clients pay us very well to keep those secrets safe, or to be able to bury them whenever there's a threat that it may get leaked."

"I understand, James. Your concerns are mine as well, so rest assured that I'm closing in on our source," Irvin said.

* * * * * * *

From his security camera, James watched the stretch Hummer pull up in front of his law firm, Johnson and Johnson's. The chauffeur stepped out, strolled around to the back door, then opened it. His sister Deon stepped out of the back of the limo. Every man passing along the sidewalk stopped. She was simply stunning, looking as if she'd just stepped off the cover of *Vogue*. Her caramel skin color had a golden shine to it. Her face was lovely, with high cheek bones that could have only been passed down from her ancestors in Africa. Her dreads reached her shoulders, with little seashells sprinkled throughout them. She wore a navy blue skirt suit by Michelle Woo and baby gator blue Chanel slip-ons. Her neck, wrists, and ankles were dripping with about a million dollars in diamonds. She strolled into the law firm, all six feet one inch of her, with the style and grace of a goddess. James saw the way the men would only drool and shake their heads. The chauffeur now held the firm's door open as Deon walked into the lobby, and he too, shook his head. *I hope I don't have to kill somebody over my baby sis,* James thought, shifting his eyes to camera two.

The minute his secretary Barbara saw Deon, they ran toward each other.

"Girl, look at you!" Barbara said, hugging Deon like a sister.

"I miss you too." Deon giggled. "What you still doing behind that desk, girl? You should be upstairs."

"I'm waiting for the catering company to finish setting up their arrangements, then I'll be up there, sweetie," Barbara replied. "I know you have some juicy information, so crack open that safe."

"I know you'd better have something for me too, with your sneaky self," Deon shot back with a smirk, as if she'd heard something.

Once she and Barbara parted, she stepped into the elevator, pressed the top floor button and smiled. "Barbara always has the juiciest secrets to tell."

"I've gotta make sure I keep my baby sister focused. She doesn't have time for meaningless small-talk," James said aloud to camera three, which covered all elevators. On camera two he spotted his brother Troy strolling into the lobby with a box of Popeye's chicken in his hand, smacking away. James smirked and shook his head and turned up the sound.

"What exactly are you doing?" Barbara questioned Troy.

Troy looked behind, then beside himself. "You referring to me, sugar?" he inquired.

"Yeah you, unless there's an imaginary friend that followed you in here, playa," she offered with a laugh.

"Oh, you got jokes, huh? Well, for your information, Ms. Secretary of the Year, I'm trying to keep my cholesterol level at soul food standards. Is that a problem?"

"There's no problem, lil man. Go right ahead and do you."

"Lil man? Hell naw! Maybe your *boyfriend* is somewhere in the vicinity, or your imaginary friend is loose again. Because I know you're not referring to this 210 pounds, all muscle, six feet four inches, as lil man."

"You're right. I can't be talking about that description of a man. 'Cause that's not what my eyes are witnessing at the moment, *sugar*," Barbara replied.

"Oh yeah. Then perhaps you're in need of an eye exam also," Troy suggested.

"What do you mean *also*?"

"This is where you fill in the blank, lil mama." Troy locked eyes with her. Then he walked to the elevator, chewing on a chicken leg, while seductively licking his lips. He looked back one last time, then pushed the button activating the elevator.

"You'd better get your lil mannish self away from here before I spank you," she said, grinning.

"You would like that, huh?" Troy questioned, then stepped on the elevator, saluting her with the drumstick in his hand.

James scoffed at Troy's image on the security camera. "And I'm supposed to implement the greatest caper ever in US History with this guy on my team." He shook his head in disappointment.

Quickly he went back to camera one, but two caught his eye.

Luqman entered the firm with two of his Arab friends. Both men were dressed in traditional turbans and baggy linen clothing. One was a short, burly man in his early forties. He was carrying a leather shoulder strap attaché case. The other was a slender, young man about thirty, but possessed the persona of a much older man. His shoulder bag was twice the size of the other.

"Ahmed and Hasan," James said with a half-smile. "Luqman, you're focused and I can see that animal instinct in you," he said, now watching the camera with an intense gaze. James had called him right before Luqman had left the mosque with some disturbing news. He took it all in stride and remained calm.

James watched Luqman speak to Barbara with a nod, then he kept it moving toward the elevator. As Luqman and the Arabs entered the elevator, the catering company was delivering the many expensive dishes prepared for all guests and employees. James knew that after the celebration ended, the real purpose of his siblings and Luqman being there would begin.

They were all there to celebrate the inauguration of the nation's first black President. Both executive rooms were equipped with seventy-two inch plasma TVs for their viewing pleasure. James and the family were on the top floor's executive room. The employees were in the executive conference room on the ground floor.

James looked around the room and noticed everyone there but Julio. At the last minute, Julio decided a moment like this only happened once in a lifetime. He boarded a plane to Washington in hopes of being a part of history. He expressed to James that when he became old, he wanted to tell his grandchildren about how he was a part of the ceremony for the first, and most likely, only black President.

Irvin strolled over to James, then stated in a hushed tone, "There's something I've been meaning to ask you."

"Be my guest," James said, setting his champagne down.

"Whomever this person is, has to be close to this family. Once I verify who it is, do I have your permission to terminate?"

A sinister look appeared in James' eyes as he thought about the question. He then smiled, as if in front of a camera.

"That's a good question. However, let my answer today be the same to you for as long as we're still friends. This goes for family, friend, or foe," he said with emphasis. "Treason is punishable by death! All my people signed on knowing this. Our cause is bigger than any one person's reasons why they would betray the cause. Am I clear on this matter?"

"Crystal clear," Irvin emphasized.

James picked up the phone and punched in an extension.

"Hello?" Barbara answered.

"Would you care to join us in a toast?"

"I'm on my way."

The two Arabs were seated by the door of the conference room in silence, as if in prayer, as everyone else chatted like old friends. Barbara walked into the room, then sat beside Deon. Deon quickly pointed, then started giggling, indicating to Barbara how funny the Arabs looked.

James interrupted everyone as he now tapped the fork against his champagne glass, indicating a toast. The caterers began passing out glasses of champagne, but the two Arabs declined.

"Barbara, would you show these two gentlemen to the kitchen so they can get something non-alcoholic to drink?" James asked.

"No problem," she stated, then left with the two Arabs.

James continued. "My family, we have arrived! This journey has been a long one, and it has been a difficult one as well. However, anything worth having always comes with difficulty. I want to thank all of you present today for believing in me. I know a long time ago, I asked all of you to do things that would not have been what you would've chosen to do or become in life—but you did it anyway. That shows me one thing: we all share the same common interests. We have torn down many walls and kicked down a bunch of doors. But there remains much more kicking and tearing down to do. There were many lives lost for us and against us, but I promise you, they weren't in vain. Yet, for the lives lost in opposition to us, their families will reap the benefits of the movement that their lost family member tried to stop. And for those who were amongst us fighting, then lost their lives; their families also have benefited. However, through this process of forwarding our agenda, there will be opposition amongst even the people we've held dear to us also. Some of them will call themselves family, and us being true to our beliefs of unconditional love for family, we'll be betrayed by those people."

James walked over to the conference table, then picked up the remote. He pressed the button, then a conversation could be heard in a hushed tone. It took a few seconds before anyone realized it was Barbara talking. Yet, they could not make out the male voice. The conversation lasted about a minute before they understood the nature of it. Barbara was being asked about company business concerning I-Max and the law firm. She had provided the caller with various codes and dates of meetings, as well as client names.

After James ended the presentation, he threw the remote against the wall; it broke into several pieces. He pounded his fists on the table. "This must not happen to our family again!" James emphasized in a dangerous tone full of evil and hatred.

Everyone's attention was on high alert. No one had ever experienced this side of James. But if walls could talk, they'd say he was Satan.

Suddenly, Ahmed and Hasan appeared through the door without Barbara. Ahmed, the big burly man, slung a body bag from over his shoulder and onto the floor. It made a loud thump. They glanced at Luqman and nodded. Luqman looked up at James with venom in his eyes and nodded. Deon, noticing everything, got up from the table and headed for the door. James took hold of her before she made it.

"I'm not finished," he stated as Deon studied him for a moment. She turned and walked back to her chair.

"Let me reiterate this to everyone once again," James said. "Nothing, or *no one* is more important than our cause! Not even me. I'd kill *myself* before I allow everyone else to fail because of me. And if anybody here feels different about what we're attempting to accomplish as a family, there's the door!

"But James—" Deon said with watery eyes, but was cut off.

"You see, for the past twelve years I've plotted and planned 24-7 in an attempt to: first, do what's right for family; and secondly, make sure we don't leave our people stranded and struggling without hope! I've dealt with the physical and emotional scars of death and more death, wars and more wars. I went through it, so you wouldn't have to. And I'm not expecting awards or accolades. My visions are real! What I want for my family more than anything, is to focus their attention on a cause greater than themselves; then let's achieve it! This is much bigger than what I've ever imagined possible. But, I've also learned if you can envision something, it's achievable.

"So," James continued. "Today those visions are manifesting into what we're about to witness. My good friend, Malik Quinn, will be inaugurated as the first black President, as a result of a conversation we had about change years ago. But on the other hand, we have a young lady who came to us looking for work, looking for a chance to make a difference, she said. And she was given that chance. Nevertheless, we somehow failed in providing her with what she thought she needed, or wanted, and in return, she failed us!"

"I really don't think she had to die for what—" Deon said, but was again cut off by James.

"But more *importantly*, though it's *necessary*," James said, locking his intense gaze on his little sister, "this ending must not be consistently repeated against our own people. It's *still* genocide. You see, today we face problems and stereotypes of every kind. And those problems may not be met in a short span of time, because there are many. But I stand here today assuring you that they will be met!"

Deon wiped away her tears as James strolled over to the 72-inch screen TV, then turned it on. A graph appeared with the faces and names of ten men. All looked rich, powerful, and dangerous. He picked up the infrared pointer, then strolled over beside the monitor. Deon recognized a few of the men from the Harvard campus. Malik was at the top of the graph with President beside his name.

"These are the men responsible for Malik becoming president.

But as I stated earlier, this vision started with two men. I'll now share this fact with you all, and don't forget it; these men are not your friends, my friends, nor Malik's friends!" James looked around the room to see if everything registered. "Just as a normal relationship will have two users, so will this one. These men are only looking to forward their own agenda." He pointed the infrared beam at the graph.

"The conversation you heard earlier was this person, George McNamara, the president's top advisor. The guy next to the president is the Vice-President, Craig Shueberg. He was picked by George. These other men are the money men who funded the campaign, too. They are tycoons and owners of billion-dollar corporations, and they are our enemies. They will expect generous favors in many areas, such as gun laws, insurance, tobacco litigation, etc. They were all picked by Mr. McNamara, and will claim to be on your side. But trust is a foreign word to these men. If we are to accomplish our goals, we must come together and stay together. These people are poised to destroy us the minute they've concluded that we won't give them what they want." James stood quietly for several seconds to let the message soak in. He thought about the assassins now relocating from foreign countries, awaiting the signal to pull their triggers on sniper rifles in hopes of ending Malik's life.

We must get stronger to protect him, James thought. *After all, this political thing was my idea.*

CHAPTER 13
The Hit

"Don Alberto made a grave mistake when he made a play for a portion of James' territory," Julio said. "I just learned this a little while ago."

"Don Alberto? Which territory?" Tray asked with concern.

"The up-town area from Washington Avenue on back to Eastern New Orleans, then everything north of Saint Charles Street on back to the ports. The business district, as well as the Saint Thomas Projects."

"Damn! Don Hamas ruled the same territory a year earlier before he was indicted. Got hit up with racketeering charges . . . and then was sentenced to life in a Supermax Federal Penitentiary," Tray said, with his thumb and forefinger on his chin.

"Right. So he knew those were James' spots, but still decided to assume control of the Magnolia Projects. He positioned his men in and around the projects, tapping into James' clientele."

"And he's suddenly out of Supermax, huh?" Tray stated, more than questioned.

"Yeah, suddenly. Sales dropped off drastically. So, about a week ago James disguised himself as a dope fiend, then took to the streets. His street general Alonzo explained that the shooting galleries they'd set up had dropped off also. The fiends were in fact, going to get high somewhere else," Julio said.

"I can pretty much sum up the rest. He found a fiend to show him where and whom to score from."

"Right. Once James had a clear picture of what was going on, and who was behind it, he started planning his massacre. There's a total of eight drug houses pumping weight, on down to rocks. Right under James' nose. He said the day he'd planned would always be remembered in the minds of the entire underworld as D-Day."

"I already knew that was coming." Tray contemplated his contribution to the impending war.

"James began planning like he was General McArthur, with maps of the entire uptown and Garden District on back to the ports, all of Don Alberto's territory."

"He's a methodical guy. So I didn't expect nothin' less."

"Nor did I. When I left, he was retrieving information and formulating strategy against Don Alberto's entire organization."

After Julio alerted Tray of James' intentions, Tray sensed James may need some behind-the-scenes assistance. Tray immediately called upon one of his up-and-coming henchmen.

"Hello," Dip answered.

"Hey, Dip. What are you doing right now?"

"I'm in Slidell at this moment. What's good?"

"I need you at my club in about thirty minutes. If you can get here, I'll personally deliver that new Range Rover you was asking about at the dealership the other day," Tray promised.

"You don't mind if I leave a little time on the clock, huh?" Dip asked,

"Do what you must, but I do need you here in one piece!"

* * * * * * *

"Roger that, old man. Sit tight, and watch the youngin' do his thing! Oh yeah, do call that dealership and confirm the color. I like platinum," Dip suggested as he down-shifted the Porsche, leaving Slidell with the quickness. He was twenty-five miles away as he weaved through traffic, pushing ninety miles per hour. Still checking his rear-view for po-pos, he accelerated past 100 miles per hour, in and out of lanes, he pushed. He then turned the volume up on his favorite song, and sang along with Lyfe Jennings:

♪ *And they're killing me with these twenty-threes and these DVDs in their rides.* ♪

Suddenly, his phone vibrated. He unhooked it from his belt, glanced at the number he didn't recall, then pressed "Ignore." Dip passed by cars as if they were sitting still, as the engine in the Porsche sent the speedometer passed 130 miles per hour.

As Dip switched lanes again, weaving through traffic, a clear lane appeared about five miles of highway. No traffic! Dip couldn't resist, he punched the pedal to the floor, unleashing all the horses available. He was amazed at the power under his control, as the speedometer stood at 180 miles per hour, slicing through the air like a ninja sword. He peeped at his Rolex: fifteen minutes left. He smiled because he knew the Range Rover was in the bag.

The Porsche glided over the hill on I-10 west bound now approaching his exit a mile away. He began slowing down, and lucky he did. The po-po was ducked-off on the side of the Interstate with his radar gun in hand. Two minutes later, Dip pulled into Club Baller's huge parking lot alongside Tray's 760 BMW.

"I see you made it on time, so I owe you something, right?" Tray asked, smiling.

"You got that right, old man. So what the business is?" Dip questioned.

"A little something has come up that's in need of immediate attention in the worst way," Tray began.

"What's up, Jaafar?" Dip nodded briefly.

"You got it, Dip," Jaafar said from the passenger seat of Tray's car.

"What's the name of that crew you put together for that mission in the Lower 9th Ward?"

"Oh. I named them the Goonies," Dip said, smiling.

"I like them niggas. That job was done real professional-like: in and out, like a robbery, no witnesses. Nobody even knew you niggas was there until the bodies began stinking," Tray reminisced.

"I'm glad you liked that, homie. I decided to go with them silencers, then ordered them lil microphone ear pieces like the Feds have, so the job wouldn't be so messy like the other ones that led to me having to fight them murder charges," Dip considered.

"That's called homework," Tray indicated. "Another thing, Dip. As long as you prepare for a test, the answers will come easy when it's time to take it. You may think at times someone out there may be better than you, but that's not always true. They've just figured out how to win. They're better prepared to win. More importantly, is that you understand this and apply it to everything you do in life, and do it every day of your life," Tray concluded.

Dip nodded in agreement.

"Speaking of homework," Tray continued, "I have to do something on a very short notice, but it's major, and it's as serious as cancer. It involves a friend of mine who's more like a son. Just so you understand the effort I'll need from you in pulling this off."

Dip continued listening, as his adrenaline began building, knowing people would have to die from the tone of Tray's voice. He was now poised like a cobra, ready to strike at a moment's notice.

"Look, my friend is about to declare war upon Don Alberto. He's done his homework, and it's evident, because he's striking without notice. His goal is to wipe out everyone within the Don's organization. Active or inactive! If they were once generals, hit men, lieutenants, etc., they should be deceased after this is over.

"My friend is taking over Don Alberto's territory in retaliation for the Don moving on his territory. Simply put, we're going to war alongside him, only he won't know we're there. We have the same information he has, but we'll get to them before he does."

"James is planning his assault at 8:00 p.m. We'll start at 7:30 p.m. I've gotten police clearance between 7:00 to 10:00. The only police in those areas will be ours. This must be done quietly, but efficiently," Tray emphasized.

Tray looked from Dip to Jaafar, making sure his orders were clear. The two men nodded.

"Very well then," Tray continued. He handed Jaafar a list of names consisting of three generals, as well as addresses to their homes and businesses. He then handed Dip a list consisting of all drug houses, stash spots, and places Don Alberto's men occupied. "Are there any questions?" Tray inquired.

Jaafar looked at Dip. "I work alone! No disrespect to you, of course," he stated, eying Dip. He made his exit from Tray's car and approached Dip's car.

"None taken, Jaafar. I can appreciate why you work alone; it's what makes sense. You're one of the best at what you do. Perhaps in the future, if the opportunity presents itself," Dip offered optimistically.

"Perhaps," Jaafar agreed with a smile, then a pat on the back.

"Well, gentlemen, if there isn't any last minute details about your mission, don't hesitate to call. This hit goes down tomorrow, and is of great importance. We mustn't miss," Tray insisted. "Once you've completed your hit, do confirm it with me ASAP. Don't forget, we're working on a time limit. Everything is riding on this operation, fellows. One shot, one kill. So everybody must go! If they're in the wrong place once the drama unfolds, no prisoners," Tray insisted.

CHAPTER 14
The Enemy

"My family," James continued, "George McNamara is an avowed enemy to what we will attempt to change. It is no surprise that he has infiltrated our organization. He needed only to find the weakest link."

"So, James, if you knew all along who turned against us, then why not let us in on it?" Irvin questioned.

"The most important issue at that time was to find out exactly what information they were inquiring about. It was on a need-to-know basis, with no disrespect to anyone. The fewer people who knew about the investigation, the more comfortable Barbara became with spying; that's when she would likely make mistakes," James reasoned.

"I'm puzzled, James," Irvin said. "How was Barbara able to obtain a Level 4 security clearance that you and I only possessed?"

"Good question. Actually, I left my pass-code card out one night when we were about to leave. I purposely left my computer on in my office, and asked Barbara to close everything out. I faked an emergency, leaving her all access to any information on the computer. What made me set up the sting was, I received a call from a friend of ours in Washington. They intercepted her call through their investigation of George. So, once she got the clearance, they were talking more and exchanging more information I fed her, which was incorrect."

"How long did this go on?" Deon asked.

"The last six months of the campaign. But let me emphasize that this fight will get ugly, and many people will die once what I've been working on is completed. And then, long after its completion, people will continue dying in an attempt to sabotage something relevant, to not only our people, but the world as well. We will soon be at war with George and those people that wish to control our friend, the president," James assured them.

"Irvin, soon after the inauguration, we're going to switch five of our best men with Secret Service around the president. Also, we're going to need you running the show on a daily basis. Can I count on you?"

"Without a doubt, James. Just let me know when you're ready."

"Very well, that's covered. Deon, it's time for you to step up into the position I assured you, you'd one day hold, remember?"

"You said one day you'd need me to lead the family when you couldn't, right?"

"That's right, baby sis. This is your cue."

"But, where are you going?" Deon asked sadly.

"Nowhere far. But today we all are going to be taking on more responsibilities. This is for all the chips. You will assume control of the law firm's daily operations at the conclusion of this meeting. There are some dangerous people out there, and I need to be exactly certain of where they are. When I leave here, my destination will be Afghanistan to see an old friend," James said with an evil grin.

"Afghanistan? What's over there?" Troy inquired.

"It's not what; it's who."

"Well, who's over there?"

"Osama bin Laden," James stated.

"So, you're friends with America's most wanted?" Troy asked, with bulging eyes, and a smirk that indicated he highly doubted it.

"Why would that be so far-fetched? Osama was schooled in the United States and has family here," James stated.

"So what's the plan once you get over there?" Irvin inquired.

"As you know, my message has been about war being around the corner, right?"

Everyone nodded.

"Well, who better to consult with and recruit soldiers from, than Osama?" Nobody questioned that fact, so James continued.

"I'm returning with a hundred of Osama's top Taliban fighters to assist me with the ground wars that are sure to come after the election."

"In a scary way, you seem to have been through this before,"

Deon suggested.

James laughed. "Not quite, but make no mistake in assuming that I haven't. I've been in wars and ordered the assassinations of many. The art of war is ever present in my mind and heart. The destruction I want to inflict upon these people will be brutal in every way imaginable. The casualties will be many for them, and will send a harsh message to those willing to oppose us. My return to the streets will solidify our stance by showing the world we're willing to get down and dirty. You see, if word gets out that we're weak, then every small-time peddler with a crew will be gunning for our territories.

"From the Mafia and their La Cosa Nostra to the cartels, no one is safe from our reign. I'll be damned if what I've accomplished over all these years, fall into the hands of scavengers. There are no more checker games in my world. I play chess, and I look forward to playing the best! I expect to challenge the best and most treacherous minds. Because challenges in life should always be looked upon as an opportunity to do great things. Therefore, we mustn't always sit back then wait for those challenges. We're bringing the fight to them, so there's no mess for us to clean. Everything accomplished thus far, is peanuts compared to the bigger plan. This discovery is like nothing anyone could've imagined, and it's ours! And once we let the world in on it, there will be many haters. And everyone over-stepping their boundaries, will get dealt with immediately. Retaliation is a must when you're sending messages that say: you fuck with us, you die," James said.

"What specific role will you be playing in the streets, if we already have an army to throw at our enemies?" Troy asked.

"Another good question, lil brother. But let me ask you a question before I answer yours."

"Okay, shoot."

"When you're in a court of law facing criminal charges, where is court held?"

"In the courtroom," Troy confidently stated.

James shook his head as if saying correct. But then stated, "Not necessarily so, Troy. Court is held in the chambers," he assured him.

"Look, ninety percent of what you see has been already talked about in the chambers. The other ten percent you see and hear inside the courtroom is theatrics. So, to answer your question about me coming to the streets, I'm actually going into the chambers. The streets won't see me, and that's the essence to having the element of surprise on your side. Nevertheless, once I leave the chamber, that ten percent you see will seal the fates of many men. So my advice to them is, if they ain't at peace with Allah, they need to get straight."

"It gets no clearer than that," Luqman stated, ending the momentary silence. "James is right. There has been too much of the same people doing the same shit to the same people. I say James has done his homework from a strategic point, and he's one hundred percent correct in assuming that the once predators will not enjoy being prey. They are arrogant, selfish, and have unlimited power. And that's their weakness to the right planners!"

"But you know how the old saying goes: ain't no fun if the rabbit got the gun," Troy said, laughing at the thought of them being in the driver's seat and calling the shots now.

James, on the other hand, stood thinking of the cliché Troy just spoke of. Now, one very important question popped into James' mind. "So, Troy, when do we know the rabbit has the gun?" He clicked on the seventy-two-inch screen, then dimmed the lights. He looked around the room and felt extra proud that all of his family was present for this historical occasion.

President-elect, Malik Quinn sat relaxed on the screen proudly, minutes away from becoming the nation's next president. His wife, Janice, was as beautiful as ever, seated beside him in a dark blue dress made by Vivian Zorlosky, and draped in a $100,000 emerald necklace set, a gift from James.

The weather was beautiful in Washington, as a couple million people traveled to witness the historic event. Some of the most powerful and influential people in the world were stopping to shake Malik's hand. Malik was decked-out in a traditional navy blue presidential suit, white shirt, and burgundy tie. Anita Baker began singing the National Anthem as the fighter jets flew overhead.

James and family were now witnessing Malik take the oath in accepting the job as Commander-in-Chief, on a chilly January day. James had come as close to Malik as he was to Troy, since they'd met years ago. Finally, their day had come, and it felt good! They sacrificed a lot of themselves for the greater good of their people. They constantly challenged the other in finding solutions independent of personal views. They understood that successes in life couldn't simply be measured by money, but by the lives one touched in positive ways within that lifetime.

The moment Malik shifted his gaze toward George McNamara and his wife Beverly, seated next to him, James smirked. Malik glance down the row at George, who seemed to be in deep thought. When Malik smiled, James did too. They both knew a snake by sight. George was not trustworthy. Yet, Malik was now well-versed in the game of politics, thanks to James. Their investigations of George had indeed revealed that he was a dangerous man. James already knew George had asked Malik to renew talks about the trade embargo. But Malik was no fool. He knew that would mean more drugs entering the United States. James and Malik were always talking about the advancement of the black race, and drugs wouldn't help that advancement. Besides, the plan James was about to unleash would be hell on drugs! The trade embargo would be lifted, but only after the plan first went into effect.

"Our people will begin to have opportunities never imagined in the 400 plus years of their existence in America," James and Malik had stated simultaneously once they realized how close they were to accomplishing the goal of all goals. Now Malik understood the importance of choosing his buddies wisely. For a second time Malik glanced at George. Though the men were far apart physically, their thoughts were in sync. They both wondered just how far the man George would go to get what he wanted? Once Malik squeezed his wife's hand, James guessed he must have been thinking about the dangers that would come with holding the nation's top post.

Now he wondered how long it would be before he'd have to take George off the shelf. Yes, he had in his possession taped conversations between Pablo and George and their "if all else fails" plan to eliminate Malik. James promised himself to never let that plan get close to happening. He'd make George wish he was never born!

* * * * * * *

George was basking in the glory as he thought about how he'd pulled off the most historic election ever. He looked at Malik, crossed his leg, then smiled like a proud parent. He squeezed his wife's hand, then kissed her on the cheek. He was thinking about how important she was to the campaign.

Life was great at this time, the best he'd felt in years. He then thought about the conversation he had with his Colombian drug lord friend, Pablo Hernandez, about getting the trade embargo lifted. George had received twenty million dollars based on the promise that he could get Malik to agree. Another drug lord, Rafael Fernandez of Cuba had invested ten of that twenty. Rafael knew that if they could increase shipments of drugs into the United States, it would mean billions more in profits. George had sent assassins from Cuba and Colombia to set up shop in the States, just in case President Quinn didn't agree with their plan.

CHAPTER 15
Street General

Dip was really feeling like a street general, as he'd coordinated his men inside the targeted areas equipped with the latest DEA Law Enforcement vests, helmets, weaponry, microphones, and infrared imaging goggles that can see through any structure. He'd also positioned three other vans at other locations, deep into Don Alberto's territory. It was 7:15 p.m. As the day had begun to be replaced by the night. His stopwatch beeped fifteen minutes till show-time. Dip reminded his troops again to only use silencers.

On the other side of the Garden District, Dip gave orders for the assassination teams to spring into action. The men poured out of the vans at every location, already knowing who's who. They'd been stalking them for the past thirty minutes, counting down. Dip and his team took control of the block within minutes, and with very little struggle. They forced all the soldiers, lieutenants, and workers inside of the drug houses, as if they were DEA, like their uniforms said. Once inside, Dip methodically checked off the names as captured, then everyone accounted for were executed.

From another location, Dip received a call. "Boss, everything is packed inside the van, and the streets are clear," Lil Bo reported.

"We're on our way out," Damond checked in from another location. "And what about your list?" Dip asked.

"Everyone on the list is now off the list," Damond replied.

"I roger that," Dip said through the microphone. "What about the product?"

"Everything is in our possession, and we're on our way home."

"See you in a minute," Dip replied, then looked at his stopwatch.

"Let's get out of here," he stated. It had taken him forty-five minutes, but as he was en route home, he wondered why his other two crews hadn't checked in. Then, as if reading his mind, his lieutenant, Bee-Bop, who he'd done time with in Angola, checked in.

"Yo-yo, this is Bee-Bop headed to the house, roger that?"

"Yeah, I roger that," Dip replied. "I thought we had to come back for you and the crew."

"That's a negative. You would've been wasting precious time," Bee-Bop insisted. "The delay was because there were a few on Santa's list that didn't want their presents, so they tried to skip Christmas. So, the elves and myself brought them back home and made sure they accepted those gifts!"

"That's the Bee-Bop I know. How about those spoils of war?" Dip inquired.

"They paid us everything owed before they receive their presents," Bee-Bop confirmed.

"That's what I call a white Christmas," Dip stated, as he and his men shared a laugh at Bee-Bop's joke.

"Hey, what's all the excitement about?" Javon came over the radio asking.

"Oh, we was thinking about throwing you a rope. I thought you might be drowning in pasta from all those Italians over there," Dip suggested.

"Man, I got to admit. That project was a muthafucka to contain once the shit hit the fan. Them pasta-eating cocksuckers were cramping my style for a second. Shit, it got messy for a minute, then that list you gave me got longer. Just consider it an investment for the future. Oh, yeah. They'll be picking up bodies until tomorrow morning," Javon boasted.

"Did they give you something for your trouble?"

"That's what took me so long. Them muthafuckas stopped speaking English for a second, then started speaking that Italian shit. But once I pulled out my pliers, then broke out some of them cocksuckers' teeth for the tooth fairy, their English came back with pin-point accuracy. Man, you would've thought they were English professors." Javon laughed. "We're on our way back to home plate now with plenty of goods."

* * * * * * *

Three miles away, Jaafar quietly entered a tobacco shop on Saint Charles Avenue. The rich aroma of the different blends filled his nostrils, now reminding him of the pipe tobacco his uncle smoked. He walked around the shop, secretly eyeing everything, watching nothing, to make sure not to arouse suspicion. The young man behind the counter continued to ring up the guy at the check-out. Jaafar quickly made up his mind that the young man would also become a casualty. He strolled over to the counter as the old guy in front of him purchased his products, then headed for the door.

"May I help you, sir?" the young man asked.

"Yes, I would like to speak to the owner of this establishment," Jaafar stated in his most professional version of English.

"Is there anything I can help you with?" came the reply.

"I have just a couple of questions that are of great importance to me and possibly the owner," Jaafar shot back.

"Maybe I can answer them, sir. I am the manager."

"Okay, does your boss want to sell this business?"

"Ummm, I don't know, but I don't think so," the young man stated.

"That's why I asked to speak to the owner," Jaafar said with a cordial smile.

The young man spun around and headed for the back of the store in search of the owner, Nikoli Clemente.

Suddenly, an older guy of about sixty years old and in perfect shape with broad shoulders, huge forearms, and about six feet tall, appeared from the back room.

"May I help you?" Nikoli inquired.

Jaafar smiled as he realized he would have to be precise in his

118

movements, because a mistake would surely result in him being the underdog.

"As I was telling your manager, I had a couple of questions. One, were you interested in selling this magnificent place, and do you have any surveillance, in case I need to purchase some, if you agree to sell?"

"First off, I have the best in surveillance equipment, and secondly, I have no interest in selling this place for any price," Nikoli admitted. "There happens to be too much valuable product in this shop, my friend."

Jaafar looked around the shop as if he were looking for the valuable product. But he was really creating some space in between him and the two men. When he spun back around, the ten-millimeter Sig was in his hand breathing fire continuously, as both men suffered bullet holes to the forehead, then chest as they slumped to the floor, side by side. He quickly locked the front door, dragged the bodies out of plain view, and then hurried into the office in search of the surveillance equipment. He located it and popped out the DVD. Jaafar headed for the side door. Two minutes later, he was seated behind the wheel of his rental car, typing the coordinates to his next victim into the GPS system. Cortez Silva was only two miles away.

After a ten-minute drive, Jaafar had just jumped the gate that led to the back of the small Italian Café's back door searching like the trained assassin he was. The young dishwasher continued to spray down dishes with his back turned. Jaafar silently crept down the small hallway right past the dishwasher and toward a door that was most likely an office.

A male voice could be heard talking forcefully through the telephone. Jaafar slid down the hall toward the room, then peeped into the room and found his target. He slowly eased the razor sharp machete from its case hidden underneath his shirt.

As he stepped into the room, catching Cortez Silva by surprise, the man realized he was in trouble once he saw who was stepping through the door. Cortez Silva was an assassin himself, and as he searched his memory for exactly who this man worked for, everything got dark. Jaafar hit Cortez with the machete three times in a split second. The first slice went across his chest, exposing his heart. The second came as he reached for something, which caused him to lose that arm. Then the third beheaded him. Jaafar worked the machete with the accuracy of a ninja as he wiped the large knife on the jacket of his victim, then replaced it in its case. He then peeped out of the office he'd been in only two minutes, seeing the coast was clear. He casually walked toward the dish room, then turned the corner, only to find the dishwasher hadn't moved an inch, or knew how lucky he was as he walked out the back door en route to his next victim's house.

A few minutes later, he was steps away from Mario Lopez's home located in the Garden District. He walked past the home, confirming the address in his memory, as he noticed the two men sitting on the porch in deep conversation. Jaafar surveyed the area, then noticed a few bystanders outside across the street from Mario and his friend. He knew he needed a distraction to get the potential witnesses away from the future crime scene so he turned, then walked back a half block, aimed his silenced ten-millimeter Sig across the street at a car traveling not far from the witnesses. He fired three shots from the weapon, and the silencer made it sound as if he had spat on the ground three times. The driver was hit, then instantly swerved into a light pole, exactly in front of the witnesses.

Jaafar spun back around, headed in the direction of Mario Lopez, creeping at top speed. Once he arrived at the home, he opened the gate, walked up on the porch, and then fired his weapon twice at the heads of the two men, slumping them over on the porch as if they were sleeping. As people began to crowd around the accident across the street, Jaafar slipped away then dialed Tray's number.

"Hello," Tray answered.

"I'm coming home," Jaafar stated.

* * * * * * *

On the other side of town, Don Alberto's limo was parked outside his favorite pasta restaurant, Miguel's. He had been there over an hour and was finally about to leave. His bodyguard Sam had also eaten his fair share. The two men now longed to enjoy a big fat cigar and to rub some nice, tender breasts and asses. They were scheduled to go straight to the casinos for some superstar treatment, but James had made other plans for them.

The valet and Don Alberto's driver, Andro, were outside the restaurant. Minutes later, Don Alberto and Sam walked out the front door engulfed in conversation, not noticing the valet that opened the door to their limo. Both men eased into the limo, as did James.

"What the—"

Pop, pop!

Before Sam could get the words out his mouth, he was dead. The silenced 9-millimeter in James' hand was still smoking.

"Drive us to that address I gave you, Andro, then call me in the morning," James stated.

"Who the fuck are you?" Don Alberto asked.

"You mean to tell me you don't know whose toes you stepped on?"

"What is this idiot talking about? He must be mistaken," Don Alberto was thinking.

"That's right. You're the powerful Don Alberto, and you can do whatever to whomever you want to, right? You're looking at me and probably thinking, *This nigger must think I'm one of his drug connects through someone else. I've never dealt with him. How does he know me?*

James continued, "Well, Mr. Alberto, I think if there was ever a time in your life that you should've asked before you took, it probably should've been this time. The only bad thing about disrespecting me is that you don't get a do-over," James assured him. Don Alberto only stared at James, wondering if he'd lost his fucking mind.

"You see, Don. You can't be allowed to simply apologize and we become friends afterward. You made a play for my territory, and that rendered yours spoils of war, if I can take it, right?" James asked.

Don Alberto smiled at the absurd suggestion of James taking his empire.

"I'll take that silence as a yes," James stated. "I know you've figured it out by now. So, I'll let you in on where we're going. You were operating eight houses within my territory, and by now those houses are closed. The men who worked them are all gathered in one place. The same place we'll be in a few minutes. You placed thirty-five men inside my territory, and they will die tonight. But they'll watch you die first!" James promised.

Don Alberto chuckled. He had cheated death many times and faced it like a man. "I died a long time ago, my friend," he stated, smiling. "Today will be no different."

"That may or may not be the case, but someone didn't finish the job. After tonight, you will no longer live to tell anymore stories about death."

"And what do you think the Commission will do to your piece of organization?" Don Alberto asked.

"They will do what they have to, and I'll do what I must do."

"You will be no match for the power associated with La Cosa Nostra, my friend." Don Alberto let out a loud, annoying laugh, then stopped. His eyes were bulging. "The day you wage war against La Cosa Nostra, the Commission doesn't just plan on killing you, they'll kill your generations before and after you! We possess the power to wipe out your entire bloodline, so choose your enemies carefully, friend. You don't possess the authority to sanction a hit such as this. You're simply out of your league. We've been here since the beginning of organized crime, and when all others have been reduced to fly-by-night organizations, we're still at full strength. We are no trend, as your organization will one day be reduced to. We're embedded in the fabric of all societies on every continent, still standing strong! So, if I do die tonight as you have assured me, I'll die satisfied, knowing my bloodline is continuing when yours will no doubt be at its end." Don Alberto paused for a second as if to take a picture. "You see, my friend, we are the Capones, Lucianos, Gambinos, Morellos, and Gottis of the world. There is no end to us. The bloodline is only enhanced by the death of an old man such as myself. There will come a younger and more deadlier one to take my place," Don Alberto insisted, then sat back, folded his arms and peered out of the window of the limo. James leaned back in his seat across from Don Alberto, laid the 9-millimeter pistol on his lap, and started clapping.

"That was a nice reflection on the history of your Italian heritage. I genuinely applaud you. However, although your history has much relevance to societies all over the world, they don't supersede history itself. You speak of your Commission and your bloodlines. But the fact still remains, you muthafuckas die too! You are no better than what me and my people are today. You speak of the unity within your bloodline, but you are at war against each other, remaining the number one cause of death within your own race. The Capones, Lucianos, Gambinos, and Morellos were at war against each other, killing each other. So that rich tradition you speak of is only a beneficial reminder for me on how *not* to build an organization. I don't glorify your stories, I pity them! I look at your ability to obtain power over the years, and today think about what it could've been. Your little Commission won't even exist in America's future, unless someone goes to a library, then read about it in a book. History will forget about you as it forgot about the ones before you. I will build conglomerate powerhouses instead of numbers rackets and drug empires for my people. Intelligence will make sure my bloodline reigns supreme, not territorial wars such as this one. This war won't define me, it belittles me, and the very essence of what I hope to become. But it's necessary! Men like you think as they have centuries ago, never changing those strategies of old and expecting different results. The truth about your bloodline that you so masterfully spoke of, is that it will only exist if they adopt my new changes. As for your death, I am well within your laws to do as I will, once you crossed those territorial lines. You should know this," James concluded.

The limo came to a stop in front of a warehouse in the business district owned by Don Alberto. Julio then opened the back door of the limo. "After you," James insisted.

The two men exited the limo, then Don Alberto was escorted into the building. Julio grabbed James by the shoulder as he strolled by. James spun around with a look of pure terror in his expression.

"What's on your mind, Julio?"

"Just so you know, all of Don Alberto's generals, active and inactive, were put to death, along with his territory seized. Everything now awaits your full control, courtesy of me and a friend of ours," Julio expressed.

"What friend is that?"

"He wishes to remain anonymous at this moment. However, we've had police clearance since 7:00 p.m. We need to be gone in thirty minutes, before all hell breaks loose after 10:00 p.m.

James glanced at his watch, turned, and started walking toward the entrance of the warehouse. Julio followed, now wondering what was weighing so heavily on his friend's mind. If he only knew, he'd stay outside . . .

Once inside, Alonzo and his crew had all thirty-five of Don Alberto's men on their knees in a line side-by-side. James picked up the five-gallon exterminator spray canister, then strolled over to a table placed in the middle of the floor.

"Gentlemen," he began. "You are gathered here today because you were somehow led to believe that you could violate my territory, for the amount of time you did, without repercussions. You were wrong," James assured them. "I know it was not your plan, and to you, it's not your fault, and I have considered this. Nevertheless, I've asked myself, what's the punishment for such a crime when a soldier is under the command of a captured general? First off, you men signed on knowing the possibilities and probabilities that you may die in defense of your oaths to this person. That time has come," James insisted. "Yet, I've decided to first let you men witness the captured general's death, so you would get a glimpse of what yours will look like."

Alonzo led the Don to the front where the men knelt about half-way down the line, so all of them could witness.

James picked up the exterminator canister filled with gasoline, then walked in front of Don Alberto. He pumped the canister, walking around and spraying the gas on the don, soaking him from head to toe. Don Alberto's short, fat body trembled uncontrollably as he attempted to plead his case through the duct tape across his lips. James continuously moved down the line, pumping and spraying the rest of the men. Each man's legs was strategically tied to the next man. After all the gas was gone, he set the canister down, then went over to Don Alberto, flicked the lighter, and set him on fire.

The thirty-five men were now frightened shit-less, knowing in minutes, they'd receive the same fates. James pulled his 9-millimeter and pumped two shots into the head of the charred corpse. He then strolled down the line, then lit a fire to the last man and watched it travel down the line, ending with the first man. Everybody else in the room had walked away from the fire and smoke, but James stood there enjoying himself. Suddenly, as if he was brought out of the trance, he went down the line with two 9-millimeters in his hand, pumping a shot into the head of each man wiggling violently from the blazing inferno. He then walked toward the entrance of the warehouse where Julio stood.

"You need this warehouse for anything?" he asked Julio.

He stared at James for a second, then replied, "Not really."

"Tell them to burn it down when they leave," James commanded as he strolled out. He then jumped into his Range Rover and headed home.

* * * * * * *

With amazement, Julio watched the huge SUV until it was out of sight. He now wondered how the young man James could've developed such extreme tactics. As James had stood peering at the burning men, his eyes twinkled with something sinister but gratifying, as if he had been enjoying the show. Julio's stomach clutched, then sank with trepidation of James' next act.

* * * * * * *

Dip and his crew were now located at Tray's club in New Orleans east. Don Alberto's drug houses lost twenty-six kilos of coke and $250,000 to the raid. Each of the other crew members received a kilo and $10,000. The rest went into their equipment fund.

Tray sat behind his desk, having just gotten off the phone with

Julio, who confirmed Don Alberto's death. He then dialed James' number.

"Hello," James answered.

"Congratulations, my friend. I hear everything went well."

"Oh, yeah," James said carefully.

"I know you're still concerned about who I am, but trust me. It's better this way, at least for now. However, I have a young friend that has just helped to secure territory that belonged to Don Alberto but now belongs to you. I'd like to see him inherit a piece," Tray lobbied.

"Is that a proposition or demand?" James shot back.

"It's a request, no more, no less."

"Who exactly is the friend, and is he going to become a thorn in my side?" James asked.

"His name is Dip, and he will not interfere in your affairs in any way. I'm only requesting the Saint Thomas Projects."

"Very well. That's his spot as long as he keeps it in a respectable manner."

"Thank you, and see you around, my friend." Tray hung up.

"Gentlemen, look here for a second," Tray suggested to the young crew of assassins. "Look, we're having a birthday party for Dip next week. So, you lil niggas don't be in nobodies prisons, and you won't miss these dime pieces I have coming in from Atlanta. And please don't be broke, 'cause I won't let yo' asses through the front entrance without that hundred dollar admissions fee, believe that! Remember, loose lips sink ships, and must be eliminated."

Tray made that statement because he noticed the shitty attitude of a couple niggas that didn't think putting money up for equipment mattered. *Shit, those niggas only see the glass as half-full, never considering the emptiness is about the same,* Tray considered. *Perhaps they would never see the logic in using strategy to win a war. Uninformed street niggas.* Tray chuckled. *But one thing is for sure: they are the ones to be watched, and then eliminated.*

CHAPTER 16
The Meeting

Three months later, James was seated comfortably in his 737 jet en route to Afghanistan. He'd been flying for three hours as he checked his Rolex. His present thoughts were about his family and the way he'd be forced to deal with George McNamara.

Irvin had confirmed that Pablo Hernandez and Rafael Fernandez had indeed transferred ten million dollars apiece into accounts tied to George McNamara. Phone taps on George had revealed the plot to assassinate President Malik Quinn. Pablo and Rafael were drug lords, and President Quinn was the only person standing in their way, unless George could convince Quinn to lift the trade embargo. Yet, that was the last thing on the agenda for James and Malik.

Nevertheless, the drug lords were secretly filtering their trained assassins into the United States, continuously building up their troop level. James knew he'd need trained killers to counter their killers. He then contacted Osama. He had remained in contact with Osama through his family, because Osama's status had already been elevated to America's Most Wanted.

The huge 737 jet glided through the air with little effort as James lay back in comfort. The smell of filet mignon filled the air, along with baked potatoes, broccoli with cheese, and garlic bread. The pretty flight attendant slash gourmet chef, prepared one of James' favorite meals. He'd been so busy lately, that he couldn't recall the last time he'd eaten.

One of the pilots entered the lavishly decorated cabin at the same time as his dinner arrived. "We should be landing in thirty minutes," he stated.

"That's much-welcomed news," James said to the pilot, Bruce. "Have we contacted our people?"

"Ten minutes ago," Bruce assured.

"Sounds like you've taken care of everything. I'll just have some dinner, then get ready for that dust in Afghanistan," James admitted.

The pilot nodded, then proceeded back into the cockpit. James pressed a button on the panel of his chair, and then someone appeared.

"Salvator, has everything been taken care of that Osama requested?" James asked.

Salvator nodded and smiled. "It's been there since yesterday, and we located those missile launchers also."

"I knew I could count on you. What have you gathered on the men sent by Pablo?" James questioned.

"Honestly speaking, my friend, they are amongst the best and most ruthless killers I know or have worked with." Salvator quickly strolled out of the cabin, then returned with a printout of the assassins entering the United States through various airports.

"They're sparing no expense in this war, James. However, we have the intelligence to counter every move, and it allows us to take them out anytime. They only think they're under the radar. And that, my friend, is one of their biggest mistakes. I think us acquiring soldiers from Osama will further tip the scales in our favor. We need men trained in extreme tactics, because you can bet your bottom dollar, their men will be."

Salvator slid the list to James, then went down the list name by name, giving James a complete history on each man. Salvator had built his reputation fighting against and alongside men such as these. There was no way they could ignore the killing machines secretly migrating into America.

On every continent, Salvator was well known; he was simply the best the world has ever known in regards to killing. The underworld was his backyard, and he was allowed to venture wherever he needed without any questions as to why he was in your country, or why he wanted to come there. Everyone knew that if Salvator wanted you dead, he wouldn't notify you of his coming. The assassin had the ability to get in and out of countries known to have impenetrable borders and safe-havens for many wanted men, until Salvator took the hit. The other men in his profession called him when all else failed and special talents were needed.

James and Salvator became friends after the Don Alberto hit. The Commission, made up of the most powerful Mafia families in the world, sanctioned the hit against James. They brought Salvator in for the job. He watched James in his home as a predator would his prey for three full days, then made his move.

The mansion was equipped with fifteen rooms, a basketball court, tennis court, theater, helicopter launch pad, and gun range, all sitting on forty acres of beautifully manicured lawn.

James had been home for a couple hours, now relaxing in his circular library. He sat in the middle of the room at his desk reading *33 Strategies of War*. The lighting inside the room held a soft glow that was gently illuminated by a desk lamp positioned directly on the pages of the book.

Salvator waited in a corner of the room, crouched behind a large box of recently delivered books. He now studied James as he did the last three days, just as he studied all the other hits over the years. He decided, just killing these powerful men wasn't any fun. He wanted to know what made these men so unique. These men were the few who tried to obtain power, and succeeded when many others failed. He watched them and recorded their tendencies to get a better understanding of what made them so special. He believed that if he studied these men's tendencies, it would reveal their strengths and weaknesses. He now pitied having to kill James, because as he watched James, he felt they were playing chess, or a cat and mouse game. James never did the same thing twice, never ate consecutively in the same places, never went to work at the same time, never left at the same time. Nothing with James seemed to bore him, like his other targets. Salvator began to envy James because of his natural killer instincts. James could fool the world with his noble demeanor. However, Salvator knew there was more to this man. He wished he could've known him under different circumstances, but the decision had been made by the Commission and written in blood! There simply had to be death that followed.

He eased out the wooden handles connected to the twelve-inch string of wire. The Commission voted that James' head should be brought to them as compensation for the death of Don Alberto. As Salvator rose from behind the box on James' blind side, he picked up his pace, closing in on his prey with each fluid step.

Suddenly James said, "Take a seat, Salvator Dovinchi."

Salvator stopped in his tracks, not sure of what to do. His eyes now roamed like a caged panther. He didn't know if a welcoming party was there, but he knew he'd been check-mated, for the first time! *How could this be?* he thought and continued to search his memory for answers to where he'd gone wrong. Nothing surfaced. He'd killed many men on every continent. He always was the one with the upper hand, the only man left standing.

"Salvator Dovinchi, born June 16, 1975 to Iranian immigrants," James began. "Your parents migrated to America in 1985 during the Iran-Iraq war. You're an only child, been on the street since the age of fifteen. You killed your first man that same year, five more before the year was out. You were the leader of a three-man hit squad that wreaked havoc on many families, until you met an old boss, Don Corlona. He took you under his wing, then you, Leandro Sardini, and Pedro Garzinez began terrorizing again after Corlona's death, but respecting the Commission's rules. Leandro was killed while executing a contract in Scandinavia, then Pedro in a prison riot in Mexico. Today, you're acting on a sanctioned hit by the Commission, who somehow has forgotten their by-laws in sanctioning this hit."

Now Salvator stood in full view of James, but still carried an unstable look. He now wondered why James felt the Commission violated by-laws. James, no doubt sanctioned, then carried out the hit on Don Alberto, a sitting Don and member of the Commission.

"What law did the Commission break?" Salvator inquired.

James smiled at the question, sensing the Commission never told Salvator about the violation Don Alberto committed against his organization. James waved his hand toward a chair seated in front of himself.

"Have a seat, Salvator," he stated.

Salvator hesitated. Then looked around the room curiously, with the wire still hanging from his hand.

"If I needed you dead, I would've killed you three days ago, when you first began watching me!"

"How did you know?"

"It's my job to know! Just as it's yours to know when is the best time to move on your target," James insisted. "However, don't strain your mind in figuring out where you went wrong. You were perfect! But, so was I," James admitted "Your skills are second to none. In reality, you were a formidable opponent."

"If that is so, how were you able to detect my presence the day I began watching you?"

"Because I was watching you first," James admitted. "For instance, what was the most visible discovery you noticed about me?"

Salvator searched his mind, then snapped his finger. "You never ate at the same place, never went to work, or left for work at the same time the previous day, and you seem to be aware of all you did," Salvator concluded.

"That's correct," James stated. "You're very observant, and that's why you were perfect. If you understood that I never did anything the same way, then I shouldn't have noticed the same person as I changed my time and places, right?"

"Yes." Salvator shook his head as the light in his mind clicked on.

"My memory caught you in different places at different times, and that could only mean I was being followed. You see, there are no coincidences in my life. Everything has a significance. But, back to your question about your Commission. As you know, within every organization, there are rules that govern the actions of its participants, right?"

Salvator nodded in agreement.

"Well, Don Alberto crossed my line as well as the Commission's, when he negligently opened eight drug houses within my territory. He moved without the Commission's knowledge, and that means he moved without the Commission. He acted alone and put him, along with his territory, at risk. I accepted his challenge and as you very well know, I won. It was fair and square, within all the rules. I always have respected the Commission, but I'm in no way a weakling! I actually don't owe them an explanation, because I simply defended my laws as they would theirs," James said.

Salvator shook his head, indicating that he understood his position. *If put in the same position, I'd do the same.*

"I must say," Salvator began. "I didn't know this side of the story, and just maybe, the Commission never knew either. You wiped out everybody, as a true general would. There was no one left to tell the story. This changes things. I am a man who doesn't kill for the sake of killing. My allegiance is to my profession and the structure of its laws, just as I was taught." he said. "My aim is to leave the profession as it was left to me. Never changing any of the integrities associated with it. The law will always override men, because the laws were put in place because of men."

James laid the book down, then asked, "Where do we go from here?"

"It all started with the Commission, and now that I know the reason Don Alberto died. I'll see if they knew. But, I would like to know one thing before I am allowed to leave your home," Salvator stated.

"I'll be as honest as humanly possible," James insisted.

"I've kept my life as much a mystery as possible, even my name, which wasn't Salvator Dolvinci when my family entered America. How could you have known who I was before my family came to America, and that they were immigrants in 1975? You see, there's no possible way for you to know any of this. Our documents were destroyed."

James stood up from the desk, reached for a book, then opened it to the first page, turned it around, then handed it to Salvator, who reached for the book, then read the writing on the blank page written in Arabic by James: *The Art of War is the Love of War*. Then under the Arabic, James wrote on that same page: *By the time you finish this book, you'll have the answer to that question my friend, Muhammad Allam.*

Because James had provided Salvator with his birth name, this further fascinated Salvator. He stood in amazement. Somehow, James had known he was coming, knew everything about him, and then knew exactly what he was going to ask.

From that point, Salvator knew this man whom he had come to kill, stood for much more than what other powerful men had been willing to. This man's thoughts were relevant and needed in the world he existed in. Someone he could match wits with, and change a lot of what was wrong within his profession.

The massive 737 jet finally landed on the runway somewhere in the mountains of Afghanistan, jarring Salvator from his daydream of how he and James had met.The two men looked over at each other to see if the other was okay. The flight attendant unbuckled her seatbelt, then prepared the men's property for their landing. They had exactly three hours to unload the cargo, meet with Osama, load the men onto the jet, then leave Afghanistan before they were attacked by U.S. forces.

The door opened, then James and Salvator exited, dressed in all black with hiking boots for the mountain run. Immediately, the plane's cargo was unloaded by Taliban fighters. They arrived in trucks, but most of the cargo was being packed on, then carried away by camels.

"This way," a young man said, waving for James and Salvator. He was dressed in white with a black turban on his head and an AK-47 strapped to his shoulder. They both jumped into the jeep and were off. On their way, truckloads of men were headed in the other direction.

"Those are the fighters you requested. They'll be on your plane when you get back," the guide assured.

It was dark along the route in Afghanistan, prompting James to look at his watch. "What time is it here?" he asked the guide.

"You have at least three more hours until daylight, my friend. You need to be long gone by then," the guide insisted.

The road was long and bumpy, with dust continuously mixing in the air. James loved the magnificent view of the huge mountains they traveled between. Rocky caves were carved out into the mountains and were used as tunnels to travel through. The air was dry but cool, and the dust made you feel gritty as it clung to your skin. After traveling for twenty minutes, the jeep came to a stop alongside a trail that led up to a cave entrance carved out in a humongous mountain that almost reached the clouds.

"You have an hour and a half. He's up there," the young Taliban stated, pointing at the cave.

Salvator and James began jogging up the mountain at a record pace. Both men were in tremendous shape, making it to the cave entrance in five minutes. They entered the cave and were surprised at the amount of lighting inside the cave. Crates of guns, ammunition, grenades, and rocket launchers were stacked four crates high throughout the cave, lining the walls.

James peeped into an opening, which was a room softly decorated with oriental rugs and smelled of scented oils. Osama was seated in a corner in front of his *Quran*.

"As Salaamu Alaikum," he greeted.

"Wa Laikum As Salaam," James greeted him back. The men then individually embraced. "How have you been?" James inquired.

"Every day is another blessing from Allah," Osama stated. "And how are you?"

"As you know, it's not always easy to implement concepts of change when the most powerful are advocating the opposite to stay in control by themselves," James insisted.

"A journey of a thousand miles begins with one step, my friend; so just keep stepping," Osama encouraged. "However, change isn't always going to happen in the minds of people."

"I agree," James stated. "Because our epidemic is in dealing with the effects of genocide strategically placed within our society. Poverty and lack of knowledge plague our people in every way. And it seems like any progress we make doesn't even tip the scale, because we're failing in so many other areas. Nevertheless, I will continue to fight whomever I must, so the seeds of change are planted in the minds of our young. My organization today, will bring about changes for tomorrow," James assured

"Yet, there are many rumors of war," Salvator admitted.

Osama shook his head in agreement, then stated, "That struggle, my friend, has been going on since the beginning. Good versus evil, right versus wrong, and in between comes the truth. Because who's right is dependent upon whose point of view is being told, and even more important is, which will be accepted. The tragic realization will ultimately be that nobody will want to do what's right, for all the bickering about who's right.

"The balance of power will always be an issue never agreed on, and the primary cause of wars. The powerful have developed a thirst for more, even though they're already in control of everything. The poorest man must defend being poor in order to hold on to what little he possesses. You never hear of the rich at war with the rich. They simply team up against the little guy. It's always the little guy with the little life, trying to hold on to a little home for his little family with a little job, that inherits the biggest problems. The rich want to run your life, then run you out of their life when you're of no more value to them," Osama concluded.

"That's why this war we're about to fight means so much," Salvator stated angrily. "They, too, will die in the streets like dogs alongside the men they've sent! When we're finished killing them, we'll kill their ideas so that their legacy will never live on. We will stack coffins to the heavens once we're finished."

"However, war, is only as effective as the purpose behind it. War is also fought in the minds of both sides. Death isn't always the only result of war; in many ways, the threat of death is usually a definitely deal breaker," James stated in reference to Salvator's conclusion

"Just remember what's important, my friends. Allah knows best, and he's the best of planners," Osama pleasantly stated. "And whatever we do, it must be in total agreement to what Allah has willed, and not our personal glorifications. Because any knowledge that fails to reveal its Creator, can reveal no truth! Such a man's intellect and reasoning always run astray and will meet with failures all the days of his life," Osama assured them.

Suddenly, the young Taliban appeared. "It is time, my friends. Daylight is upon us. We must leave."

Osama nodded, then looked over to James and Salvator. "Hopefully, one day soon and under different circumstances, we'll have a meeting of the minds again," he suggested.

The three men embraced, then Salvator and James exited the cave as their guide hurriedly escorted them back to the jeep; and twenty minutes later, to the landing strip.

The sun began to cast a golden glow over the horizon as the huge 737 jet lifted up over the mountains, leaving Afghanistan in its wake.

The two friends were now seated, peering out of the windows of the jet in their own thoughts of the recent conversation with Osama, as well as calculating their next move. Both individually came to grips, or an understanding that their next move would amount to some mass killing once they returned to the States, considering their cargo—the Taliban fighters, aboard the 737 jet with them. They were some evil-minded muthafuckas.

CHAPTER 17
The Defiant One

Although it had been months ago, Troy remembered clapping as his brother James stood in deep thought after thanking everyone for attending the meeting during President Malik Quinn's swearing in ceremony. Troy had witnessed a passion like nothing else he'd ever felt when James had spoken about the goals they planned on reaching in the future. They also often spoke about politics and business. "There's a fundamental difference in politics," James said. "The difference is having elected officials as friends, and not having them as friends after electing them. That's the position the poor has always found themselves in. Victims of the campaign speeches and the promises, followed by the pat on the back."

Then he expressed the need to turn over his street empire in order to deal with the drama affiliated with Malik's presidency. Troy and Luqman had been controlling every aspect of the drug trade in a limited role since they'd been home from the penitentiary. But now, there would be much more to consider. James, however, always stressed the importance of them finishing the colleges they enrolled in, as well as having legitimate businesses.

Troy exited at I-10 Chef Menteur Highway in New Orleans East, pushing his new Hummer with his partner Luqman seated next to him. He made a left on America Street, now cruising through the neighborhood, observing all the activity going on. Suddenly, Troy made a left into a driveway and pulled into an open garage that closed once the Hummer entered. Both men exited, then entered the home through the side door.

"What's good?" Kane asked, as he reached out to each man, giving them a fist pound.

"Business as usual," Troy responded.

Kane strolled back into the other room, then came back with three duffle bags. He tossed them on the floor, then stated, "That's $10.8 million for this month's take on four spots."

"How much product you have left?" Luqman questioned.

"I divided the forty kilos left between the four spots. That'll last for the rest of the week."

"I'll send another hundred kilos tonight," Troy assured. "Have you looked into those investments?"

"Nah, not yet, but I'm working on it. Just never decided what I want to do," Kane admitted.

"You do understand this isn't an option, right?" Luqman inquired.

"Man, you niggas killing me," Kane shot back, getting frustrated with these niggas sweating him about nothing. "Be cool. I said I'm going to get a business together when I figure it out! Shit, since you niggas left Angola, y'all been on some other shit!"

"Oh, now we the niggas on some other shit, huh?" Troy asked. "How soon a nigga forget from whence he came. I remember a nigga that agreed to all the stipulations associated with being a part of this here money we getting! You remember that, nigga? You know what, don't answer that, fool," Troy stated. "Look, as I stated before, ain't no options. Only niggas that are staying, are those obeying. Nigga, this not no ball till we fall operation here! We have rules and regulations in place so we don't have to go through that. You right. We on some other shit since we left Angola. We on some never going back shit. What you on?" Troy questioned.

Kane gazed at an annoyed Troy as if he were unconcerned about whatever the discussion was about.

"That's exactly what I'm saying. You don't know what the fuck you in it for! Nigga, you just in it, and that's dangerous for not only you, but everyone involved with you." Troy's murderous eyes said he wanted to jump down this nigga's throat.

"Be easy, Mr. Big Man, with the big words. We all in this together, right?" he asked with his arms spread out, waiting for an answer. Yet, Troy knew that in Kane's mind, he really didn't give a fuck!

"I thought we were, but you seem to have found a new set of rules you're playing by," said Luqman, looking mean as a muthafucka. "Fool, it's been three years since we put you down on this hustle. Just so you know, we weren't allowed to have no parts of this type of money until we established legitimate businesses, and nigga, you're not an exception to the rule. There was no choice for us, only a big, fat ultimatum! Take it or leave it.

"See, this game won't be here forever, and we won't be in it forever, either! Only a fool would make this game his profession, and we're no fools. Sure, playboy, you've had a nice lil run of fate. Got your money up something serious," Luqman stated, and began clapping to give Kane praise. But then he stopped, and his entire complexion changed. "But, don't think for a second that you're just that good, playboy, or that you're untouchable! You see, the protection from the law you're receiving is only because it's within our operation. However, even the po-po know that all good things have an ending, and they learn to retire, and not expire."

"All right, all right, you niggas got your point across," Kane said. "Look, I'm on that just like when we were in Angola, remember? So be easy like I said. And you niggas need to be doing something with all this bread, 'cause I need to be making rounds." Kane held out his hand for some dap from Troy and got it, but Luqman just stared at his hand with a "don't fuck with me" look. Luqman casually picked up the duffel bags, then headed for the door, seriously wanting to smash Kane.

Troy exited the garage, headed for the loan company they owned located inside the Lake Forest Plaza. He looked over at his friend as he stared out the window. He understood why Luqman wanted to let Kane go, so he decided not to bring up his name as he navigated through the heavy traffic.

"That nigga putting us all in jeopardy," Luqman stated out of the blue.

Troy took a deep breath before speaking about the subject. "I understand that, and this the nigga's last straw. That's my word," Troy said.

"Oh, don't worry. You ain't gots to give your word again, 'cause I'm not asking no more. I'll be damned if I touch them gates to Angola because of a nothing-ass nigga. Fuck that! We made this nigga, Troy! You should be more concern about who's at the top that the Feds gon' be asking about when this reckless nigga gets knocked off. Like I said, his days are numbered," Luqman assured him, then leaned back in his seat gazing out the window.

Troy's phone rang, breaking the silence.

"Hello," Troy answered.

"What you doing?" James questioned.

"The usual pick-ups."

"I'll be landing with our friends in a couple hours. You have everything together?"

"Yeah, we got the entire hotel, and the charter buses are at the landing strip waiting too."

"That's perfect. Is everything okay down that way?"

"Just like you left it. How's Osama?"

"Same ol' Osama. Still fighting. Where's your shadow?"

"He's right here," Troy replied. "You want him?"

"Nahh, just wondering about him. Tell him I have something for him."

"Will do. Call me when you touch down."

"Be careful. I'll see you in a few."

In a daze, Luqman continued to gaze out of the window, knowing his instincts were telling him right about Kane, and him being the cause of their entire empire possibly crumbling. He knew he had to do something, and do it fast!

* * * * * * *

Club Ballers was jam-packed that Saturday night. The parking lot was the size of two football fields with not a parking space remaining. It was filled with expensive vehicles, such as, Mercedes, BMWs, Bugattis, Ashton Martins, Maseratis, Hummers, and candy coated Old Schools. Vehicles not in that category were parked along the highway, no questions asked. Club Ballers was the most exclusive spot in New Orleans, and there was a one-hundred-dollar entrance fee, no matter who you were.

Tray managed to recruit Young Jeezy, Rick Ross, Trina, and Lyfe Jennings to perform at Dip's birthday party. There were three floors, and all were packed.

Dip sat in the VIP section, sipping Moet, reminiscing on how different his life had become since he had met Tray. He reflected some years back when he was in Angola planting squash, corn, okra, and other nasty vegetables at the plantation. Prison wasn't for him, he'd decided. No one had ever been more real to him than Tray, not even his family. Suddenly, his phone began to vibrate. Dip opened the text message, then smiled. It said "Happy Birthday!" and it was from Tray. Then another text appeared from Bank One.

"Huh . . . why would Bank One be texting me?" he stated out loud, then hit open. The words, you have just received a five million dollar transfer into your account 760564 were printed across the screen.

"No shit!" Dip stated, unconvincingly. "Somebody thinks it's April Fool's day instead of my birthday. Probably a misprint, a five dollar transfer would have been more likely." He tossed the phone on the table after enjoying a laugh at the joke.

"Hey there, lil mama, looking for me?" he asked a pretty young Toni Braxton look alike strolling past him. He ran game well enough to get her attention and keep her at his table, determined to take her back to his place. They sipped on drinks and listened to music. Dip was leaned back bobbing his head to the sound of Young Jeezy, as a nigga with shoulder-length dreads walked toward his booth, standing every bit of six feet five inches and 280 pounds.

"What's up, birthday boy?" Kane asked.

Dip looked up at Kane with pure hatred in his expression as he reflected back to the fight they had in Angola. Actually, it was more like a war! Neither man would give up. The fight went into the record book as one of the most brutal ever without a weapon involved. When the fight was stopped, both men lay in the infirmary with broken noses, black eyes, and Dip broke his left hand. They tried for three years to get back around each other to do it again, but administration wasn't having it. *Now we meet again,* Dip considered, reaching his hand into his waistband for the 45 automatic.

"Chill, homeboy. It'll be another time for that. I come in peace today," Kane suggested, sensing Dip had his hand wrapped around that iron. "How's life been treating you?"

"Everything lovely on my end, as plush as possible is my motto," Dip responded.

"It's good to see that. And life isn't treating me so bad either." Kane spread his hands out, flaunting the diamond necklace that hung from his neck with the letter K drenched in diamonds. "I just wanted to drop off a bottle of what you were drinking for old time's sake." Kane grinned widely.

"That's mighty nice of you, ol' boy. Thanks. But if you ever in need of that two hundred back, it'll be at the bar," Dip reminded him. *Now you better get'cha dumb ass out of this hornets' nest before it becomes your coffin.*

Sensing it was a good time to leave, Kane threw up the deuces, then strolled away with his dreads swinging, now listening to young Jeezy spit "Thug Motivation."

"Pardon me, sweetheart. Can you give us a few minutes?" Tray asked the young lady sitting at Dip's table?

"Sure, no problem. I'll be on the dance floor," she told Dip. "Make sure you come get me."

"So, who's your friend that's built like a line-backer?" Tray asked. "Yeah, I was in my office watching behind the two-way mirror."

"Oh, that ain't no friend."

"I can get him out of here if you want," Tray suggested.

"Nah, that nigga ain't ruining this night. I'm having too much fun for that to happen," Dip assured him.

"In that case, take a walk with me," Tray insisted.

Dip grabbed his phone, then both men walked through the club, being greeted like celebrities. Tray reached the elevator, slid his key inside, then the doors opened. They rode down, then exited on the first floor, where Rick Ross stood holding the stage down with Trina. Every baller and ballerette were dancing out of their shoes, singing along. Bobbing their heads to the music, Tray and Dip exited the back door.

Surprised by the sight before him, Dip asked, "What the fuck is this!" Excitement danced in his eyes.

"This is your truck I promised you," Tray insisted.

"This that new Range Rover!" Dip stated eagerly.

"It's armored too. Get in." Tray tossed Dip the keys, then went around to the passenger side. Dip chirped the alarm, then opened the door, sliding into the seat, looking around the truck like a kid in a candy store.

"Look, Dip. You have your own territory now. This means you're in charge of a kingdom," Tray stated.

"What are you talking about?" Dip asked.

"The Saint Thomas Projects is your territory, courtesy of James Johnson, for your assistance in securing the territory from Don Alberto, and winning a strategic battle that ended in victory for James. Every general should be rewarded, Dip. Get used to it. That's how I roll. Feel me?"

"That's what's up."

"However, you must also prepare for those who'll come up against you for the money that territory will bring. You're no longer playing checkers. It's chess. You now have something someone else wants. So in essence, you're not the hunter anymore. You're the hunted. Feel that?"

Dip shook his head yes.

"The name of the game is to not get comfortable at the top, to the degree of losing sight of who and what's lurking at the bottom," Tray emphasized. "Oh, yeah. Did you get your text message?"

"Yeah. I received yours and one from Bank One that probably was a mistake," Dip replied.

"Why do you say that?"

"Because it mentioned that I received a five-million-dollar wire transfer. That would be *nice*," Dip stated, laughing.

"What would you do with it?" Tray inquired

"Hmmm. Never figured I'd be in a position to see that much money, let alone have it in the bank. I really wouldn't know, honestly." Dip dropped his head a second. "Man, look. I was always told I wouldn't amount to shit. So as long as I stayed a step above shit, I felt I was in good shape. There wasn't an elevated level of expectation for me, or from me. That's just how it was. Feel me?"

"Yeah. I feel you, young blood. Expectation didn't live on my block either. Sometimes poverty took the place of potential. But it doesn't have to end this way," Tray encouraged. "And not every story has to be a success story. It's what you do with your life going forward that'll determine success. If you had the opportunity to be someone important, who would you be?"

"Man, I just want to be rich and out of this rat race. Could I think about that after I'm rich?" Dip inquired.

"It doesn't work like that. You must first become someone in order to become rich."

"I probably would just hire someone to invest for me and triple my money. So, I'll be rich without being someone important," Dip reasoned. "Don't they have people who make money for people investing?"

"Sure do. But how do you stop them from stealing your money or making bad investments?"

Dip shrugged.

"Chances are, you'd end up right back where you came from because you're too lazy and brainwashed to actually believe you can be somebody," Tray emphasized.

"I guess I need to start making some plans, huh?"

"If you plan on holding on to that five million dollars in your account, you'd better," Tray suggested.

Dip's eyes grew to the size of Bo-dollars as he registered what was just said. "You can't be serious?"

Tray smiled. "You earned every penny of it, and now you have the task of keeping it away from the thieves."

"I thought we were the thieves?"

"You've just moved up to a different class of thieves. But don't think you're rich yet. You're only hood rich."

"Not by your standards. But with this much money, my weight is definitely up something serious!"

Tray laughed. "Man, I know people that spend five million on a vacation without asking how much it costs. Look, tomorrow we're going shopping to get you some business attire."

"Man, thanks. You've blessed me like a father, and I'll never forget this."

"Thank me when you're a successful businessman, and not a day before," Tray insisted. "I know the dangerous territory you'll be traveling. You'll be tested at every level, and a failed test could cost you your life, Dip. Always keep that in mind and stay alert."

Dip took all that Tray said in and let it rest on his mental. He wasn't sure he had what it took to live up to Tray's expectations. But he would give it one hell of a try.

CHAPTER 18
Justice Served

Luqman crept alongside the home of his next victim. The home was one of the nicest in the neighborhood, eighteenth century Antebellum. It was in fact, the oldest in the neighborhood, and it also represented old money. The walls and floors were graced with the finest surfaces, mahogany and cypress, stained, then glossed to perfection.

Vinny Pachero, the son of a once prominent DA in Jefferson Parish twenty years ago, was now one of the most feared DAs. Inheriting his father's by any-means-necessary approach to convict strategy, he'd sent many guilty and innocent men to Angola State Penitentiary. Tonight, however, there lurked the repercussions of an innocent man's wrath! This would prove to be a serious problem for this gated community.

Dressed in all black, military-issued everything, Luqman made his way down the long trail that led to the back of the home. He patted his side, feeling for his hunting knife. It was there, and the 9-millimeter pistol too.

"I've waited for this day too long," he whispered to no one. He made it to the back door, then slid his key into the doorknob, turned it, and it crept open. Luqman remembered the distinct smell of the home from his visit there two days before. He posed as an electric maintenance man, and it worked like a charm. That would be the day he stole the key impression, enabling him to gain access, then subsequently steal the alarm code.

Tick, tick, tick, was all that could be heard. The sound of the grandfather clock signaled the age of the home's contents. The wooden floors creaked every couple of steps as Luqman made his way toward Vinny's bedroom. Vinny had little private life, other than his lover, whom Luqman witnessed him kissing on many occasions.

Creeping alongside the bed, Luqman silently watched Vinny sleep for a few seconds, until the rage and thirst for revenge overrode his thoughts. "Wake up, muthafucka. It's time to die!" Vinny jumped up into a sitting position, but was immediately knocked back down from the mighty blows thrown.

"What you want? Take everything, it's yours," he began offering. "How'd you get in here?" He tried to focus to get a visual of the perpetrator.

"That doesn't matter, muthafucka. I'm in here and that's all that matters. Don't you agree?"

"That's a very good point," Vinny thought. What do you want? Are you going to kill me? I have a safe with plenty of money in it. Just take it, then leave!"

"You would like that, huh? You gay muthafucka," Luqman said. "Fuck your money, muthafucka! That don't erase all them years I lost, due to your bitch-ass prosecuting me for something I didn't do!"

"But son, I could not have known I was sending an innocent man to prison. I swore to uphold the law."

"Open your mouth!" Luqman commanded.

Vinny began visibly crying crocodile tears. "Son, let's just talk about this, please. I'm sure we can find some common ground."

"This cracker don't follow instructions well," Luqman said, sliding his hand to his side and unclamping the huge hunting knife. He brought the knife down with tremendous force, and its butt came crashing down upon Vinny's head.

"Owww!" Vinny exclaimed, grabbing his head.

Luqman stuck the rag into Vinny's mouth, pulled out the duct tape, and then wrapped it twice around his head and mouth.

"Now it's time for you to listen, cocksucker! You will die today. No questions asked, or doubts about it. I've watched, plotted, and planned for this day for years. Tonight, you're going to get what you truly deserve. Since I left the penitentiary, I've visited the courtrooms and seen you still in action, still at work. You and your detectives fabricate the stories, get on the witness stand, and lie on a stack of Bibles. It only shows how much you believe in that Bible. The truth is that you muthafuckas don't believe in God or the law, if you did, you'd respect the law, then have respect for the God you pray to."

"But . . . I-I have upheld the law, and—"

"The only thing you've upheld is injustice. There has existed a secret society in Jefferson Parish for a long time. The DAs, judges, and lawyers have failed to administer justice as they swore to. Lawyers sell out their clients to free another client. Then, I've personally witnessed the destruction it has on the wives, children, and families that have struggled to make payments before and after the sell-out. An already struggling family is now left with thousands of dollars in debt, and broken promises by crooked-ass lawyers. Today, I get some of it back for them too, starting with yo' bitch ass!"

Luqman continued. "Sure, you crackers bring some of those lawyers to trial on hand picked cases you know they can win, but that's only to make more inmates lobby their family members to hire these bum-ass lawyers. Everyone thinks this lawyer is king of the hill after your manufactured win, instantly guaranteeing him hundreds of thousands of dollars for a verdict you bought by design." Vinnie's eyes grew larger after the last information was revealed. "You basically didn't lose anything, being that the charges should've been dropped anyway. But the name of the game is to accept the charges, then the client has to hire an attorney. That attorney, nine times out of ten, will be one of your boys who'll convince the crooked judge to set an outrageous high bond, so the client can't get out of jail. That means the monthly payments will continue as long as the client is in jail, and pose little risk in discontinuing those payments. Then every time the client's court date comes, there's another set-back by the attorney. Anything to keep that money coming. Right, Mr. District Attorney?"

Vinny's eyes now watered as he slowly came to grips with reality.

"That's what I thought, bitch! You cocksuckers have sent your children to college, and your children's children off this lil scheme. But the sad part is that you crackers are not smart. You cheat! You may be smarter than ninety percent of the people you scheme on, but ten percent get away because they're smarter than you, and buck the system, then never get caught up again. However, the easiest lives to take are those fresh off the porch from the playpen. The wannabe thugs who are dropouts and possess very little of anything in the brains department, right?" Luqman questioned.

"Aarrggh! Why won't you just get this shit over with!" Vinne yelled out of frustration. "No, no, no. I'm sorry. I didn't really mean that. Look, I don't want to die."

"Am I, right, Vinnie?" he asked again, but received no reply. "I'll take that silence, or no eye movement as a yes. I know you're wondering why you're still alive, right?"

Vinny's emotionless gaze spoke for him.

"I just needed to break down the little scheme you crackers have in effect, so you'd know from a life you tried to take, that your judges, lawyers, and DAs aren't that smart. Because if they were, I would've never got out of your trap, uncovered your scheme, then be in your bedroom, you faggot!" Luqman plunged the knife into Vinny's chest as sound attempted to escape his mouth, but to no avail. Blood leaked instead. Vinny's head slowly fell back onto his pillow with his eyes opened as wide as they could stretch. Then Luqman jumped into the bed and dragged the knife from his chest down to his stomach. His guts were hanging out and intestines leaked shit into the bed, making the scene even more gruesome.

Cautious of the time, Luqman slid his knife back into its case, then reached into Vinny's chest and yanked out his heart. Blood gushed everywhere as he hurriedly wrapped his heart, then placed it within a black sack. He jumped off the bed and stood there, staring at Vinny's body violently jerking.

"Now, you're truly who I thought you were, one heartless muthafucka! Today, another one of you low-life racist, muthafuckas has perished. But there's much more work to be done! Get ready. On my way, Jefferson Parish," Luqman stated as his smile widened. He walked around the home wiping clean anything that he may have touched, or any shoe prints he may have left. The bloody mess was confined to the bedroom, and the king-sized bed held most of the evidence, as the body was encircled in crimson.

At the back door, he visualized his exact steps, again. Satisfied with his performance, his message was sent. He now felt confident that he left nothing for a forensics team. So he let himself out of the back door.

Luqman placed another used pair of latex gloves in his black backpack. He retrieved another pair, then crept alongside Vinny's home to the front yard. Once there, he retrieved a can of red paint from the backpack. He lurked in the shadows a moment to let his eyes adjust to the darkness. It was approximately 2:30 a.m., and his next move needed the cover of night to execute.

This meant the occasional old lady seated at the big picture window peering out, needed to be discovered. The guy and girl seated in the car parked along the road making out, needed to be spotted.

After surveying the neighborhood, Luqman sprang into action. There was no fence, so accessing the front of the home required only a casual walk up to the wooden front porch. He shook the can with the marble rattling around inside, then went to work.

Out of his peripheral, he caught a ray of light from the headlights of a car turning onto the street of Vinny's home. He quickly dove behind a nearby flower bed. The vehicle moved slowly up the street until it was in plain view.

"Shit!" Luqman said, seeing the white and blue police car moving toward the home.

Standing as still as he could, the adrenaline began to heat up his body. He was 60% finished with his masterpiece, but the temptation to flee from a possible murder arrest seemed pretty appealing. The car slowed even more when it neared Vinny's home. *Do they see the message?* he thought. His body was betraying him as he felt the urge to run. But his mind had slowed to a halt, and was thinking of angles to determine the best decision. *Patience,* he thought.

Just as the thought occurred, the patrol car sped up as if there was suddenly an emergency. Luqman sprang into action once more as he sprayed the home in graffiti style. He was nearing the finish line, when he heard something or someone. He hit the dirt once again, ending up behind the flower bed.

An old white guy on a bicycle was coming down the street. He crept through, looking from home to home on each side of the street as if he were the neighborhood watch. Luqman lay still as the Peewee Herman look-alike stopped dead in his tracks. He stared at Vinny Pachero's home, then squinted in an effort to read the graffiti writings. After a few moments, Peewee Herman jumped on his bike, then peddled away as fast as he could.

Luqman sprang into action once more to complete his masterpiece, knowing his time was limited. *Just a few more strokes.*

"Finished," he stated, then stood back to admire his work.

Moments later, the sound of engines running at top speed was closing in from all directions. Luqman dropped the can in the backpack, then ran alongside the home toward the backyard. Red and blue lights were twirling everywhere. He quickly jumped over the back gate, then peeped from behind the new home with the two flood lights that popped. The oversized German shepherd in the next yard began barking. Luqman sprinted down the alley in an attempt to distance himself from the dog and Vinny's home. He jumped another gate, then crossed another street. The morning light was almost peeking out, threatening his cover. Frantically, he looked in all directions, hoping the vehicle he arrived in was in the direction he was headed. After a moment, he saw no more red and blue lights, nor were there engines roaring. Luqman reached out and checked for an unlocked door on an old white Econoline van, just as screeching tires were heard and the red and blue lights twirling. The door was locked. He then ran to the passenger's side. Locked also. The patrol cars were racing up the street toward him. *Last chance,* he thought as he ran to the back of the van. He gave one good pull on the handle, and to his relief it opened, and without the interior lights coming on.

Once inside, Luqman lay down as the patrol cars sped in all directions. *How long can I stay here? What are the chances they'll send the chase dogs after me? How long should I stay?*

Luqman had achieved his goal after he painted his masterpiece. The words, "Justice Served" fit the occasion perfectly. But would his masterpiece cost him his own life?

* * * * * * *

Troy and Ray-Ray stood outside the armored Suburban as James' jet landed at their private landing strip. The 737 jet engines roared to a halt as the plane came to a stop in front of them, then James and the Taliban soldiers stepped out and down the stairs.

"Where's Salvator?" Troy inquired.

"He's here already," James acknowledged. "We dropped him and some fighters off to take care of a few loose ends, then he had a meeting with the Commission."

"We've secured the hotel in eastern New Orleans for our friends," Troy stated. "How was your flight?"

"Interesting, but needed for what I've been told. It seems we have some company down here that didn't get my permission before they came, and to top it off, they aren't even good for the economy," James joked.

"So, they're not tourists?" Troy questioned.

"Nope, and that's going to cost them more than they imagined."

"So, what's the plan?"

"I need you to get with the special ops team Irvin's sending this way. They'll be monitored for now, but our goal is to let all of their people in, then make an example out of them for future references," James assured.

"What exactly are they coming here to do?"

"To kidnap me," James replied, laughing. "They're a part of George's team. We received confirmation he was wired ten million each from Rafael Fernandez and Pablo Hernandez as part of their war fund. They've hired the best and are willing to pay generously, as we now know. You see, the trade embargo is very important to

152

Cuba and Colombia. These men stand to profit billions if they can sway Malik to do as they want. Apparently, my name has surfaced, due to their search, and an assassin team has been sent my way.

"They clearly didn't know who they were dealing with, but they'll wish they'd passed on the job. I promise you," James said. "Look, call the morgue and pick up fifty body bags! When all their forces get here then die, none of them will be buried here. I want them muthafuckas sent back to their countries, special delivery," James said furiously, while seated in back of the Suburban. Sweat beaded up on his forehead as his blood pressure spiked.

"If war is what they've come for, it'll come swift, no questions or excuses. It's on," James assured. "I've ordered identification papers on our friends in the back. The next phase will happen a few days from now. We have four training camps that are located at the major entrance points in the United States. At least twenty-five of these vicious muthafuckas will be set up in each state." James took his thoughts off the assassins infiltrating his city.

Moments later, the convoy of Suburbans and coach buses turned into the Days Inn hotel in New Orleans East. James stepped out, then strolled into the office where his long-time friend stood waiting.

Rudy and James were really close, like brothers. They met on the streets and stayed friends because of the streets. Rudy soon needed a way out of the streets, and James made that happen. He now owned the hotel, and had a family that consisted of a wife and two kids.

"What's good, James?" Rudy inquired, happily.

"Business as usual," he stated as the two men approached each other, then embraced. "Look, these are the friends I told you about."

Rudy looked out the window at all the Taliban fighters with turbans on their heads looking like Osama Bin Laden. He then looked back to James.

"They're not about to start blowing shit up, huh?"

"Not our shit," James assured. "How's the family?"

"They're doing fine, all praise be to Allah. And how are the siblings?"

"Troy's outside. Deon's running the firm."

"No shit! And what about you?"

"Pinch hitting, that's all. You know me. But look, I really need to be going. If you need me, don't hesitate to call."

"You've already done enough. I got this, James."

James then strolled out of the office with Rudy in tow. Rudy needed to lie down his no explosives rule. He knew as he witnessed the Taliban soldiers de-boarding the buses.

CHAPTER 19
Business or Pleasure

Where the hell is he? Fidel thought, awaiting his friend, Pedro Sanchez. Fidel stood up and reached into his pocket, retrieving a five-dollar bill. He placed it on the table, then strolled out of the coffee shop. Suddenly, a sharp object pressed against his back.

"Don't turn around or you'll die," someone stated.

What the fuck is happening? Is this a hit in the middle of an airport? Fidel wondered, searching his mind for anyone this bold. No one came to mind but himself. What about his mission? And James Johnson? And the $500,000 George McNamara would pay him to kidnap James?

"You can turn around, now," the voice commanded.

Thank God, it's Pedro, Fidel thought. "One day, you're not going to be so lucky, my friend," Fidel said.

"Loosen up, friend. Welcome to New Orleans," Pedro greeted.

Fuck New Orleans, you piece of shit! "Where are you parked? So we can get the hell away from all these agents."

"Just outside over here," Pedro stated, tapping Fidel on his back, hoping he'd loosen up.

Pedro made New Orleans his home five years ago after taking a hit on Colombia's last president. Since then, he'd managed to stay off the radar, but was now anxious for some action.

"You know where to get some heavy artillery?" Fidel asked.

"You must've forgotten what I do, or do you think you're the only assassin? That'll be the easy part, my friend," Pedro replied as he threw the luggage into the back of the Tahoe. Both men then jumped in, and Pedro pulled away.

"So, what brings you to these neck of the woods?"

"Someone by the name of James Johnson," Fidel informed him.

"Is it business or pleasure?"

"Both," Fidel shot back, thinking about the five hundred thousand he was going to make to kidnap this chump.

"I mean, do you know this Mr. Johnson, or what he does?" Pedro pried.

"Does it make a difference? He could be an oyster fisherman. What the fuck do I care? Fidel stated, slightly losing his temper. "Look, I'm here to kidnap this muthafucka, then hold him until further notice."

I know this fool's not talking about kidnapping the James Johnson. Maybe I need to be taking a long vacation to Florida, Pedro thought. *Holy shit! And he came by himself?*

"So, does this Mr. Johnson own a law firm on Canal Street?" Pedro asked. *Please say no, you fuckin idiot!*

"Oh, so you know him?" Fidel inquired.

You idiot! Someone sent you to kidnap the most powerful black man on this side of the equator and you ask if I know him. You should too. "Not personally, but he's a very popular man down south." *That's just putting it mildly, in hopes that you think about giving that money back, or just staying away from me,* Pedro thought.

"It makes no difference to me how popular he is!"

It should, you damn fool. "So, Fidel, how many men are you using on this mission?"

"Hmph! I have five of my best men on their way as we speak," Fidel said with pride.

That many, huh? Pedro shook his head. "You sure this is the right guy, this James Johnson?" Pedro inquired, hoping a mistake had been made.

Fidel retrieved a picture of James from the file provided by George, then handed it to Hector.

Someone must want Fidel dead. This is a suicide mission, Pedro thought.

"My friend, my family and I were just about to take a long trip, a much-needed vacation. I will help you obtain the artillery, then we'll be leaving." Pedro forgot about the much-needed action he wanted before James' name was mentioned. He also had no family, but still needed that vacation.

"What's the problem?" Fidel asked, observing Pedro watching his mirrors regularly, and with a hint of nervousness.

"Look, my friend. You're going to need more than five men to kidnap James Johnson."

"Okay, then I'll send for five more. That should do, 'cause my men are the very best in the whole world! There will be no escaping my well-trained assassins. I trained them myself in the jungles of Colombia under extreme conditions and heat," Fidel bragged.

And you'll bury them yourself, too. I'm outta here, Pedro thought. "My friend, you're going to need more than ten," he said. "Ten men trained in the jungles of Africa wouldn't get you into a restaurant if James were eating!"

"Okay. How many do you suggest I send for?"

"You're going to need an army, my friend. James Johnson has men around him that are the very best at what they do. These men are legends, and he is also. I don't know who assigned you this job, but chances are good he knows you're here; he knows everything about who enters or leaves his territory."

"You talk like James is a damn superhero. I am a legend myself! No, I will take him with my ten men," Fidel concluded. "If what you say is true, my friend, then I'll become a legend or a corpse. I know for sure that no one can ever tell a war story if they've never been in one, and that is what I've come here for. To go to war! I respect your input and advice, but a war is only won in battle."

"Oh, well. Can't say you weren't warned. It was good to have known you, but one must also learn that every war isn't fought; some are negotiated," Pedro said finally.

* * * * * * *

Don Hamas strolled through the Airport in a $5,000 Davinchi Gardana Italian-made suit, looking like the second coming of John Gotti. The only difference was that Don Hamas didn't die inside the

Federal prison as Gotti.

His focus was that of a cobra about to strike an unsuspecting victim. He paid attention to all sights and sounds within the airport. The woman running after her child, the young man impatiently waiting in the ticket line, the police curiously looking for anything out of the ordinary. He honed his skills while in the penitentiary. It was now paying off, because he noticed everything and took pride in the attribute. Especially at his age, an age whereas these attributes would traditionally begin diminishing. The last fifteen years he prepared his mind for everything and underestimated nothing. Now, many men would ultimately pay a non-negotiable price for what his friend Don Alberto, had to endure.

The meeting today would be a formality, as he'd made up his mind a long time ago. The Commission, in Don Hamas' mind, had been reduced to a joke. They betrayed him! How could he be loyal to the same Commission who turned their backs on one of their very own? He entrusted his territory to Don Alberto, and he now knew two things for sure. Don Alberto was no longer living, *and* his territory was in the hands of a *nigger*! That was a problem. His thoughts were suddenly interrupted by someone calling his name. The man standing before him was Mario Catino, a member of Don Cordona's family, Don Hamas remembered.

"Welcome Don Hamas. The Commission has sent me to accompany you back to their location. How was your trip?"

"About the same as all others on a plane. Very shaky," he replied.

The snow-white Bentley was parked curb-side as the chauffeur stood beside it. Dressed in a black tuxedo, awaiting their arrival. Once there, the chauffeur opened the door, and both men slid into the top-of-the-line in elegance vehicle.

"Would you like something to drink?" Mario asked, as he waved his hand toward the miniature bar with various wines and liquor bottles stacked in it.

"I never drink before business," the don answered. "So, what's been going on with you, Mario?"

"Same ol' shit," Mario stated, careful not to say more than he was supposed to.

Don Hamas immediately sensed it from his body language. Knowing that Mario wouldn't reveal much about anything, he kicked back and enjoyed the ride in silence. He was steaming inside, but learned to manage his emotions through meditation and yoga classes. The ride took ten minutes as they now pulled up to the Royal Sonesta Hotel on Canal Street. The chauffeur opened the door, then both men stepped out the back of the Bentley. They strolled into the hotel and onto the elevator. Once at the presidential suite's door, Mario slid the electronic key, then the door snapped open.

Mario led the way through the spacious suite lavishly decorated and stocked full of caviar, sushi, and champagne, courtesy of the hotel. Seated at the table were, Don Cardona, Don Santos, Don Deandros, Don Silvas, and Don Giodana. They all noticed the difference the fifteen years had made on Don Hamas immediately. Gone, was the arrogance that followed him around like a halo. Everyone figured he'd harbor negative feelings about the Don Alberto fiasco, but what's done is done, they decided amongst themselves long ago. They never retaliated once their forces came before them to share the circumstances surrounding Don Alberto's death. Simply put, he broke the laws and it led to his demise. The commission accepted Salvator's reasoning; how could they not? He was the most loyal enforcer the Commission had ever known. His evaluation was unquestionably 100% right, 100% of the time, they concluded…

"Greetings, Don Hamas," Don Cardona stated. "Take a seat and make yourself comfortable."

Don Hamas did as he was told.

"First of all, it is the Commission's unanimous view that you remain a respected member. Many years have passed and a lot has changed, but much remains the same," Don Cardona expressed. "True, you most likely have questions about territory that once belonged to you, and we will address these concerns."

No shit, Don Hamas considered.

"However, your rights to various gaming entitlements for the past fifteen years have continued to be put aside in the event you were released." Don Cardona slid Don Hamas an envelope. He opened it, then read the print out with enough zeros that made him do a double take.

"I hope those figures prove to be around what you figured," Don Cardona expressed, knowing fifteen-million to a broke man was the difference between living and dying.

"Don't spend it all in one place," Don Santos joked.

"I'll keep that in mind," Don Hamas stated without a hint of distaste for the remark made by Santos. *I'll keep you in mind too,* Hamas promised himself. *My first enemy has shown his true self; how many more are there?*

"Have you any questions or concerns about the money?" Santos asked.

"Should I have any?" Hamas shot back.

Don Santos shrugged. "Look, gentlemen, I'm very grateful for the consideration by this commission if that's what you're wondering. Don Santos," Hamas continued after giving Santos a wry smile. "The money is greatly appreciated also, and just know that if the shoe was on the other foot, my support would have been the same. But let's reflect for a minute. As we know, everything created has its time, then it moves on. Life, friends, family, health, etc. Absolutely nothing is promised, except the death of it! The Commission today has proven stronger than any of the examples given from a loyalty perspective, and that's how it should be. It's how it's always been," Hamas emphasized, with the clenching of his fist. "Nevertheless, I won't get into our history, but I'll make this point. We have survived generations of wars, politics, and prosecution by generations of law enforcement families designed to disrupt and ultimately, annihilate our way of life. Yet we've remained here, and in many cases, remained loyal to the codes and by-laws that have kept us surviving and steadily building momentum. So, Don Santos, I remain grateful to be a part of the traditions that made me the man I remain before you!" *I wonder who has something to say about that,* Don Hamas considered.

"Don Hamas, you said in many cases the Commission has

remained loyal. Do you wish to elaborate on such cases where we haven't?" Don Deandros questioned.

"That is true, Don Deandros. I do feel that Don Alberto's death could have been avoided had the commission stepped in. I also feel that I should've been contacted about the decisions that followed in relations to the territory," Don Hamas expressed.

Don Silvas laughed out loud. "What rights did you think you had to any territory sitting in a Federal penitentiary?" Silvas inquired.

"Blood, sweat, and tears," Don Hamas insisted as his temper began to reach its boiling point. Perspiration beaded on his forehead and nose as his temper told these muthafuckas how he really felt, but now was not the time.

"But your blood, sweat, and tears are no different than any other member of this commission, past or present, who lost territories in wars. What makes your territory so precious?" Silvas questioned.

Another enemy has surfaced. Don Hamas paused so he'd choose his words carefully. The commission had missed the point. The source of Don Hamas' frustration wasn't the loss of territory itself, but rather who he lost it to …

"Obviously, our views on this issue are different. I hope no less important, but maybe had it been the loss of *your* territory, our views would be the same," Hamas suggested.

"Perhaps not," Don Giodana offered. "Your rights to this commission and its decision or its by-laws didn't exist when you were in the penitentiary. Do you honestly think anyone with this commission was obligated to conduct its business through channels afforded to you by the Feds?" Don Giodana questioned, then lean back in his chair, folding his arms across his huge belly and waited on a reply from Don Hamas.

"Look, there existed other channels, as we very well know, Don Giodana. Yet, I can only speak of the respect I would've afforded the next member of this commission, had it been their head in the lion's mouth," Hamas concluded.

"Then, you would have been a fool! Would it have been worth another's head in the lion's mouth, too?" Salvator inquired as he stood up, then adjusted his suit jacket. "Many men have come before you, then found themselves in your position, but none as unaccepting of the consequences as you. It's as simple as this. In order for you to lose your position of entitlement, you had to lose your freedom. The Commission followed protocol and named Don Alberto heir to your territory and stake in the commission's daily governing as you wished. Your obligation to the Commission was transferred, and so was the Commission's obligation to you," Salvator said. He had been seated in back of the room, clad in a black suit, black sunglasses, and carrying a black gun. He now knew this man would mean trouble down the line for his friend James. But this also meant trouble for Don Hamas!

Who the fuck does this assassin dog think he is? How dare he lecture me on how the commission works! Don Hamas thought as his blood began to seethe. "You speak as if you're part of the Commission, Salvator. Maybe since I've been away, your status has changed. Do enlighten me. Who are you now, and from what position do you speak?"

"I am who you've always known me to be, Don Hamas. My status will never change. It's against the codes set forth before any of our existence. However, my role is no less important than anyone seated at this table. I am the blood, sweat, and tears you spoke of so eloquently! Whose blood pours into the streets when territorial wars are being fought against families and for the Mafia families? Whose sweat drips from every pore in their bodies as they wait in scorching heat on rooftops, trying to kill assassins before they kill a member of this commission? And who sheds the tears when a fellow assassin loses his life to protect a life that views our profession as, only assassins? Are we now unworthy to speak amongst the lives we protect? Can you recall a time when you did any of these things, Don Hamas?" Salvator angrily questioned.

Don Hamas stood in a daze. There was nothing he could do or say, other than take revenge.

"I'll take that as a no! And to answer the question of who I am? I *am* the by-laws! Whenever someone crosses the line, who does this commission call? Exactly! But, if you want them to call you instead, be my guest. Nevertheless, I am the law at this time. What happened to Don Alberto was all his doing. He acted alone and intended to profit alone. He moved without the Commission, by making a play for someone else's territory, and it backfired! A victim of his own scheme. Greed got the best of him, simply put. Your former territory became spoils of war through Don Alberto being outmaneuvered, and we knew nothing about what happened until after it did. The Commission ordered the hit on the man responsible, but it was rescinded once it was learned why Don Alberto was killed. The contract went against our by-laws and infringed upon the road never traveled by wise men. That would have caused conflict had we moved negligently."

"And what conflict would that be?" Hamas questioned.

"The only violation that had occurred was done by Don Alberto, who knew the by-laws and the chances he took in acting outside of them. We support laws, not greed. That's your conflict! The gentlemen had every right to defend what was considered his territory. And he knew enough about our by-laws to counter Don Alberto. It took him four hours to gain control of the territory, a flawless operation. Many men died along with Don Alberto, and because of him," Salvator concluded.

"So, is this information about this gentleman available to me?" Don Hamas inquired.

"What's the matter? You don't trust the Commission's decision?" Salvator asked, anxiously awaiting the reply.

"It's not a big issue, but maybe I wanted to one day meet him." Hamas stated with a devious sneer.

"Maybe we can set up a meeting with you gentlemen," Salvator said.

"That might be a good idea, Salvator. Why don't you do that," Don Hamas stated with malice.

Chapter 20
The Indecent Proposal

James received the news on his way home from his earlier flight. The three world renowned scientists he hired five years ago, had pulled it off. They listened as James proposed his idea, studied it objectively, then made a collective decision amongst each other, to begin work on the highly-complexed experiment. This technology, if perfected, would revolutionize the world, and possibly bring James in consideration for the highly-coveted Nobel Peace Prize.

Perfect timing, James thought.

The armored, platinum-colored Bentley rolled up to the curb in front of Harrah's Casino on Canal Street. The chauffeur exited the vehicle, hurried around to the back passenger side, then opened the door. Salvator stepped out of the vehicle, looked around, then was handed a black attaché case. He stood at six feet, four inches, 250 pounds, wearing a black suit, black sunglasses, and concealed a black gun. Nothing had changed.

Suddenly, James appeared from inside the back of the Bentley. He stepped forward donning a platinum Armani suit tailored to his six feet, four inch, 222-pound frame. He adjusted his suit, then his tie. After glancing at the presidential diamond bezel Rolex, then the platinum big block gator shoes, he began his stroll, satisfied with his flawless appearance. Salvator followed, still peeping from behind the sunglasses.

WILLIE GROSS JR. WITH WAHIDA CLARK

James walked into Harrah's, then continued down the long strip filled with poker machines and dice tables, etc. People stopped what they were doing as James walked through, looking as if he'd just been plucked off a limited edition copy of *GQ* magazine. Women whispered amongst themselves as James walked toward the elevators. His shoulder-length dreads were in sync with his long, graceful steps, making him even more irresistible to the gawking women.

Moments later, they reached the elevators, then out of nowhere, a young lady approached James, only to be turned away by the huge assassin, Salvator. James smiled at the young lady's boldness.

The elevator arrived and the two men boarded it. The door opened on the penthouse floor, prompting Salvator to step off, look in both directions, then signal James to step off. They approached the door to the suite. Salvator slid the key, then they walked into the room.

The Dons were all seated in the living room area, casually talking. They were now seeing James for the first time and were noticeably impressed.

"Gentlemen," Salvator began. "I was asked by Mr. Johnson to set up this meeting while you all were here on business. He wanted to meet, then discuss some future opportunities that may exist for you men. I'll let Mr. Johnson take it from here," Salvator proposed.

"Gentlemen, thanks for agreeing to meet with me, and I hope you'll find the accommodations to your enjoyment during the rest of your stay. The casino has been notified that each of you can play up to one hundred thousand dollars on my tab, not that you need it, but for hospitality purposes."

"Today, I'm offering you gentlemen first-hand information about an investment you're pumping a lot of money into, that'll soon become a loss instead of a viable investment. That investment is the drug trade. Namely heroin and cocaine," James emphasized.

The Dons immediately refocused their attention.

"Nevertheless, I've summoned you gentlemen out of respect to this Commission for not intervening into my affairs many years ago. So, in return, I've come to save you hundreds of millions of dollars, then help you make hundreds of millions of dollars, with no strings attached."

James noticed the expression on Don Giodana's face. His wrinkled forehead seemed to be asking, *Who does this muthafucka think he is? The government can't stop drugs. So how can he?*

"I know, it doesn't seem real, but before you leave here tonight, hopefully I can convince you as a friend would another. Pull out now and don't invest another penny into the drug game. I've been working on a project that has been approved after five years of scientific research. I won't get into the specifics, but this is my proposition to you." James took a sip of bottle water from the ice bucket. All the Dons were baffled about the revelation, as their relaxed posture had now become tense.

"Don Giodana," James began. "You oversee the drug trade in New York, Wisconsin, Nevada, and Utah, right?" He nodded, then James reached into his attaché case and retrieved paperwork with figures printed out. "New York's monthly take is fifteen million, Wisconsin is ten million, Nevada is ten million, and Utah is ten million. Am I correct?"

Don Giodana nodded yes.

"Don Santos, Washington's monthly take is ten million, Missouri is ten million, Indiana is ten million, and Arkansas is ten million. Am I correct?"

Don Santos agreed with a nod.

"Don Silvas, Pittsburgh's monthly intake is fifteen million, Colorado is ten million, Maine is ten million, Rhode Island is five million. Am I correct?"

Don Silvas also nodded, impressed with the man's ability in researching their private information.

"In three months, you will not be able to purchase a kilo of cocaine or heroin anywhere in the world," James stated. He paused just to get a read on their body language. He knew their attention was his.

"Not a coco leaf or poppy seed will be picked without my approval. I purposely left out three states that will be under my control. Louisiana is already mine; Texas and Florida are the others." A brief silence passed before James made his next statement.

"Your guess is correct, gentlemen. Those are the entrance points. But, I won't need them for what you may be thinking. The drugs won't even make it to the shores of the United States. As for my proposition, I'll get down to the business portion. All of you can still receive those monthly figures, but not from the drug trade."

"Oh, so that's what this is about. You want to take over the drug game. A hostile takeover. And so, what are we supposed to sell now, insurance?" Don Giodana asked.

"No, I'm going to deposit those figures into your accounts every month, *not* to sell drugs," James pitched.

"What's the catch?" Don Cardone questioned, knowing something had to be sacrificed, an arm, a leg, or something.

"The catch is, if you don't sell drugs anymore, my people can no longer buy drugs." James paused. *They think I've gone mad.* "I'm going to buy them instead, so, the drugs never make it to our neighborhoods, then destroy lives."

"So, what do we do in the states where we no longer sell drugs? They're still our territory?" Silvas inquired.

"You invest in them, Don Silvas. I'm giving you free money, but I'm also hoping to gain a partner in my fight," James pitched.

"What do you mean? Invest?" Don Cordona asked curiously.

"Improving the quality of life in those states. What's wrong with building better housing, then creating jobs in those communities? The citizens of those communities will be looking for work now that the drugs are gone. You'd be creating a working-class community. Your states will be worth more to you in a long and short run by reducing crime. You'll profit even more once you continue building apartment complexes and businesses that will give jobs to your renters. That means your rent on time and better workers dedicated to making you money," James suggested.

"So you want us to help you help *your* people?" Silvas questioned.

"First of all, I want you to help yourselves. I could've said nothing about my plans, put them in motion, and in five months tops, gotten the states for free. What are those states worth to you without the drug trade? Nothing! This isn't an ultimatum; it's a promise of something good, or bad for you. My goal is to always create alliances, not enemies. But six months from now, all of you will be laughing at your enemies as you witness their empires crumble. They will search the world over, then come back empty-handed. Drugs won't exist anywhere." James paused, unbuttoned his jacket, then took a glance at his watch as if indicating his time was short.

"I either watch some empires crumble, or all of them. That's your choice tonight. And, I will need your answers before we leave." James walked over to the table, then retrieved some more paperwork from the attaché case.

"These are monthly contracts and figures I spoke about. If you accept my offer, fill out the accounting information, then sign the contract. There happens to be one other matter needing to be addressed. In these states belonging to you, no drugs are to be sold by you or otherwise," James stated.

"So, what are we now, honorary policemen?" Don Santos asked.

"Don Santos. Have you calculated how much money you'll receive from me yearly?"

"Yes, I have."

"Does $480 million sound about right?"

"That's correct," Santos agreed.

"That's nearly half a billion dollars, plus your investments that'll possibly flip those numbers. Now, out of that money, you're not planning on investing anything towards keeping your investment safe?" James stated curiously.

Santos shrugged.

"You're really not appearing to be a solid partner, Don Santos." James glanced at his watch again, then stood up in front of the Dons looking frustrated.

"I respect this Commission because I remember a time when I needed its respect. But, as a businessman, I will not bend any further than I have. That respect will remain, but my offer will not. I'm walking out of here headed for the airport to meet with the drug lords that are responsible for one hundred percent of the drugs smuggled into the United States. They will know a good deal when they hear one. The question before you tonight, gentlemen, is: Do you?" James knew he'd seal the deal in mentioning the drug lords, and he knew this offer was simply too good to turn down. He walked over, then retrieved his attaché case, and without even looking at the contract, he scooped the papers up from the Dons, then shoved them into the case.

"I take it you gentlemen will have a good time for the remainder of your stay, and it was my pleasure to have finally met you," James stated.

"One more question, Mr. Johnson," Don Silvas requested.

The greedy man question, James figured. "May I answer it before you ask?"

"Be my guest," Don Silvas stated.

"The deposits will begin three months from today, then continue as long as we're partners."

Don Silvas just nodded, indicating that James had once again done his homework.

* * * * * * *

"This is Channel 8 News team reporting live from the scene of a very gruesome murder in Jefferson Parish. All reports confirm that the deceased is none other than a well-known Assistant District Attorney for the Jefferson Parish District Attorney's Office. Everyone in this well-secured gated community is wondering how such a heinous crime could happen so close to home. Amidst all the drama of today's events, speculation is running rampant of a possible serial killer on the loose. Our sources confirm a pattern of law enforcement officials being slayed, and I'm joined here with a member of the Jefferson Parish Crime Task Force, Sergeant Jones, who can possibly confirm those reports."

"Sergeant Jones, what can you tell us about this latest murder as well as the possibility of a serial murderer of law enforcement officials within Jefferson Parish?"

"Well, Mitch. This is an ongoing investigation as you know. I won't speculate about any serial murderer, but we're exploring all avenues and possibilities; what we do know about today's event, is the victim is a long-standing Assistant District Attorney, Mr. Vinny Pachero. We think this murder occurred this morning around 1:00 a.m. to 3:00 a.m. There are no suspects at this time, and I'd ask that anyone having seen anything unusual between these times or otherwise, please contact the Sheriff's Office immediately. Crime Stoppers is offering a ten thousand dollar reward for any information that leads to the arrest and conviction of the perpetrator or perpetrators of this crime."

"Sergeant Jones, did there seem to be signs of a forced entry, or what's the likelihood that the victim knew his killer?"

"I can't get into the specifics, other than the deceased's name and his location within the home, which was the bedroom."

"What do you think was meant by the words, 'Justice Served,' painted on the outside of Mr. Pachero's home?" the reporter asked, who'd just walked up.

"Ladies and gentlemen, we're not clear on why the killer did anything as of yet. Our goal is to process all the possible evidence found at the crime scene, and maybe it'll point us in a direction. But until then, anything at this time would be pure speculation," Sergeant Jones concluded.

"There you have it, ladies and gentlemen. Another murder in Jefferson Parish, possibly linked to the others. Or, that's what our sources are speculating. We'll bring any new developments to you as we receive them. But until then, thanks for tuning in to America's number one news team, Channel 8 News."

Within the home of Vinny Pachero, investigators feverishly combed the horrific crime scene in an attempt to uncover any possible leads. Detective David and Officer Rosotti agreed that the suspect was good. He took his time, then tortured the victim, as he did his last two victims.

* * * * * * *

Miles away, Luqman stood in front of the TV in his home, monitoring the broadcast. Suddenly, he flicked it off, once he observed his handiwork. He then strolled over to the refrigerator, retrieved the sack that contained Vinny's heart, then headed for the backyard. His pit bull, Treach was anxiously awaiting the treat. Luqman played around with Treach a few minutes, then emptied the sack into the bowl.

The feeling he received was just as gratifying as the actual kill. Vinny Pachero was now off his list, and the detectives involved with his case were in his sights. *Beware, muthafuckas. I'm coming.*

* * * * * * *

Kane had been uptown making a drop that turned into him chilling with a couple fellows he'd done time with, until he received a call from a jump-off from the Saint Thomas Projects.

Last time he'd gotten with ol' girl, she blew his mind with the tricks she performed with her big, juicy ass while riding his dick. He loved his girl, Diamond, but, Wanda was the truth. *The bitch said she was home playing with the pussy, thinking about me.* "I'm on my way," Kane stated. He hurriedly threw up the deuces, then left the homies hanging. He was now rolling down Washington Avenue in his lime-green Charger. Then, under the cover of limo-tint, he lit a cigar full of purple haze.

His attention was suddenly distracted, so he slowed to a creep, but conscious enough not to stop traffic. *That's Dip bitch ass,* he thought. He pulled over to the side of the road, then began stalking his prey.

Repeatedly, his phone went off, as Wanda continued calling. But Kane continuously pressed IGNORE. *What this nigga doing posted up at the Spur Station as if he own it? Maybe this that nigga spot.* A man exited the Spur Station with two duffle bags, then threw them into the back of a Range Rover that Dip was leaning against. *That's got to be money! Either way, I must have it!* Kane began dialing.

"Yo, Lil Killa. I need you like a fish need water, homie," Kane said.

"What's good, playboy?"

"Man, there's this nigga over here at the Spur Station by the Saint Thomas Projects with two duffle bags of money and dope," he lied. "We needs to get it."

"You got-damn skippy we do," Lil Killa stated.

"Where them niggas at you run with?" Kane inquired.

"They right here."

"They have artillery?"

"Shit, we have enough artillery with us to shoot up the Saint Thomas Project for a month straight, and it's in the car with us now."

Stupid niggas dot com is where your pictures should be posted, Kane thought. "Look, I know this nigga won't be here long with all that loot, so you niggas need to hurry. Do you have another car so you can hit the station, that nigga, then get everything?"

"Yeah, we can pick up one along the way."

"Look. I want you to spin on this nigga by yourself. Let them other niggas go get what's in the station. The nigga is sitting in a platinum Range Rover like he's King Midas."

"On everything, playboy. They won't have to do an autopsy on this nigga!"

"How far are you away?"

"About five minutes, we pushing it, fool!"

"Hurry up before this money gets away." Kane leaned back in his seat behind limo tint, anxiously awaiting his goons to come put an end to Dip. *Yeah, nigga. Today your ass about to meet your maker.* He inhaled purple haze and turned his music up a notch. *That old-school shit, Scarface.* Kane began singing along.

♪ *I started small-time dope game cocaine, pushing rocks on the block, never broke, man.* ♪

Ten minutes later, Kane watched Lil Killa pull up to the last gas pump. Three niggas pulled up to the other end, then headed inside carrying major heat. Lil Killa walked up to Dip's window with an AK-47, then tapped on it with the barrel.

"Hey, nigga, it's time to die with your bitch ass," said Lil Killa, as he began pulling the trigger. The AK-47 roared and spit shells everywhere as they ejected for what seemed like eternity, but the glass didn't budge. Lil Killa pulled back from a wider distance, then began the assault on the Range Rover again.

Braca! Braca! Braca! Braca! Braca!

Nothing but sparks flew, but again the window never gave in. Suddenly, gunfire erupted from inside the Spur Station. Lil Killa began walking off from Dip, who seemed to be laughing the entire time. It was now his turn. Dip slid his window down enough for the .45 Desert Eagle to obtain a clear shot, then pulled the trigger.

Boom! Boom! Boom! Boom!

The powerful gun sounded off. Lil Killa's head exploded on contact.

"Fuck!" Kane stated, slamming his fist against the steering wheel of the Charger. He then witnessed Dip's position his Range Rover in front of the door of the station.

Dip waited there like a buzzard on a fence, but with his passenger window rolled down. There was nothing Kane could do as he watched the two men coming out, dragging another man. Two duffle bags were being carried by the two men, right before he witnessed the flashes of light and the booming sounds of Dip's Desert Eagle. The three men dropped to the ground along with the duffle bags.

Hurriedly Dip exited the vehicle, walked around the truck where the three men lay, and retrieved the duffle bags. He opened his back door, threw them in, and drove away from the crime scene as if nothing happened. He passed by Kane's vehicle with his foot on the pedal, and with the focus of a cobra in making sure he didn't get pulled over.

Kane heard the sirens whirling from a distance. He pulled away, still replaying in his mind the drama that had just unfolded. He knew with absolute certainty what he was up against at the expense of Lil Killa and his crew. *Better them than me.*

* * * * * * *

"Tray, where you at?" Dip questioned, his voice laced with urgency.

"At the club. What's wrong?"

"Niggas just tried to get at me and rob the station," Dip replied.

"You need a doctor?"

"Thanks to the Range Rover, I don't. But that lil nigga's AK

174

beat the truck up pretty bad."

"That's replaceable. You're not! They got away?"

"Not on my watch," Dip assured.

"Were there any witnesses?"

"Didn't see any, but I'm having this sinking feeling there's more to this," Dip alluded.

"I have an idea," Tray stated. "I'll call the police chief and see who the victims were. This way, we'll find out who they were affiliated with, and maybe there's a big fish lurking behind the scene, feel me?"

"Yeah, I feel ya."

"How many dead?"

"I left four bodies outside. I don't know what's inside. Too many sirens speeding to the scene."

"Do they have cameras outside?"

"Yeah, we installed them once we bought the store, why?"

"Because we need to get that DVD before it falls into the wrong hands. I'll see you when you get here." Tray hung up.

Chapter 21
The Schemer

"George, my friend. How's everything going in Washington?" Pablo inquired from his home in the Bahamas.

"Everything is going according to the plan," George lied.

"That's very good news, George. Yet, I haven't heard anything on the news reporting that your president is lifting the embargo. Am I correct?"

"Rome wasn't built in a day, either, Pablo," George shot back. "Look, these things take time and strategy. You must be patient. This administration is new. They're not going to move at warp speed to undo policies in place, without laying the necessary groundwork first." *These foreigners don't understand politics.* "Besides, these policies have been in existence for over a century," George added.

"Fuck policies," Pablo emphasized. "You just received twenty million dollars to make this thing happen, and that's what I'm expecting. No questions asked. You shouldn't have promised me things out of your reach. You didn't speak of policies when you asked for that twenty million, remember?"

"That wasn't the issue at the time, Pablo. I told you to give me a little time so I could work out the kinks. I'm actually on my way to meet with the President about this very issue. So, when I hear something, you'll be the first to know."

George hung up the phone, then reclined in his comfortable chair. *Fuck Pablo. Who the fuck does he think he is?*

Minutes later, George exited his office en route to the Oval Office, finding Malik standing with his back to him, peering out of the window. *Why does he always stare out of that damn window?*

"Knock, Knock," George stated, standing behind the President, jarring him out of his daydream. "What's on your mind?"

Malik spun around toward George, now wondering what scheme he'd been working on.

"Oh, nothing much," Malik lied. "The usual. Signing and making calls," he added. "Then, there's them old, worn out Republicans that are still out of touch, time, and ideas, but insist on telling us how to, or how not to run a country," Malik joked. "Hell, the last time I checked, they ran the country into a depression and a recession. Have you heard anything different, George?"

"No, sir. They're the same Republicans we defeated in November . . ."

"That's what I remember too," Malik insisted.

I really don't have time for this little game. Fuck the Republicans! "Mr. President, it's like you said, they're out of touch with reality," George responded.

"Maybe they've located scientists that created a super smart pill that works super-fast," Malik suggested.

Who the fuck cares? George was growing more impatient. "I don't recall the FDA approving such a drug, Mr. President. As a matter of fact, they're still who we thought they were. No smarter!"

"They had me fooled, George, judging from the press conferences they're scheduling. Then talking about what we should be doing when they've done the opposite for the last eight years." Malik got a better look at his advisor. "What's on your mind today, George?"

"I've been getting messages from other countries attempting to begin talks about our international trade policies that I still think we need to explore," George said.

"I'm still considering talks with some of those countries, George. But today, they're not a priority."

"Mr. President. What don't you like about the options in lifting the embargoes on those countries, that'll allow them to build up their countries' struggling economy?"

"I don't like the fact that those countries single-handedly account for one hundred percent of drugs smuggled into the United States. And if the embargoes were to be lifted, it would increase their export, then cause a stockpile of those drugs here."

What about my fears, Mr. Goddamn President? What about these assassins over here ready to kill my ass dead if Pablo doesn't get what he wants?

"Can't we set up stations from within those countries to monitor and search what's being shipped out?" George desperately asked.

"Let me explore some other ideas, George. But this project is going to take more creative ideas than what you're presenting. I need pros and cons, commitments from governments, etc. Do I make myself clear?"

"Crystal clear, Mr. President!" George left the Oval Office feeling like he'd accomplished something.

Malik, however, had only grown tired of the discussion of his ludicrous idea.

* * * * * * *

FBI Agent John Cage and U.S. Attorney Roy Striker stood on the steps of Jefferson Parish Courthouse, preparing to address the media on the rash of recent killings of law enforcement officials.

It was 12:00 p.m., perfect timing for the live broadcast on all news stations present. Agent John Cage strolled up to the podium and was joined by U.S. Attorney Roy Striker and two other agents.

"Today, we begin a probe into the recent attacks on the law enforcement community of Jefferson Parish. We ask that the public continue to bear with us as we attempt to bring the perpetrators of these crimes to justice. It will, in no way, be an easy task," Agent Cage said. "But you will receive my undivided attention for the duration of the investigation. There will come an end to these cowardly and senseless acts of terrorism. Whoever they are, they will slip and our efforts will catch that slip, then put an end to this nightmare for the citizens of Jefferson."

Behind the scenes Jaafar was on top of a nearby building,

patiently lurking and methodically monitoring the build-up of law enforcement. Jaafar had assembled his high-powered rifle, and now the cross-hairs of the scope were trained on John Cage speaking into the microphone. He'd been waiting for Luqman to make his move against the law enforcement of Jefferson Parish. And now that he did, it was his turn! This war was declared when they railroaded Luqman and Troy for murder, and now it was their time to shine! Those same prejudice crackers who took Luqman and Troy's life for all those years, would now get their issue.

Agent Cage stood on the steps with the air of a very important official, and Jaafar decided he wouldn't kill him yet. He determined that Agent Cage was the brains, so what purpose would it be to kill him first? Even Al Capone had Elliot Ness to chase him around, and he loved the attention, the thrill of being chased. A shadow that follows your shadow, that keeps you on top of your game, and always watching.

Jaafar refocused his attention through the scope at the men standing behind the podium, then with two fluid motions of his trigger finger, the bullets left the rifle, then entered the skulls of the two agents standing beside Agent Cage and U.S. Attorney Roy Striker, and exploded on contact. Quickly, Jaafar gathered his tools, then made his getaway.

* * * * * * *

Salvator sat in the back of the limo, peering out the window as they passed the leaning tower of Pisa in Italy.

"How many times have you been here?" James asked him.

"Only once. A mission many years ago," Salvator responded. "I didn't know the scenery was so breathtaking."

"When things settle down in the States, maybe you can buy an estate over here," James suggested.

If only I'd chosen another profession, that might've been possible. Salvator thought. "No, it'll never work! There's a beast inside of me that needs to be fed. My understanding of the world is filled with nothing but darkness, destruction, and death. It's the way of the world, the nature of the beast. It is also why you won't retire either, James," Salvator said. He also knew James only wanted to

179

give him a way out because he couldn't get out himself. A better life, or a safer one. Thanks. But no thanks, friend."

"I don't think the coroner would be too happy with me on the loose over here, James. I'm certainly not good for tourism," Salvator stated.

"I would've figured you to just lay back and enjoy those breathtaking views you spoke of earlier," James said.

"Breathtaking for me once I got bored with the scenery would mean someone being thrown from the leaning tower."

"In that case, let's not keep you in this beautiful city too long," James offered. "On second thought, I think the States would be a little more at home for your taste, my friend. Shit, the officials over here may take my visa if you're allowed to fly in and out of the country with me, then leave a trail of bodies."

"That won't be me, James. That'll be my evil twin," Salvator stated.

"Well, keep the evil twin at home today. We're tourists, remember?" James joked.

Salvator shrugged with a smile.

"Besides that, I was wondering how you convinced Pablo Hernandez, Rafael Fernandez, Felix Estrada, and Ali Mikheil to agree to this meeting on such short notice?"

"Let's just say I offered to come visit them, but they thought about the mess I leave when I'm inconvenienced."

"So, they know there's a chance they may not make it back home if my offer is rejected?"

"They don't know you're here," Salvator stated. "I thought I'd give them a little surprise, especially Pablo and Rafael. Those fools are already down twenty million dollars. You should've just let me kill them, then replace them with our people in Colombia and Cuba."

"That would mean a bloody war in both countries, then we'd have to deal with the police. It takes time to infiltrate, and time isn't on our side. We need cooperation now! This way means less time wasted, less lives lost, and less money wasted. We're going to kill two birds with one stone. I have a beautiful plan. Trust me," James assured Salvator.

"You always do. That's why you lead and I follow," Salvator admitted.

The limo pulled up to the Ritz Carlton Hotel. The sun was at full throttle, instantly reflecting off the polished chrome of the limo. James and Salvator slid out as the chauffeur held open the door. Minutes later, the two men strolled into the hotel past the front desk. The regulars seated around the hotel lounging, stared at James and Salvator as if they were royalty, judging by the confidence they exuded.

The elevator appeared, then they entered it. They exited on the top floor. James punched in the code given to him, activating the lock that popped the door open. As they walked in, all the other men were outside on the balcony enjoying exotic drinks and talking business.

"Gentlemen," Salvator joined in. "Glad you all could join us on such short notice."

"I'm sure I speak for the rest of us also, Salvator. The pleasure is all ours. It's not like we had a choice. Either meet today, or our families end up floating onto a shore somewhere in South America," Pablo accused. "Who's your friend?"

"I think he can do a better job at introducing himself, but you all may want to come in and take a seat so you don't miss something that may turn out to be fatal later on," Salvator insisted.

Pablo studied James as if he were a test.

"First of all, I'm here on business and that alone. I don't care about what you do, or who you are, only that you be a part of history or be history," James said.

Felix Estrada's blood pressure rose instantly from the threat.

"The world is about to change, and I will be the cause of it," James explained, in a promising tone.

The drug lords began to look amongst the others for clarity.

"Today, you men are only looked upon by the world as drug lords, the scums of the Earth. Maybe that's what you aspired to be. But I'm here to change that title to legitimate businessmen. With my assistance, your governments will recognize you as companies.

They will allow you to produce and sell all the dope your little hearts' desire."

"You claim to have a lot of power to say we never met you before today, ay, mister?" Felix Estrada stated.

"James. James Johnson," he said.

They suddenly lost their edge. Ali Mikeil had been briefed about James through Osama and knew James was a friend of Osama, and that sealed the deal with him, whatever it was.

"For those of you who know a good deal versus a great one, I propose you seriously consider mine. You have many problems that'll put that good deal in jeopardy; not the case with me. I'm offering a partnership that'll expand your operations to new heights."

"How are you proposing to get our government in on your plan, Mr. Johnson?" Felix inquired.

"As we speak, gentlemen, your presidents are preparing to meet with my president tomorrow at the White House. There will be many things discussed that are designed to help your countries. Jobs will be created, taxes will be paid to your governments from the drugs sold, then bought, and that means the economic impact would be felt instantly. So, I come with ultimatums; they will save money and lives by not having to declare war on drugs against you gentlemen. But if you reject my offer, they will replace you, not me! I won't have to. My proposal to them is like a cold glass of water to a man in hell. They won't turn it down, gentlemen!"

"So, what exactly are you proposing?" Ali inquired.

"Basically, that you sell me everything you produce, no matter how much it is, not a crumb goes to anyone else. If so, your product will be considered illegal, and will only become legal as long as you ship it to Johnson Industries. You will be paid in full upon the arrival of your product. No questions asked."

"So, you'll be distributing our drugs into the states for more money, instead of us, right?" Pablo questioned.

"Not hardly, Mr. Hernandez, I have no intentions of *ever* seeing another kilo of cocaine or heroin reach the shores of the United States."

Now the men were confused. Pablo stood up, then walked to the balcony and peered out, as Rafael and Felix were shaking their head as if to say, not possible.

"Then, why buy it? And for what price are you considering we sell it to you?" Pablo inquired.

"That's a couple of good business questions, Pablo. I like that. Maybe I can make a businessman out of you, yet. That reminds me. I have something for you and Rafael." James reached into his attaché case and retrieved two envelopes, then handed one to each man. They both opened them, then looked at each other, then back at James.

"I take it, it's all there?" James asked, winking at both men."Now, to answer your question of why I buy drugs. I'm buying them so that they don't reach the States. And by me doing so, this contributes to the growth of my people, who are being destroyed at every level because of your product. Sure, I can pump money into rehabs and centers for junkies, then sit around and hope they don't end up right back where they started. But those are only remedies that help a very small percentage of the whole problem. I've created a solution! Rehabs and methadone clinics are only sticking points for politicians to say: 'Hey, we're combating drug addiction.' In reality, they're no more than junkie handouts. As long as drugs are around, people who use them will remain socially, economically, morally, educationally, and spiritually dead. No matter how many schools you build, TV commercials you advertise, drugs will always be the focus of drug users. As for your second question, I'm considering the purchase of your drugs at a fair price. Because I'm a fair man, Mr. Hernandez, as you already know," James indicated, referring to the ten million dollar checks he'd just given them. This was money they'd given George McNamara in their plot against himself and the president. *I should've killed them both,* James thought.

"However," James continued, "I expect my constituents to be reasonable as well. So, don't make a mistake in thinking you're helping me. As I've stated, you will be replaced, so consider it helping yourselves. Then, I'm proposing to make you men legitimate. Something you've never been. No more wars, no more raids destroying your crops, and no more of your shipments being seized. You simply bring your product to one of my factories that are now in the process of being built in your countries, then get paid, gentlemen. I've made your lives easier than you ever could've imagined," James concluded.

He then reached into his attaché case, retrieved two more envelopes, and handed one to each of the remaining drug lords. The envelopes contained ten million dollar checks, along with a note. It read:

A small advancement on the product already processed. Do not ship another kilo, or all bets are off
Salvator

James handed Pablo and Rafael the same notes, but no money.

"My plan begins today, gentlemen. There existed a time when business was sealed with a handshake. Yet, those days are long gone. Greed has replaced respect, loyalty, and honor. Contracts are how business is conducted now." James began passing out contracts. The men scanned over them, but their minds were already made up. This was the deal to die for. No matter how much they disliked being told what to do, everything was made easy for them. Almost too good to be true.

"Just so you understand the contracts, men, before you sign them—you violate them— it's war! That's my word, and it's never broken. Not even for me," James assured them.

Salvator immediately began collecting the contracts, preparing to leave.

"Anything else, gentlemen?" James questioned.

"How do we get in contact with you?" Pablo asked.

"You don't. I'll be in contact with you for business purposes only. I take it you and Rafael will be disposing of the garbage in Washington, right?"

"As soon as possible," Pablo agreed without hesitation. Just that fast, George's fate had been sealed.

"I'll be sending you another package in a day or so, Mr. Pablo and Mr. Rafael. You'll find it at the airport," James promised.

Little did they know, the men from their country had invaded James' privacy, and would now have hell to pay for doing so. They also didn't know that if George wasn't disposed of immediately, Salvator had orders to terminate them immediately.

CHAPTER 22
Check Mate

"What do you mean, Camacho?" Fidel asked.

"I'm saying this guy James isn't in any of the places my contacts claim he frequents," Camacho stated.

"You said your fuckin' connect was this and that. So, what you think about him and his so-called pull now?"

"Probably the same thing you're thinking. That's the answer you want?" Camacho questioned. "Shit, it still don't change the fact that this James dude is not sitting around waiting to be kidnapped." *He must think this James guy is stupid.*

"How fuckin' hard is it to find this sucker, kidnap him, then be on our merry fuckin' way?" Fidel inquired, with his hands raised in the air as if the answer would fall out the sky.

Fidel and his crew had been hiding out at Pedro's old place. Pedro had left Fidel his entire arsenal along with a number to call in case he needed more equipment. Immediately, Pedro left town after convincing Fidel to send for more men. "Okay, twenty men. No more," stated Fidel. "Just in case ten won't do!" Fidel transformed the house into a torture chamber. The windows were blackened, ropes hung from multiple positions, and tables were full of knives, scalpels, and syringes. All they needed was to find James.

* * * * * * *

"Everyone locked and loaded?" General McCloud asked through the small ear-piece microphone. He was there to execute a flawless operation, just like other countless missions he'd overseen. McCloud was one of the black soldiers in Fort Lejeune to make General in Louisiana. General McCloud enlisted in the armed services at the age of eighteen. He hadn't left yet, even at the age of fifty-seven. No wife, no children, a career military man in every sense of the word. No mission was too large or small.

The entire team responded "yes," dressed in full body armor and fitted with high-powered silenced rifles.

"This is to be executed quickly and quietly, men. I want all the gas shot into the house at every point. So, let's drill holes first into the floor, insert the canisters into the rooms they're in, and one sniff will do. This shit will drop an elephant to its knees, so use your masks. Jason, I want you to stand by with the big truck. Once everyone inside is knocked out, we go in. Remember, there's a zero chance of you surviving a sniff of this gas, so be careful when we go in. Jason, pull the truck up to the house blocking the view of anyone passing. We clear?"

"Crystal clear, General!"

"Troy, you bring the body bags when I give Jason the signal, understood?"

"I'm on that, General," Troy insisted.

"Are we on the same page, gentlemen?"

The men inside the SWAT truck all nodded as they sat parked down the street from Pedro's house.

* * * * * * *

"Camacho," Fidel began. "What other information does your connect have on James, other than where he's not?"

Reluctantly, he offered the next information, knowing Fidel wouldn't want to hear this part. Yet, Camacho figured this would stop the questions.

"Oh, he said this dude James is some kind of a legend and is always with this guy named Salvator," Camacho said.

"Who?" Fidel asked, hoping he had not heard right.

"Salvator," Camacho curiously answered. "Why? You know this other guy?"

You fool, Fidel thought. *If you don't know Salvator, then that's*

WILLIE GROSS JR. WITH WAHIDA CLARK

your blessing. At that moment, Fidel was ready to leave.

"Shit!" he cursed, banging his hand against the table. "That's why Pedr got out of town so fast. He also knew Salvator and James were friends. *Wait until I see that piece of shit again. That's why he said I would need an army.* Fidel glanced around the room at his men, then shook his head. *What have I gotten myself into?*

"Yeah, I know him," Fidel said. "I'm just going to regret having to kill him," he lied.

Fidel now desperately peeped out the blackened windows. He didn't notice it at first, but now he did. The big truck parked down the street had been there too long.

Shit! He wished it were the police, but somehow he knew better. He glanced back for his men again, only to find them collapsing like heart attack victims. Canisters of gas had been pumped into the front and back of the house and were rapidly spreading about the house, silently seeping into room after room.

At that moment, he cursed the ground George and Pedro walked on, as he felt himself slowly slipping into unconsciousness.

Fidel hadn't known that they'd been under surveillance the minute they landed. The special ops team had received the order from James to execute, then have their bodies in the air ASAP.

* * * * * * *

Dip and Tray were seated at the bar inside Club Ballers, awaiting Chef Ryan's arrival. Their goal was to obtain the highly exculpatory DVD. The wrecker truck had just left with the Range Rover to be repaired and repainted another color. The telephone began ringing behind the bar.

"Hello?" Tray answered.

"This is Chief Ryan, Tray. Look, I couldn't make it. This shit is huge. But I got my guy over there now trying to maneuver, but the Feds are all over the damn place."

"Man, I need that DVD!"

"I understand that, but the scene inside is a bloody mess. There are many civilian casualties. These guys mounted a small war in there. Look, my guy is in there, and he's very reliable in these situations. If anyone can get it, he will. Keep you updated, Tray."

188

Then the phone went dead.

Tray laid the phone back into its cradle, then began massaging his temples.

"That bad, huh?" Dip questioned.

"Fuckin' Feds crawling everywhere. Them fools killed plenty civilians inside the store, Dip." Dip dropped his head. "We've gotta get that DVD, man. That's four first degree murders, if your face is on that DVD," Tray reminded him.

"The jury won't hesitate to convict me on those charges, then sentence me to death. Fuck! Just when things were finally going good in my life," Dip said. He grabbed the remote, then turned the on TV.

"Reporting live from the scene," a reporter said. "This is Dan Dixon of the Channel 4 News Team, and I'm on the scene of a vicious robbery that took place only a couple hours ago. Reports confirm that three suspects entered this Spur gas station armed with guns, taking control of the station while robbing it. Gunfire erupted that resulted in a standoff inside the store with the gunmen prevailing over several employees. There is a lone survivor, who was hiding in a walk-in cooler at the time, witnessing everything. The motive was, in fact, robbery, according to the witness. Ten innocent civilians were executed as were six employees. However, in a bizarre twist, the three gunmen were found dead outside the door of the station, gunned down as they attempted their getaway. Also, a man armed with an AK-47 was found outside, dead of apparent gunshot wounds. Our sources confirm the robbers made it out of the store with duffel bags of money. Yet, none were recovered. The question in everyone's mind is, did the robbers get robbed, or betrayed? I'm now joined here by FBI spokesperson, Mr. Raymion Morgan."

"Mr. Morgan. What can you tell us about this bizarre turn of events that transpired today?" the reporter asked.

"Well, Dan, I'm very limited because the investigation is still ongoing. But we're attempting to reconstruct every piece together as we go. So, the case will continue to produce leads. What I can confirm, is that there are sixteen dead, and one survivor. There are many theories, but the FBI report facts, not theories."

"So, Agent Morgan, is there a possibility you're looking for an additional suspect because of the four bodies found outside?"

"We're exploring all avenues, Dan. So, we encourage anyone with information to come forward. Maybe someone saw something that may link our existing leads to others, so please contact us on the FBI hotline," Agent Morgan said.

"One more vital question, Agent Morgan, before you go. Do you know if the station had any surveillance equipment?"

"At this time, we're not commenting on the evidence in this case, other than we're still gathering it."

"There you have it, ladies and gentlemen. Reporting live from the robbery that went bad, then fatal for the robbers. We'll bring you any further information as we receive it," Dan Dixon reported.

* * * * * * *

Inside the Spur Gas station, Sergeant Nixon frantically searched the office for the video equipment. He moved a jacket that hung from a rack, and then the equipment appeared. *Bingo!* Sensing the Feds would be headed this way in search of the same thing, he hurried. Then suddenly, all the color was removed from his face. The DVD was missing! *But who? How could they have slipped past me? This isn't good,* Sergeant Nixon thought. He knew a promotion would have followed him in finding that DVD. Now he had to explain to the chief that he'd been beaten by someone better, and the DVD was in their possession.

* * * * * * *

"They think the robbers got robbed, Tray," Dip reported, now satisfied that there was no mention of his platinum Range Rover on the news.

"It's not what they *did* say that hurts you with the Feds, Dip. It's what they *didn't* say that haunts you to the end. You're now playing chess with the best, my friend. The Feds don't say much about anything. But when they move, empires crumble," Tray assured him. "Just the fact of them being on the scene speaks volumes. Trust me. Behind the scenes, they're working a hundred different scenarios. If there are any leaks, they'll continue pounding until that leak turns into a crack. I need you to go back to the scene. You're the owner. But in no way are you to answer any questions on your whereabouts until your lawyer is present. Tomorrow we'll go retain one of the best firms in the South to represent you from here on out.

The telephone began ringing.

"Hello?"

"This is Ryan, Tray. My man just informed me that the DVD wasn't in the machine."

"You gots to be kidding me, Ryan."

"I wish I were, Tray. The machine was turned off and the disc was gone. But, he was sure that no law enforcement got there before him."

"What about *before* he arrived?"

"He's not sure. But he know the Feds arrived around the same time he did. He's shaking down a few agents now for possible info on any evidence seized. This is all I can do for now, my friend."

"I know, Ryan. That's why I called you. One other thing . . ."

"What's that, Tray?"

"Who was the lone survivor?"

"A foreigner by the name of Akbar Lakee. You know him?"

"Nahh. But I'm sure my friend does. Where is he now?" Tray inquired.

"Most likely with the Feds. They'll re-enact that scene a thousand times before he gets any rest."

"Hopefully, your friend isn't on that DVD, my friend, or he's burnt toast!" Chief Ryan muttered.

* * * * * * *

The scene in Jefferson Parish was pure pandemonium as the news crew and civilian crowds flocked to the courthouse in protest of the crimes happening to law enforcement.

FBI Agent John Cage rewound the video again, trying to get an idea of which way the sniper fire came from. As he viewed the three news stations' footage of the sniper attack, he knew his fight would be like Sisyphus, rolling a boulder up a mountain. What was evident is this was another message, and the messengers were professionals. *Bringing these animals to justice is my only concern,* Agent Cage thought. They had declared war, and he had accepted their invitation. But why would the sniper kill two agents, but not the ones in charge? *Does he want to play a cat and mouse game? Why didn't he kill me? Yes, Jefferson Parish is regarded as a very racist place, with many enemies. To find these avengers, would be like trying to get Don King to cut his hair.* Then Agent Cage thought about the clue left by Vinny Pachero's killer.

He picked up his phone and began dialing.

"Hello?"

"Roy. This is Agent Cage. I need you to send me some case files of the ADA that was killed recently."

"How far back you want? The guy's been around for a while?"

"I'll tell you what. Send me the high-profile cases for the last ten years."

"You on to something?" Roy asked.

"Just a hunch. Need to see where it takes me. I think the ADA is the key to cracking this case."

"Oh yeah. Would you like to share that hunch?"

"Look. The words, 'Justice Served' were painted outside of his home. It seems deliberate, and overkill. This guy had already been tortured, no doubt dying a horrible death, right?"

"It certainly looked that way to me," Roy agreed.

"Then why take the chance of getting caught spray painting a house after you've committed this horrible act, if all you intended to do was kill him in the first place?"

"Maybe he's sending a message?" Roy stated.

"Right. But to who else?"

"Jefferson Parish!"

"That's right," Agent Cage agreed. "The entire system is this person or persons' focus. He was alerting us that he's still out there at the press conference. I say, Mr. Pachero must have prosecuted him, or them."

"What about the others that were killed?"

"Pull any cases they worked together, then see if Mr. Pachero prosecuted and convicted these people."

"Anything else?" Roy asked.

"Yeah. Pray that we're on to something, 'cause we're chasing a ghost who doesn't leave evidence," Cage concluded.

CHAPTER 23
The Taliban Soldiers

"Luqman, you get the rest of them identifications James sent by UPS?" Troy asked. "There were fifty of them, right?"

"Yeah, that's them. Have you given the Talibans their credentials? The bus is waiting to take them to the airport."

"They waiting on you, Troy. All fifty passports, identifications, social security cards, money, etc."

"Twenty-five are going to Texas and twenty-five to Florida. Plus, their compounds have been built, so its show-time!"

"So, James thinks there's going to be some trouble at the entrance points?" Luqman inquired.

"That, plus a few organizations will need to be taught a lesson. They're not going to listen at first. Plenty of bloodshed will be the end result. So, we equipped those compounds with chemical and explosive laboratories. Then, our first unit leader is, Mahmoud Alzare, and that's one devastating individual. His torture techniques make Hannibal Lector look like Little Red Riding Hood," Troy joked.

"And, we received information that local law enforcement have their hands in on the drug trade in Florida and Texas. So, James wants this situation dealt a devastating blow, if we're going to stop the flow of drugs into the communities. That's why Mahmoud and Ahmed Wali are overseeing the two states. They're Osama's torture experts."

"Osama must be kin to the devil," Luqman thought out loud.

"What about the Mafia who always manages to keep their hands into everything," Troy asked.

"James said they agreed to pull out of the entrance points, then turn over the streets in exchange for a very good business proposition." Luqman considered that James probably gave them no choice other than the graveyard or sinking into the Gulf of Mexico with cement shoes. "That serves them right, because if the Gulf could talk, the Mafia would be *under* the penitentiary."

The bus load of Taliban fighters pulled out, headed for the private landing strip in Houma. But an hour ago, the Colombian and Cuban governments received the cargo plane full of dead bodies from that same landing strip.

The families of the assassins were notified to pick up the remains of their deceased family member, immediately. They were outraged, but could do nothing about it! James had simply got some—that got many. They just got the short end of the stick today.

"I hear the assassins arrived back in Cuba and Colombia," Troy stated.

"Yeah, I wanted in on that shit. I never killed a Colombian. Man, they actually thought it was going to be that simple to just come here, kidnap James, then ride off into the sunset. Then, this guy Pedro walks into the law firm and reveals the entire plot. Deon said he was begging for his life the minute he stepped through the door." Luqman laughed as he relived the conversation with Deon. "She also said he kept saying he was sorry."

"What was he sorry for?" Troy asked.

"Sorry that he knew the man who was plotting to kidnap James."

"You're kidding, right?"

"The God's honest truth!"

"So, who exactly is this guy anyway?"

"He's from Colombia, but apparently got into some trouble years ago, and was hiding out down here!"

"What he do in Colombia?"

"Assassinate their president!" Luqman offered.

"Stop lying!" Troy shot back.

"Everything checked out. He's who he says he is; name, picture of him from the report in Colombia, the works. He ultimately showed the Special Operations Team the house where the twenty assassins were held-up in, looking for James, too."

"What does he want in return?"

"His life, and to be considered for work, if we ever need his expertise."

"Where is he now?"

"In a hotel. His home is full of the gas used to take out those supposed assassins trained in the jungles of South America. From what I hear, when Pedro heard who Fidel was coming to kidnap, he told Fide, he was about to leave for a vacation."

"He's a smart man. I like the sound of this fellow. He enjoys living." Troy laughed.

"Maybe I'll put him on a job over there in Jefferson Parish, where them rotten racist muthafuckas live," Luqman suggested. "Speaking of which, did you see those two agents get whacked at the news conference?"

"Yeah, but that wasn't your work?"

"Hell no. I'm more of a knife kinda fellow," Luqman assured him.

"Then, who in the hell else Jefferson Parish done pissed off besides us?"

"Shit, they don't care until it's their blood being spilled, but whoever it was, I like their style," Luqman said. "It's about time those folks start hitting back instead of turning the other cheek. When I finish, they'll have to purchase more land to build more cemeteries to put those lowdown scoundrels into! It's about time the predators know what it feels like to be prey."

* * * * * * *

James and Salvator arrived at the White House on schedule. President Obdel Karzi of Afghanistan, President Felipe Esdoza of Colombia, President Santiago Valdez of Mexico, and President Fidel Castro of Cuba, were all in attendance at the request of United States President, Malik Quinn.

The men were all gathered inside the presidential conference room. Malik thanked everyone for coming, then expressed his positive thoughts on the giant steps each country would benefit from the meeting today. Malik strolled over to the door, then closed and locked it. He knew George was somewhere around. Besides, today's meeting would also seal his fate in the upcoming weeks.

"Gentlemen," President Quinn began. "This is my friend, James Johnson of Johnson Industries. What he has to offer today is important. It's needed, and it's going to revolutionize the world in many ways. You see, when most companies are thinking about profits, this man is thinking about people! I hold my present position of president, because he was thinking of me when he could've easily been in this position. His motto is and always has been "to search for something greater than yourself." He still lives by that creed! He's a remarkable man in a sense that people such as he, only exist once in a lifetime. Some people find one cause in life to be a part of, but James Johnson keeps on looking for more after conquering countless others. Today, gentlemen, he has conquered yet another, and most likely isn't finished, because he's still thinking about people instead of profits," Malik said, then took a seat.

James stood up to address the presidents. "Thank you, Mr. President, and all of you distinguished gentlemen for joining me today in an attempt to bring about some positive changes in all our countries. I want to give you a brief summary of the new technology I'm about to introduce. It's a chemical solution to a worldwide problem. Drugs! My team of scientists have been studying ways to turn cocaine and heroin into fuel for cars. We've found a way, gentlemen," James reported.

The presidents looked at each other, wondering if this was a big joke.

"Gentlemen, the drugs you want to rid your countries of, we want to buy them. Straight from the producers, then manufacture it into fuel without the drugs leaving your countries. My plan is to build factories within your countries, then ship the fuel back to the United States once it's converted. I will now explain to you what I need. Then, what you'll get in return, if you agree to those terms. First of all, the drugs would have to be legalized in your countries in order to be sold to me. But, they become illegal when sold to anyone else other than me, and punishable by life in prison! This turns your drug lords into legitimate businessmen. These are the type of people I want to do business with. Your rewards will come in the form of taxes made off the sale of these drugs to me, and of the drug lords' portions of what I pay for the drugs. So, you're being paid twice in one transaction. There will be no more war on drugs in your countries, so there's more money saved to invest in other things. Your prison population will dwindle. The factories I build will create jobs for your people, and that will create a strong economic boost that'll contribute to building up your countries' infrastructure. Also, the shipping of the fuel back to the United States and abroad creates more jobs and opportunities for your citizens. That means more taxes for your government, and a better quality of life for all involved." James paused for emphasis and to gauge their interest.

"So, gentlemen, there are no hidden tricks nor agendas. This is the real thing. I have just recently met with the head drug lords in your countries, and they all have agreed to my terms and await your approval." James then reached into the attaché case, retrieved the contracts, then distributed them to each president. "I'll now gladly answer any questions, or listen to any statements if any exist," he suggested.

"When will this new technology hit the markets, Mr. Johnson?" President Karzi asked.

"In three months, our vehicles will be rolling off the assembly lines."

"When do our contracts begin, Mr. Johnson? Because from my point of view, it's a no-brainer. My only wish is that I could've come up with an idea such as this," President Valdez stated. *I see why his president is so proud of him.*

"As soon as I'm allowed to build those factories, the quicker I can begin hiring and shipping fuel," James insisted.

"What about the independent groups that produce these drugs and smuggle them into the United States, Mr. Johnson? What if they do not like, or want to accept your offer?" Valdez questioned.

"That certainly is a possibility, President Valdez. However, there must be an understanding that this is an opportunity for *your* country. If you want your country to prosper from this partnership, you must act on it. Are you now asking me what should you do if they don't accept?" James questioned with a confused look.

"Yes, Mr. Johnson," Valdez stated timidly.

"That's what I thought you were asking! Look, who are you?"

"I'm President Santiago Valdez," came the reply.

"Then, muthafucka, act like it!" James shouted.

Everyone else tensed up in the room for a moment, trying to digest what just occurred. Salvator smiled.

"Stop being so damn weak! If them muthafuckas don't want what you're offering, you kill them! Do you all understand what killing means?"

All the presidents nodded.

James hated weakness, and especially hated weak people in powerful positions. "Muthafuckas get in the way, we kill they asses over here in the United States, plain and simple! There will be nothing but slow singing and flower bringing when you step out of line here. Oh, what you thought? We're about morals over here? Fuck that. We about results, fuck the dumb shit! If we want something in your countries, what do we do?"

The presidents now looked confused, but they knew exactly what the United States did.

"You take it," Karzi stated boldly.

"Thank you, and don't you ever forget that either! We don't give a lovely fuck about how you feel afterwards! If it's over there, we coming to get it. Fuck the consequences!"

"But, that doesn't make it right," Malik stated in an attempt to calm down the negative energy in the room.

"Who gives a fuck about right or wrong anymore, Malik? Besides the poor suckers that have been wronged?" James questioned.

Malik stood silent as everyone else did.

"We have an opportunity to begin work on a broken promise guaranteed centuries ago. These governments in this room today can begin to right a wrong done by the same people sworn to protect the rights of its citizens. They've failed where we'll succeed, but I'll be damned if I let some independent low-level drug smuggler get in the way of that success. You men need to grow some balls if that small of a problem will get in your way. If your forces can't handle the problem, then I will. But it's going to cost you dearly," James promised.

"Yes," Salvator said to himself, as he noticed how frightened the presidents became once James showed the flip side. He could smell the fear! There was blood in the water, and James was the shark. *Go for the kill, James,* Salvator thought. *You can run all their countries. They're weak!*

James, standing erect like a soldier, glanced at Salvator and winked, sensing Salvator's thoughts. *Maybe another time,* he had communicated to Salvator without a word spoken. But the seed of fear had been planted, so James smiled.

* * * * * * *

Tray and Dip strolled into Johnson and Johnson's law firm. Tray had made an appointment with Deon Johnson to discuss retaining their services. Dip had been mentally pre-occupied with what was going on, in relation to the gas station massacre. He and Tray showed up at the murder scene, but most of law enforcement had left, and the questions asked were limited, but he was still spooked. He knew at the blink of an eye his life could take a turn for the worst.

"May I help you, gentlemen?" the receptionist asked.

"We have an appointment to see Ms. Johnson," Tray replied.

"What time is that appointment, and what's your name, sir?"

"It's for 9:00 a.m. Mr. Tray King."

"Yes, Mr. King. I see that appointment. Can you have a seat, and Ms. Johnson will be down in a second for you."

Dip was seated beside Tray in the massive lobby, stressing. It was his first time in a law firm as big as this one. He thought, *They even have a black receptionist.* The walls were decorated with paintings of civil rights leaders such as, Harriet Tubman, Martin Luther King, Malcolm X, and Frederick Douglas. The furniture was very expensive and surrounded by ancient artifacts. The scent in the air was of expensive kid skin leather and cypress wood. The atmosphere was a cozy one. Just enough to give you a warm, fuzzy feeling about being there in the first place.

Deon stepped off the elevator, and Dip thought he'd died, then gone to heaven. She walked toward the receptionist, retrieved some memos, then walked directly to Tray.

"Hello, Mr. King. Sorry for the wait. I'm Deon Jonson," she said, then extended her soft, manicured hand. He accepted.

"This is my business partner, Quami Jones," Tray said.

Deon admiringly looked over at Dip, dressed in gray Brodana Gorbachi slacks, a gray Felipe Zambrono cashmere shirt, and gray Brodano Giorbachi lizard skins on his feet. Dip was a street nigga, but today he resembled a model for *Black Kings* magazine. He stood at six feet four inches, 230 pounds, caramel complexion, with a platinum and diamond smile worth about eighty grand. Today was not a good day for Dip, until Deon strolled out of the elevator.

Coincidently, her day wasn't going well, either, until she laid eyes on the most handsome man she'd seen since college. Dip gently took her extended hand, as if it were a fifty-carat diamond.

"Nice to meet you, Mr. Jones," she expressed.

"The pleasure is all mine, Ms. Johnson. But do call me Quami. That's what my friends call me."

"Then why do I call you Dip?" Tray asked.

"Because you're old, and sometimes you lose your memory, remember?"

"No, I don't remember no shit like that," Tray angrily stated.

"You see what I mean about his memory, Ms. Johnson?"

Deon shrugged. "Gentlemen, would you like to take a walk to my office, so we can discuss your legal needs in private?"

"Certainly, Miss," Dip replied. "By the way, you look very familiar. Have we met or hung out at some of the same places?"

"I don't hang out, Quami. Sorry," Deon stated.

Damn, I love the way she says my name. Her voice is very addictive, just like her presence. I must have her.

"Have you ever been to New York, the Manhattan area?" Dip

inquired.

"No, I haven't as of yet. Perhaps in the future," she replied.

Dip was thinking, *Don't feel like the Lone Ranger. Me either.*

"I was there last year," he said. "Are you familiar with Sothesby Auction Houses, where fine art and antiques are auctioned off?"

"Bullshit, nigga. You were here with me all of last year," Tray whispered in Dip's ear.

"I've heard of them," Deon stated. "But as I've said, I've never been there."

"Would you do me a favor?" Dip asked.

"It depends on what it is," Deon stated.

"Don't ever tell me or anyone else you've never been to New York!"

"What you doing, nigga? Embarrassing me for one," Tray admitted, whispering to Dip once again.

"Why would I not tell the truth about visiting New York? It really isn't a big deal," Deon suggested.

"It's not that it's a big deal. It's just a lie," Dip accused her.

Deon tilted her head down slightly, as if thinking, *I know this Negro didn't just call me a lie to my face?* She stood there steaming. As if really coming unglued, and losing her cool. That intelligent black woman persona was about to be out the door, and a transformation into home girl with the attitude to match was rapidly about to take control of this situation.

Dip sensed he had her where he needed her, boiling hot! "So, now let's turn that frown upside down. Peep this, lil' mama. I don't mean no harm. However, as I've stated, we've hung out at the same places. I never forget a face, and especially one as beautiful as yours. I was in New York for an exhibit on ancient ancestry, and you were there. We hung out, just like I said we did. I saw you, then I approached you. Not a word was spoken. We just looked into each other's eyes.

"Oh, we did, huh?" Deon said sarcastically, placing her hand on her hip.

"The longer I stood there, the longer you stared. What we shared in that short period of time, etched a vivid picture of timeless beauty into my mind, forever. Our time was cut short because I had to leave. And has proven to be one of my biggest regrets. But I searched for you ever since. Especially at all the other ancient history exhibits, because I knew your taste in art, but you never again appeared. I often thought of you, and the way I left you behind. There were no good-byes, because I told you I didn't like them. I'll see you around, is what I assured you. There were no waves from you nor me. Nothing to indicate that we would not see each other again."

"Okay, Mr. Jones. That's beautiful, but wee need to get on with—"

"As I was leaving, you continued to stare. I looked back once more before I exited, and you continued staring. Oh, how I wished I were that lucky man who possessed you. Then, after continuously searching for you with only that vivid picture of timeless beauty etched in my mind, I found you! I was both happy and sad, then satisfied."

Now fully engaged, Deon folded her arms. "Keep going." Her eyes took him in completely.

"Come to find out, you had gone home to a place where I've never been, but where we belonged, Africa! I found out more about you than I was told by you. I only knew what your eyes would reveal to me. I knew that you were a strong woman, and that you loved your God (Allah). Then came your family and the richness of your culture. You did not tell me your name, but I know that too, now. It's a beautiful name. Biaka Nadeema. A beautiful flower is its meaning. The entire exhibit was about you, with one simple, but beautiful word describing that exhibit: Queen!

Deon couldn't help but blush, then laughed once she saw Quami's friend's frown. "I apologize for him in advance," he said.

Dip continued. "There was a rich, African businessman at Sothesby that day I first met you. He acquired you for a record fifty million dollars. He said he needed you more, so he brought you back home to Africa."

"I don't have fifty million dollars," Dip said. "But if I did, I'd spend it on you instead! At least you could wave back to me, or talk to me. But more importantly, you'd get to know every day how long and hard I've searched for a woman who exhibits the beauty and grace of Queen Biaka Nadeema. You're an exact replica of Queen Biaka, and I just have to express my intentions to get to know you. Your beauty is magnetic, but your intelligence is frightening. I could not understand why I was so drawn to that painting at that time, but I do now. Her eyes simply, but forcefully suggested she knew exactly who she was. She was royalty! Your eyes say the same thing to me, and I'm frightened, but I need to be in order to respect you, because the threat of losing you again trumps all!" Dip said with a magnetizing gaze.

Deon eyes looked into Dip's eyes with mild excitement. "Beautiful story," she said with a slight grin. "Now, can we get to the reason you guys are really here?"

"Yeah, we can," Tray said, elbowing Dip.

"Chill, old man," Dip said, annoyed.

"Damn. I didn't know this lil nigga had that in him," Tray muttered.

"Aaaaand . . . so what about our law firm, Mr. Jones?" Deon asked, shifting her weight from leg to leg, now feeling uneasy.

"I need that too. But please don't take me for granted. I'm a man who knows what he wants, and I'm willing to make the necessary sacrifices to achieve those things precious to me, and for you, if given the chance."

"My, my, Quami. You don't give a girl much wiggle room. However, let's get the business end of your acquaintance rolling. And just *maybe*, we can speak on that personal level during *non*-business hours," Deon expressed.

"I'll hold you to that," Dip said.

"And it is of the utmost importance that we get the business part rolling. A life is at stake and possibly a whole lot of jail time and maybe, just maybe somebody forgot all about that," Tray said, glancing over in Tray's direction.

CHAPTER 24
The Jack Move

Ring, ring, ring.

"Hello?"

"Who this?" Kane asked suspiciously.

"What's up, old nigga? This Mikey, nigga. You forgot about your lil homie?"

"You know it ain't like that, playa. But what's on your brain?"

"Shit, nigga, them folks been asking mad questions about Lil Killa nem'. I loaned them niggas my car when they said you had a lick for them."

Fuck! Kane thought. *Just what I needed, a dying declaration. Why niggas can't keep their mouths shut about business?* "Nahh, them niggas ain't had no lick coming from me, fool. It must've been another nigga," he lied. *Bitch-ass niggas with loose lips.*

"I heard that, playboy," Mikey stated. "Well, these streets talking pretty heavy, and singing your name like the National Anthem. You know my car got caught up in that shit. Now these folks cramping my style. Fuckin' Feds hanging on the block more than us!"

"Sorry to hear that, playa," Kane said, but was really unconcerned.

"Shit. Them niggas had some mad artillery in their vehicle. Where you been at, nigga? That shit all over the news."

"I just got back from Texas, homie. But one of my broads gave me the scoop," Kane lied.

"Maybe you should lay low, homie. Like I said, them niggas' families talking real reckless, but they going on what they heard. I ain't that nigga you gots to convince that you were out of town, but them people probably got yo' phone number out of Lil Killa's phone and checking them phone towers to see exactly where you were."

"Yeah, I might just do that. Let me know if something else comes up. Feel me?"

"You got that, big homie," Mikey promised. Maybe Kane must not have known that he had been around when Kane first left the block the same day the robbery happened.

Without thought, Kane dialled an important number and it rang three times.

"Hello?"

"Hey, baby," he greeted. "What's up?"

"Nothing much, just working around the house. What's up with you?" Diamond asked.

"Something just came up, and we're going to be leaving town a while to lay low."

"What's wrong?"

"I can't get into specifics right now. But I need for you to pack up. We're going to head for Atlanta, and don't tell anybody. Take only a few clothes, plus all the money and dope left. I'm going to be running around for a second. But get everything together, then call me. I'm going to meet you off the interstate. Take only important shit and give the key to Carla. She can have the furniture and shit. You feel me?"

"Yeah, I got you, baby. But what's up all of a sudden?" Diamond inquired.

"Tell you when we meet up. I just need to leave for a few until shit cools off. Niggas hating as usual, but involving the po-po," Kane expressed.

"Well, give me thirty minutes, baby, and I'm on the road."

"I'll be waiting for your call."

Kane had just received a hundred kilos from Troy, plus the

other four houses had at least ten apiece. There should be about two million dollars in money he had to pick up, too. So there was more than enough to get out of town and start a new life."

* * * * *

Ring, ring, ring.

"Yo, what's good?"

"Hey, Dip. What's happening man?" Akbar inquired.

"Who's this?" Dip asked.

"This is Akbar. I work at your store, man."

Dip snapped his finger, realizing this was the lone survivor. "Hey man. How's everything?"

"It's slow man, but you can't keep a good man down."

Dip sensed something was wrong in Akbar's voice. "Did them people harass you much?"

"They tried, but I didn't see or say nothing. In my country, we don't cooperate with police. We handle everything in-house."

"So, what's on your mind?" Dip inquired.

"Well, I was taught to think fast in certain situations, and it has kept me alive for many years. I've survived many close calls, and yesterday was another one. By me thinking fast once more, I may have prevented a major catastrophe for someone else this time," Akbar suggested.

Bingo! He must have the DVD. Slick muthafucka.

"You get my drift, Dip?"

"Yeah, I got your drift. What's your price?"

"I would like to know what it's worth to you, my friend? I'll accept any reasonable offer. Shit, there were four bodies laid to rest by your forty-five automatic. Feel me?"

"Let's cut the small talk, Akbar. If you were my friend, I wouldn't have to pay for the DVD."

"That's correct. And if I were your friend, I wouldn't have to work for you, either," Akbar reminded Dip.

"So, what's your price? I never was good at putting a number on another man's property."

"I think for a man of our standards, you can afford a couple hundred thousand. Final offer."

That's not bad for a possible death sentence. But I can't see myself give over two hundred thousand to this scrub muthafucka, Dip thought.

"When can we meet?"

"Let me get back with you. I need to look at a few things first, so I can ensure that I get a chance to spend that money," Akbar stated coldly.

"Okay. Suit yourself. But be careful. I don't want that falling into the wrong hands."

Akbar hung up the phone, then put his next plan into effect.

* * * * * * *

Ring, ring, ring.

"Who this?"

"Hey, Kane. What's up, man?"

"What's up, Akbar? How you living, man?"

"Not that good, man. I'm just a squirrel in this world trying to get a nut. Feel me?"

"Yeah, I feel that, Akbar. What's on your mind?"

"Picture this. You heard something about that robbery that happened yesterday, right?"

"Yeah, I heard a little something in the wind. What's on your mind?"

"From what I'm hearing and seeing, it don't look good for the home team," Akbar replied.

"Oh, yeah. That depends on who the home team is. I'm always visiting," Kane shot back.

"I don't know, and it ain't my thing to judge a man when he claims his innocence. However, I have come across some irrefutable evidence that puts a couple of fellows on the scene that are saying different. Like I said, it may be a matter for the judge and jury to decide. Feel me?"

Kane said nothing, but realized that only two niggas walked away from the scene. Him and Dip.

"Or, we can make arrangements to keep this evidence out of the wrong hands, especially the judge and jury."

"What exactly are you speaking of, Akbar?"

"You do drive a lime-green Charger with dark tinted windows, and the name 'Kane' on the license plate, right?"

"You know I do."

"Well, my friend. You're the one seen leaving the scene after waiting fifteen minutes. So, you're either who set it up, or a material witness. Oh, yeah, the streets are saying you had something to do with killing them youngstas. But only me and this DVD know the truth. So where do we go from here, Big Man?"

"That only proves my car was in the area. So what?"

"Okay, play Mr. Tough Guy. But we both done been in them courtrooms, and those DAs paint some pretty ass pictures to the jurors. If you want to roll the dice, be my guest, but Dip won't! He's going to buy this muthafucka so fast, the money will reach my account before the bank opens."

How the fuck this nigga know Dip? He might be trying to double-cross me. I got to kill this foreign muthafucka. If Dip gets his hands on that DVD, he'll know about me. But, if I get it, Dip's in trouble. That's four dead bodies on that muthafucka. I can milk his ass for that money back and get rid of him, too. Priceless! Kane thought.

"How much for the DVD, Akbar?"

"A man in your position will always have my respect because you value freedom and the pursuit of happiness. I knew you'd see it for what it was worth," Akbar concluded.

"Man, let's cut through the bullshit. My tolerance is real low when it comes to blowing smoke up my ass. What's the fuckin' price?"

"One million dollars, my friend." Akbar trembled as he got the price out. He knew these were some dangerous dudes. But he knew they didn't want to see the penitentiary again, too.

"You're kidding me. Right?"

"Why would I do that, Kane? It's business, not politics," Akbar responded.

There was silence on the phone for a few seconds.

"That's the best you can do?" Kane asked.

"That's my final offer. Non-negotiable!"

"When can we meet?" Kane asked.

"Let me put a few pieces together first, just so I get the chance to enjoy that money, Kane."

"So, you don't trust me?" Kane felt played.

"Trust is something that has ended many things, lives in particular. I never walk into a room I don't first know how to get out of. So once I figure out how you can get this DVD and I get the money, you'll hear from me again. Don't worry about the time, my friend. There's no statute of limitations on murder." Akbar hung up the phone, feeling like a rich man. But the road he must travel could turn deadly at any moment. He was dealing with two wounded animals as long as he possessed that DVD.

CHAPTER 25
The Informant

Salvator set the meeting between James and Don Hamas right after the meeting with the presidents. The two men were walking in a park five minutes from the White House. They had been there for fifteen minutes. James handed Don Hamas an envelope that contained a five-million-dollar check.

"This is only a gift of respect for you and your contributions to a world that few are allowed to behold. Yet, many have tried and failed."

Don Hamas understood the statement.

"Thank you, and I accept your gift and agree with your analogy. However, I, or we still stand on opposite sides of the street in our interpretations of certain rules and guidelines established." He didn't accept the money as compensation for his territory, or the hit on Don Alberto.

James shook his head in agreement. He knew the man would never accept that his kingdom was lost. Especially when he didn't lose it!

"But times change and sometimes the rules do too," Don Hamas continued. "It doesn't make it right, but the fundamental question that needs to be addressed is, did those changes make things better?"

"Don Hamas, sometimes when a man makes a conscious decision about his life or business, he does so understanding the repercussions. There can be no fundamental difference when everyone operates from the same playbook that has been achieving the same results for centuries. There can be no excuses. No—I'm sorry. No—I made a mistake, especially when war is declared. There can only be a truce or victory. The Commission has been that way as long as you can remember. It has never changed for any one man. I am not a part of your Commission, but I understand its laws. I understand what the implementations of those laws by your uncles, grandfathers, and friends stood for. Those same laws provided structure and stability, so that the Commission stands on a code between and amongst its power structure. It allowed no one to step on the next man's toes without consequences. This is how I remembered it to be, and the integrity of the game will not change because of me, or on me. If someone wants something I have, he's more than welcome to try to take it. But, he must intelligently weigh the risks versus the rewards. Your friend, Don Alberto, was one hundred percent aware of the possible risks of the moves he made. Today, I stand before you with a different plan that involves a peaceful resolution to small problems and everyone still can become rich beyond imagination," James offered with his arms spread out.

"Let me guess. You're going to be the top dog in this plan of yours, right?"

"Not unless you have a way to make billions without the government sniffing up your ass every time you take a shit," James replied.

"I think I'm going to pass on that plan. I have a few of my own that will ensure me a comfortable living," Don Hamas lied.

"That's your choice." James knew Don Hamas hated him with a passion, and would never stand in line behind him, not even in a bank. "But do know that I am here to stay, and there are going to be changes in everything that I'm affiliated with, *even* the Commission. So, good luck in your future endeavors."

Don Hamas walked at an even slower pace, listening to every word, but plotting his destruction of James. He was tired of hearing

212

this garbage, so he strolled toward the gate where their separate limos awaited them.

"Today, we have discovered much about the other, and possibly the future can hold a better direction. Thanks for the gift and the perspective," Don Hamas suggested. The two men shook hands, then walked in separate directions. James entered his limo with a smirk.

"What's that look for?" Salvator inquired.

"It really puzzles me how people who've had power for most of their lives can't even think straight if they lose it." James shook his head. "They don't even explore the possible gains from that loss. Arrogance consumes them to a point that they don't see the jeopardy that arrogance puts them in. He really has conditioned his mind to think that I don't belong amongst the ranks of men deserving of power," James said.

"It's a fool's fate."

"That's right, my friend. People like him are stuck in the sixties way of doing things. They never want to acknowledge that things are changing and new ideas are being implemented. They think if you're not a pot belly, greasy Italian who migrated from Sicily, you don't matter. But, as I assured his friend before I killed him, it's a new day."

"So, what did he not say?" Salvator laughed.

"That he hates my guts, and the first chance he gets, he'll remind me by ending my life," James said with a treacherous smile.

* * * * * * *

A few blocks from their meeting, Don Hamas entered a local cafe, then walked to the table occupied by the agent who was responsible for him leaving the Supermax Penitentiary. Only after learning Don Hamas' appeal would be granted by the courts, so he made a deal first.

The two men greeted each other with a handshake.

"How's everything going, Mr. Hamas?"

"It's so-so, I guess. Even a snail gets to its destination if he stays out the way."

"So, is that what you're trying to do since you've been home?"

"That's what you'd prescribe, right?" The agent nodded in agreement.

"Only because it's best, and there is a bigger picture involved. Other than that, I couldn't care less about your secret vendettas between gangstas. Did you get anything useful toward the bigger picture?"

"Not really. We walked and talked, but the conversations were completely metaphoric."

"So, he made no mention of the murder of Don Alberto?"

With narrowed brows, Don Hamas looked puzzled at the agent, as if he belonged on the cover of *Stupid* magazine. He ran his fingers through his hair, amazed.

"Would you make mention of a murder to a man you never met, and the guy you murdered is this guy's friend?"

"Not really. But there are some pretty stupid criminals out there."

"I don't doubt that," Don Hamas suggested. "But I don't think he's one."

"You're giving him that much credit? What did you talk about?"

Don Hamas reached into his shirt and disconnected the wire taped to his chest, then handed the entire machine to the agent. "He must be out of his fuckin' mind if he thinks I'm going to accept him as being one of us. Never! His bloodline is garbage. He can never stand in my shoes. The Commission had the audacity to take this nigger's side over mine. They will also pay dearly for their transgressions against me. Can you believe he had the fuckin' nerve to lecture me on the got-damn laws my father, uncles, and grandfather created?"

The agent shrugged, only concerned about evidence, not stupid Mafia talk.

"He killed a made man, and the law states he has to pay for that mistake with his life! That's the law I'm under. All of a sudden, these niggers with college degrees wearing three-piece suits think they matter," Don Hamas remarked sarcastically.

"So, when are you meeting again?"

"I left the door for that open. So did he. I guess it's whenever we need to."

"You know this has only just begun, right?"

"What the fuck do you mean? I came to you, wise guy. I'm running the show, understood?" Don Hamas asked.

"I understand that if you don't get us what we need, you'll continue digging until you do. One hand washes the other. That way, we both get what we want."

"Just so you know, this here operation is going down the way I've designed it. You're not going to run me around here and there like a little fuckin' rat on a leash. I will get in touch with you when the got-damn time is right. No ifs, ands, or buts, understand?" Don Hamas looked at the agent waiting for him to bow down to his demands, because they needed him as much as he needed them. The agent stared back at Don Hamas, showing no emotion at first. Then, his face turned the color of an apple.

"Look, you piece of shit in a thousand-dollar suit. You ain't running a muthafuckin' thing! Talking all that gangsta shit. But I promise you this—" The agent paused a second, trying to gain his composure. "If you ever speak to me in that tone again, I'll escort your funky ass back to the Supermax Federal Penitentiary you just left. You've tasted a little freedom, but you're far from it. Now do you want to test me?" the agent asked.

Don Hamas said nothing. He only stared in silence. *He thinks I don't know about my appeal being granted. As long as the streets know it, I'll deal with this piece of shit afterwards.*

"That's what I thought. I'll talk to you real soon." The agent stood up and adjusted his suit, tapped Don Hamas on the shoulder, and then left.

* * * * * * *

Ring, Ring, Ring.

"Hello?"

"Hey, baby. What's up?" Kane asked.

"Oh, nothing. Just getting a little sleep. You okay?" Tara asked.

"Everything cool. Look, I need you to meet me by the plaza as soon as you can. How long is it going to take you?"

"Do I have to go inside?"

"Nah, we can meet in the parking lot."

"Well, in that case, give me ten minutes, baby," Tara suggested.

Kane hung up the phone, then leaned back in the seat of his Charger parked down the street from Tara's house. He had to get in and out of the house without her questioning him about where he was going, or what's going on. He didn't have time for questions or answers. Shit was critical! Kane lit up a blunt, then cracked his window. He and Tara had been tight for a couple years, even before the fame. Tara was a student at Delgado Community College, and was determined to be somebody in life. Her only flaw was that she loved her a gangsta nigga. Her last boyfriend was killed in a shootout. Kane met her shortly afterward. She worked as a secretary at a law office.

As her Infiniti sped down the street in the opposite direction, Kane crept into her parking spot, then made his entrance into her home. Once inside, he slid his key back into his pocket, then went to work. He first went for the safe he had stashed away eighty grand in and another hundred grand in jewels. Once he grabbed that, he went into the closet and took the AR-15 leaning against the wall and his vest. As he was walking out, he took twenty grand, then threw it on the table. He peeped out of the door, satisfied that nobody was around. He strolled to his car, popped the trunk, then slung the vest and laid the rifle down in the back. He pulled out of the driveway on his way to his four stash houses.

Ring, ring, ring.

"Hello?"

"Hey baby, where you at?" Tara asked.

"I just left the house, baby," Kane replied.

"What house are you talking about?"

"Your house."

"Why would you be there when you asked me to meet you at the plaza?"

"Because I'm about to take a trip for a little while, and I hate good-byes, especially when it's concerning you," Kane admitted.

"What do you mean you're leaving, Kane?" Tara asked, getting emotional.

"Look, some serious shit has come up, and I have to make decisions, not excuses. Trust what I'm telling you. It's the best move for the both of us right now."

"Nigga, you know I trust you exclusively, but did it have to come down to me not being able to see you before you left?"

"Like I said, I make decisions, not excuses. There was no time for explanations, or second guessing. It is what it is, sweetie. Look, I left some money on the table, and this is not good-bye, okay?"

"I hope not, nigga. My graduation is coming up, so I need you here on that special date you promised me," Tara reminded him.

"You know I wouldn't miss that for all the dope in Mexico, sweetie."

"You *better* not, nigga. You also need to take care of yourself. I don't want to lose you to this game, Daddy."

"I know, lil mama. That's why this decision is a rushed one, but one I need to make nonetheless."

"You know I love you, nigga. So, come back to me, or send for me. I'll be there, feel me?"

"Yeah, I know. I'll keep you informed if anything changes. Let me get back to business," Kane responded.

Minutes later, Kane arrived at the dope house in Little Woods. He noticed a couple niggas posted up on the corners as lookouts. He blew his horn as he crept by. His main guy at the house had already been notified to shut everything down, then pack up all the money and drugs. Kane was coming to pick everything up. He explained that the Feds were coming to raid the dope houses later that night, and they had got a tip from their contact downtown.

Kane picked up his phone, then dialed a number.

"Let's get it," he stated.

"On my way," the answer came back.

A big black nigga named Monster strolled out of the house with a small duffel bag, then stepped into the car.

"What's good, homie?" Monster inquired.

"It's all bad right now, my nigga," Kane responded.

"Shit, we all knew this day would come. Let's get it over, so we can get back to the money."

"That's for sho'. I'd rather be on a temporary vacation, than an extended stay in the penitentiary."

"That's for muthafuckin' sho, nigga! Nothing wrong with being that nigga who lives to see another day, huh?"

"Not unless you're the biggest sucka since Charms made the blow pop," Kane joked.

"That's what's up, playa. Anyway, nigga. You got too much heat with you in this car for me to be hanging witcha'," Monster suggested. "I'm a four-time loser, and I ain't got my tool on me to shoot it out with these bitches, so I'm gone. Get back with me whenever."

"I got you as soon as this shit over," Kane promised.

Monster gave Kane a fist pound. Immediately, Kane drove off, en route to the other three dope houses, hopeful that the rest of his pickups would be as smooth as this one.

* * * * * * *

Deon was twenty-five with only one serious relationship to her credit. That was during her college years. Although it was short-lived, it fitted her. It was the kind of relationship her mother always wanted her to consider, totally monogamous. She knew Quami Jones AKA Dip was hot, and may have a bit of baggage, hence the reason for his visit to the law firm. But his delivery of the short story resonated as him being genuinely interested in her. She hadn't felt that feeling in a very long time. It was something a woman in a position of power had to have. It was something her intuition assured her that only Quami could deliver. *Time will tell,* she thought.

After several dates and many conversations, Deon grew comfortable with Dip and dating became both fun and exhilarating.

On a Saturday night, Dip scooped up Deon from her mansion, and they rode in the back of the Phantom, sipping Moet. They conversed endlessly as the chance for them to really bond presented itself. They were both impressed with the other's style. The snow-white Phantom glided to a stop in front of the long lines waiting to get into Club Ballers. Dip tapped on the glass divider, indicating to the chauffeur that they were ready to exit the vehicle. The driver came around, opened the door, and then stood there as Dip and Deon made their exit.

Everyone in the crowded lines looked around as the others did. Tonight was R&B night, and the owner had blessed the couples tonight. Top of the line entertainers were in the house. All three floors would be packed all night long. The parking lot was full as usual, with nothing but ballers, as usual. The code in Club Ballers was that you come hard, or don't come at all. Anyone sporting knock-off clothing or jewelry—this wasn't your spot. Club Ballers had its own version of the Red Carpet.

Deon and Dip looked absolutely stunning! Deon had chosen a pure silk dress made by Michelle Woo, with sprinkles of diamonds that made up the shoulder straps. She had left the salon earlier, freshening up her dreads. The little sea shells were still there. A string of diamonds wrapped around her neck loosely. Her wrist sparkled from a diamond and platinum tennis bracelet. The purse and shoes were Prada.

Dip decided to slip into a comfortable zone with Armani slacks, vest, everything black, no shirt, to show off his massive muscles and a black Dobb on his head. His wrist game was sick. Bezzled presidential Rolex, diamond two-inch thick bracelet and a diamond pinky ring. Not to mention, when he smiled you needed sunglasses, as his teeth were made of diamonds, worth nearly a hundred grand.

"Who the fuck is that?" a short, fine, curious chick named Laura was asking the bouncer at the door.

"What you know good?" Dip asked as he and Deon walked toward the entrance.

"You got the best hand, my brother. But I'm cool with it 'cause you a cool dude."

"One does what one can, my brother," Dip replied.

"I second that motion," Big Luke stated. "Who you have with you, my brother?"

"Oh, you've never met my wife?" Dip replied.

"Umm, not that I can recall. But had I met her, I would've remembered. There's two things the mind shall always remember, someone who's real pretty or pretty ugly," Big Luke suggested

"So, what are you saying, Big Luke?"

"Well, you know she ain't ugly, nigga, so what you think?"

"Nigga, you going to let us in the club, or continue sucking a nigga's nuts up there?"

"What? Who said that?" Big Luke asked, looking through the line in an attempt to find who disrespected him. "That's what I thought, pussy!"

"You going in there, Dip?" Big Luke asked.

"Nah, I don't like skipping. I got a key, I'll go through the side door." Dip glanced down the line of people waiting to get in the club, hoping a nigga would say something. Deon grabbed his arm and tugged at it, as if she were reading his mind. *Let's go,* her eyes told him. When he looked at her beautiful face, he decided that tonight would be a special night for them, and he wouldn't ruin it. He nodded, then threw up the deuces to Big Luke. They walked a couple yards to the door marked 'Employees.' He inserted his key, and the two of them disappeared.

Inside, there was a booth set up in VIP for them, equipped with a full view of the stage. "Thank you," Deon stated, then gently placed her hands on his face, and planted a kiss on his lips.

"No, baby. Thank you," Dip replied. "You must know that women such as yourself are a rare find. You're smart, conscious of who you are, and very respectable of your personal and professional self. Where most women are struggling, you're past those stages, no identity crisis. That seems to always be the stumbling blocks in relationships. You're attached to something essential to who you are, or trying to become. There's purpose and passion always flowing through your veins. Every day is looked at as an opportunity, instead of just another day of the week to you. I can sense it, because you're always working on something or into something. But it's never outside of your identity, sweetheart. You keep it real and true to who you are, and that's why I'm ready to commit to you," Dip suggested. "Only you."

Deon was very teary eyed, but strong enough not to shed a tear. How could she? She had been taught that big girls don't cry. *No matter what emotion you're feeling, don't let it control you. You control it,* James told her. *Always guard your heart as if it were money. Because once you give your heart, it's like giving something away that controls you.*

That mustn't happen, too much is at stake, Deon concluded. "That's sweet, baby. Let's talk about that later on, okay? You've got some serious, serious things going on. That's your focus. That's my only focus." Deon kissed his lips, seeing the perturbed expression on Dip's face.

CHAPTER 26
The Hit

Dip had just picked up his freshly painted Range Rover from the dealership. He was rolling down Chef Highway, about to enter his old neighborhood, the Desire projects when his phone rang.

"Hello?"

"Dip, what's up, my nigga?"

"What's up, Kev?"

"Just cooling, playboy. How's life treating you?" Kev asked.

"Cold as a muthafucka. But it could be worse!"

"I heard from a few of your comrades about the incident that occurred, and I have a name that keeps coming up,"

"That's some welcoming news," Dip replied.

"Who is it?"

"A nigga named Kane. He fucks with them niggas out there with all the work in the East," Kev expressed.

Dip cursed himself at the thought of this nigga sending a hit on him. *That nigga wasn't man enough to face me.* However, this nigga had done homework and he hadn't, so that meant Kane was ahead of the game. *Fuck!* Dip knew he should've never taken his eyes off this nigga. Kane was simply too smart of a nigga, a street general that should've never been able to leave Club Ballers the night of his birthday party. Period, point blank!

"So, what that nigga role was in all this?" Dip inquired.

"Oh, so you know this nigga?"

"You can say that."

"Yeah, well, the streets are saying this nigga was on the scene when this whole incident went down, playa."

"Damn!" *Just when I thought things couldn't get worse. I wonder if the nigga witnessed my work.*

"What else the streets saying, Kev?"

"That the nigga called Lil Killa nem to the scene to execute a lick, which was involving some major bread. I don't know how the nigga knew your business, or what he could've possibly seen, but the lil niggas who got smashed was told to get to your spot quick."

"Where you say the nigga be at?" *The nigga had to have been out there. He had to have witnessed my pick up and that's why he called them clowns,* Dip considered.

"In the East."

"Where exactly?"

"The Goose. America Street is where he lives."

"What the nigga drive?"

"A loud ass lime-green Charger, tinted windows," Kev informed.

"Thanks for the info, playa. I owe you one."

"No problem, homie. You stay up."

Dip began dialing.

"What's up, Dip?" Tray responded.

"I received some information about the incident that happened at the station."

"You got a who with that information?"

"Oh, yeah. And it sounds about right, too."

"Who was behind it?" Tray asked.

"Remember that big nigga with the dreads that you wanted to throw out the club that night of my birthday party?"

"Yeah, I remember that sneaky-looking muthafucka"

"The nigga name is Kane. Me and the nigga go back to the days when I was in Angola. We squared off and remained enemies ever since. Somehow the nigga witnessed my pick up, then called them lil niggas to come make a hit, figuring he had the drop on me."

"So, the nigga was allowed to stroll up out of my club and do homework on you, without you ever inquiring about his

WILLIE GROSS JR. WITH WAHIDA CLARK

whereabouts?" Tray asked.

"That's about right. And, I take full responsibility for the slip up."

"That's why I bought you that armored vehicle. You next generation niggas don't play defense. You niggas not bulletproof like you think. That's your testosterone level making you think like that. So, you did any homework on this nigga?"

"I got some info on the nigga. Just need to know a few things about who he's working for," Dip replied.

"Who he supposed to be working for?" Tray inquired.

"Them niggas who got the East on lock, Troy and Luqman."

Tray leaned back in his comfortable chair for a second. He had to go through the proper channels before he ended this nigga's life.

"Look, you just play defense on that issue right now. I personally know these people, and out of respect, it must go through the proper channels. Feel me?"

Man, I feel what you saying, Tray, But, this nigga moved on me, Dip thought. "Yeah. I feel you, but what's the problem?" Dip asked angrily.

"The problem is, I made a call, for starters. The second problem would be you not knowing what you about to get into," Tray assured him. "That nigga work for the same people who gave you that territory, and you don't want to go to war with them, unless you're tired of living. I never taught you the gentleman way of conducting business. But, it'll keep you breathing longer if you learn the word respect," Tray offered. "We're going to get him, but it has to be by the rules. You're still playing chess, my young friend. Just let this be a lesson to you. Never let an enemy out of your clutches. You should've killed him when the opportunity presented itself."

"I feel you, old man," Dip replied.

"Now, is there anything else I need to know before I put this in motion?"

Dip searched his thoughts for anything, then remembered something extremely important.

"There's one other thing."

"Should I be sitting down for this one?" Tray asked.

"Don't know . . . but it's a problem that may make you want to lay down."

"What is it? And spare no details," Tray commanded.

"I got a call from the lone survivor, Akbar."

"What's the problem?"

"He has the DVD that the Feds are looking for with me putting in that work outside of the station."

"So, let me guess. He's into extortion now?"

"That's exactly what it is. And, he's playing hardball, too."

"How much?"

"He wants two hundred thousand, final offer."

"What did you tell him?"

"When can we meet," Dip shot back.

"So, what happened next?"

"He said he would get back at me with a plan, so he could get the chance to enjoy the money."

"Sounds like a smart man, too smart for me to like him," Tray suggested. "Other than that, there's nothing else?"

"Shit. You need some more on your plate?" Dip asked.

"I just don't believe in letting important shit linger, then it turn into a burden," Tray shot back. "Some major networking has got to be done, and in a hurry. Both these situations can fuck your world up at the drop of a dime. This is what they mean by 'killing time!' Let me do my thing. You keep out the way in the meantime?"

"That won't be a problem," Dip responded, then hung up the phone. He turned his Range Rover around, then headed in the East to holla at his girl, Keoka. *Fuck that shit. It's a must that I hunt this nigga down. He crossed a line . . . My line.*

* * * * * * *

"Hello?"

"James, I need to speak to you a second," Tray suggested.

For a second James paused and leaned back in his comfortable office chair. He now wondered who this mysterious person was that constantly called him. Especially while he was at the mansion strategizing.

"What you got?" James curiously asked.

"Look, there's an incident that happened the other day at the Spur gas station that some people who robbed the store was responsible for many innocent casualties. You familiar with it?"

"It's been all over the news. I take it our people still control that territory, right?" James inquired.

"Everything's under control. But, what we've found out is that the robbery was also a hit sent from your camp," Tray stated, then waited for a response.

"That's impossible," James assured. "There's never been a hit issued, and me not give the order in my camp!"

"I understand your position. But I'll let you in on what I know, and we'll figure out where we go from there," Tray shot back. "Anyway, the person who sent the hit works under Troy and Luqman in the East. His name is Kane. He and my general who you gave the territory, have had a history since their Angola days. Enemies, of course. However, Kane happened to see my guy picking up his deposits, then called for his crew to come and take the deposits, then take out my general.

"When his crew arrived minutes later, my man was seated in his bulletproof Range Rover. As three of the gunmen entered the store, one of the men stood at the Range Rover, then emptied two banana clips from an AK-47 into the vehicle, with no effect. My man caught the gunman as he was about to flee the scene, killing him, then repositioning the Range Rover in front of the door of the station and waited for the other three to exit. When they did, he killed all three of them, retrieved his money, then came to see me. We recently obtained the information that your guy was in fact, on the scene. More than likely, ducked off in his vehicle quarterbacking everything. I know you don't condone this type of disrespect, and not to mention, it's bad for business. The Feds are crawling all over the place."

"How accurate is your information?" James inquired.

"If I'm notifying you, I've eliminated all doubt first, my friend. The next phase to be implemented was death warrants. But our relationship has been forged with respect, and that's where it'll remain. So my proposition is for you to take care of this in-house, or I can send someone," Tray advised him.

James thought about his options for a second, then decided he would make this move, so that it would be clean and quiet. He would send Salvator to handle this immediately. Kane had definitely crossed a line that he would live to regret, James considered.

"Very well," James stated. "I will handle this situation my way. He has violated my rules, so he should die by my hands. Consider this done, and thanks for the *way* you presented your problem. Respect goes a long way."

"No problem. I'll be in touch with you in a few days."

James hung up the phone, and then dialed Salvator's number.

"Hello?"

"What are you up to, my friend?" James inquired.

"Checking my traps, passing through the territory uptown. Why? You need me?" Salvator asked.

"Yeah. Are you familiar with this dude Kane that runs the houses in the East?" James inquired.

"I've watched him a few times. What you need?"

"I need for him to go to sleep immediately."

"That won't be a problem. Is there any specific way?"

"Quickly."

"I'm on my way. Consider it done."

Salvator turned the Audi A-8 around, then headed for the interstate in search of Kane. He turned his radio up to six, adjusted his clock to 6:00 a.m., then turned the air conditioner up to six, and when he opened the center console, his 9-millimeter Sig Sauer was lying there, along with a silencer. He popped in the clip, screwed on the silencer, then laid the pistol in his lap. He was ten minutes away from his destination.

* * * * * * *

Dip was pulling into Keoka's boutique on Crowder Boulevard, in the East. He stepped out of the Range Rover, then strolled into the store. The buzzer on the door sounded off. Keoka looked up, then smiled when she saw Dip.

"Hey, handsome," she stated.

"How the hell are you, with yo' sexy ass?" Dip replied.

"Nigga, I ain't seen yo' ass since the party. Where you been?"

"You know I'm a businessman, sweetie," Dip said.

"Damn, nigga. Close your mouth before you blind a bitch in here."

"I see you still that same ol' Keoka, huh?"

"Shit, nigga. The last thing I heard, ain't nothing like the real thing!"

"That's why I know who to come holla at when I need some real talk," Dip stated in a serious tone.

"That's for sho. What you need to know, big brother?"

"This nigga, Kane. What's the haps on his big jive ass?"

"You dealing with that rattlesnake?"

"Nah, the nigga crossed a line that's going to cost him his life. But right now I'm just doing my homework."

"A few of his 'hos come through here talking like the nigga this and that. They silly 'hos, so they go for fried ice cream," Keoka stated.

"You have addresses on them women you speaking about?"

"That'll be a dead end. Kane would never lay his head at any of them project 'hos crib. But they got this one named Tara that comes through here claiming to be carrying the nigga's baby, and she pretty decent in the sense category. When she comes back through, I'll get that information for you."

"I'd appreciate that, baby," Dip replied.

"Put me on the VIP list, ol' pretty ass nigga."

"You got that." Dip walked behind the counter, then gave Keoka a hug.

Feeling better about his situation, he strolled out of the store. He knew if the nigga didn't do anything else, he was going to get him some pussy. He now felt like his homework would definitely pay off. However, what was troubling him was that he didn't know how much this nigga knew about where he laid his head, or where he got his pussy, and this was definitely a problem!

* * * * * * *

Thirty miles away, Kane and Diamond met up at the RaceTrac gas station in Slidell on their way to Atlanta. They shared an embrace as they met at the gas pumps.

"What's wrong, baby?" Diamond asked.

"Like I said. Niggas including my name into shit dealing with them people that will ultimately lead them to me. And you know when they come, I'm going to be dirty," Kane stated.

"So, what's this shit your name included in?"

"That shit that happened at the Spur station."

Diamond shook her head, indicating that she knew of the situation, and that it wasn't good. "So, what's the plan from this point?"

"I got a friend of mine in Atlanta. We're going to start a new life down there."

"What about this drama at the Spur station?"

"As long as there is just questions being asked, I'm cool. As long as I'm not around to answer any questions, is even better."

"What about Troy and Luqman?" Diamond asked.

"They'll be all right. Time will heal a broken heart."

"You're not scared of them niggas, huh?"

"I don't have no reason to be scared, do you? They know who I am. If they don't like the way I get down, then that's their issue." Kane grinned.

"Peep this," Diamond suggested. "As long as we look at this shit from every angle, it can be pulled off. But understand this, nigga. I don't sit on my ass all day. I know you, and I know the niggas you deal with. I'm going to roll with you and be down to squeeze triggers for you, but don't play me like I'm lame," Diamond stated.

"Where is all this coming from?" Kane asked.

"It's called experience. Every nigga involved in the Spur station shit, and us leaving town with these other niggas' money and dope are critical situations. Don't downplay this shit to me like I'm no fuckin' goofy bitch! If you got a plan, let me in on it. If not, then let's put one in effect immediately."

"Everything's under control, baby. I got us, but I never doubted who I have in my corner."

"I know you been doing your thing since coming home from

Angola. But remember who held yo' ass down. And, I let you in on whatever I was into. I didn't leave out one detail. My life is on the fuckin' line in this game we're playing. So nigga, don't keep me in the blind like I can't handle the truth all of a sudden."

"Like I said, Diamond, we good. But let's fuel these vehicles up and get on with our plan, which is to see Atlanta in five hours. Another thing, we got enough product in this vehicle to send us away for a minute. So we driving the speed limit."

Diamond nodded as she finished pumping gas in her cherry-apple red Charger. Kane strolled into the store, and she remained outside watching his every step, wondering what his plan really was. She had heard how the streets were talking about him double crossing them robbers at the Spur station, and now she wondered if he would do her the same. But she had learned how to play chess, also. So she would implement her own plans, too. Diamond smiled as she thought about her strategy.

****

NEW TITLES FROM WAHIDA CLARK PRESENTS

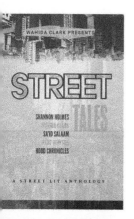

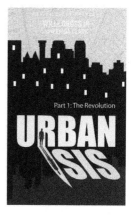

#READIT

WWW.WCLARKPUBLISHING.COM

CPSIA information can be obtained
at www.ICGtesting.com
Printed in the USA
LVHW091620280819
629259LV00002B/284/P